THE VERMILION PARROT

BOOKS BY DAVID RAINS WALLACE

NONFICTION

The Dark Range

The Klamath Knot

Idle Weeds

The Wilder Shore

Bulow Hammock

FICTION

The Turquoise Dragon

The Vermilion Parrot

THE VERMILION PARROT

A Novel

DAVID RAINS WALLACE

Sierra Club Books
San Francisco

The Sierra Club, founded in 1892 by John Muir, has devoted itself to the study
and protection of the earth's scenic and ecological resources—
mountains, wetlands, woodlands, wild shores and rivers, deserts and plains.
The publishing program of the Sierra Club offers books
to the public as a nonprofit educational service in the hope that they may
enlarge the public's understanding of the Club's
basic concerns. The point of view expressed in each book, however, does not
necessarily represent that of the Club. The Sierra Club
has some sixty chapters coast to coast, in Canada, Hawaii, and Alaska.
For information about how you may participate in its programs
to preserve wilderness and the quality of life, please address inquiries to
Sierra Club, 730 Polk Street, San Francisco, CA 94109.

Library of Congress Cataloging-in-Publication Data
Wallace, David Rains, 1945-
The vermilion parrot : a novel / by David Rains Wallace.
p.   cm.
ISBN 0–87156–630–3
I. Title.
PS3573. A42564V4   1991
813'.54 — dc20   90-22918 CIP

Production by Janet Vail
Jacket design by Sandra Dean
Book design by Richard Garnas
Printed on recycled paper in the United States of America
10 9 8 7 6 5 4 3 2 1

To Bob Leyland

"It was surely well for man that he came late in the order of creation. There were powers abroad in earlier days which no courage and no mechanism of his could have met."

Sir Arthur Conan Doyle
The Lost World

Vacation Couple Sees Moon Shot In Reverse

New Smyrna, August 1, 1969–Bill and Lena Palmer of Green Bay, Wisconsin, weren't surprised to see something streak across the sky last month as they sailed their rented ketch on a six-week vacation cruise through the Bahamas. They knew the first manned moon shot was scheduled for July. The couple was surprised to see the fiery contrail head toward the earth instead of the sky.

"We thought, oh, this must be a horrible tragedy," said Lena Palmer, 47. "It must have failed and gone into the ocean. But when we got to Nassau we heard it had been a success. We were surprised."

"There's no doubt it was something," said her husband, 47, a vice president of the Hilltop Trucking Company. "It was big. It lit up the sky."

Sources at the Cape Kennedy Space Center expressed puzzlement at the Palmers' account, and added that the Palmers' failure to establish the exact time and location of the sighting would make it hard to investigate. No similar reports have been received at the Center, the sources maintained.

TRUCKER PASSES ALIENS ON WASHINGTON BELTWAY

GIANT VULTURES RIDE IN STRETCH LIMO

Washington, D.C., May 20, 1985–"When I clicked on my brights getting ready to pass, I could hardly believe my eyes," said truck driver Pete Duhamel, 42. "Somehow the high beams passed through the smoked glass for a second, and I saw what looked like a bunch of big birds looking out at me. They had beaks and red heads, like . . . vultures."

"They didn't do anything, just looked at me. I hit the brakes, and then I couldn't see them any more. It was a big gray limousine, the kind they call a stretch limo."

Duhamel said the vehicle speeded up and left the Beltway on the Rockville Pike Exit. "I didn't get a license number," he added. "I was too flabbergasted, but it was a Maryland plate, I'm pretty sure."

Duhamel has an "excellent" driving record, said his employer, the Hilltop Trucking Company of Green Bay, Wisconsin. A Seventh Day Adventist, he does not use alcohol, tobacco, or caffeine. "If he said something, I'd believe it," said Hilltop Trucking president William Palmer, 63.

SCIENTIST: BIRDS EVOLVE ALIEN INTELLIGENCE?

Pocomoke City, Md., May 20, 1985–Exobiologist Fred Handley Ph.D. of Delmarva College said yesterday that a giant bird would be a very likely form for extraterrestrial intelligence.

"Birds are among the most intelligent vertebrates," Dr. Handley said. "The African Gray Parrot, for example, is among the five smartest animals along with apes, dogs, cats, and rats. In the Paleocene epoch, just after the dinosaurs became extinct, birds competed for evolutionary dominance with mammals. It's quite likely that on another planet like the earth, birds would have won the evolutionary race and developed civilization rather than mammals."

Asked if vultures are intelligent, Dr. Handley said he didn't think so, but added that "terrestrial standards can't be applied when evaluating exobiological organisms."

The National Space and Aeronautics Agency and the Institute of Exobiology at Cornell University declined comment on Dr. Handley's theory. An unidentified source at the Institute added that Duhamel's sighting would be impossible to investigate in the absence of physical evidence.

Eco-Activist Claims
Fed Condor Coverup

Goleta, August 15, 1985–Richard Karue of the Condor Rescue League charged yesterday that the Federal government may be covering up wrongdoing in the disappearance of eight California condors this summer.

The endangered condor has been the subject of a recovery effort by U.S. and state agencies since 1983. Four of five known breeding pairs of the birds failed to return to nest sites in May.

Speaking before a small group of self-avowed ecoradicals at Los Padres National Forest Headquarters in Goleta, Santa Monica resident Karue said, "Big birds like condors don't just disappear into thin air. They get disappeared."

Karue claimed the condors may have been killed or captured by developers fearful of strict land use controls. He called for expanded investigative efforts from resource agencies.

U.S. Fish and Wildlife Service agent Phil Conte told the *Leader* the condor disappearance is being investigated "vigorously," but he couldn't discuss details. "Unfortunately," he added, "given the millions of acres of condor habitat, the causes of most birds' disappearance will never be known."

1

There wasn't a single book on bankruptcy in the business section of the Waldenbooks in Redding, although business sections were big in 1986. I did find eight copies of *Bankruptcy: Do it Yourself* in my local library's card catalogue, but they'd all been stolen, including the reference copy. Even the *Ba* volume of the *Encyclopedia Britannica* was missing.

The stolen copies would have been shelved between *The Cashless Society* and *Property Power*, which about summed things up for me. Too much property, too little cash. In the heady days of the late 1970s property inflation, I'd plowed some windfall profits into a tree nursery business and thirty acres along the scenic Trinity River in northern California. I'd been confident that, even if the business didn't succeed, the property would be worth so much more after a few years that I'd be able to sell out and retire to Costa Rica or something. A decade later, the property was worth about what I'd paid for it, and I figured I could have sold my aging tabby cat more easily. The cat, Lewis, catches gophers, which should be worth something. At least, dead gophers show up on the property sometimes. Maybe they just starve to death.

The source of the windfall profits—growing marijuana in Shasta Trinity National Forest when I was resource officer there—might have been a source of reflection on crime's unprofitability, but I wasn't in the mood for reflection, a luxury of the solvent. Anyway, crime had been the *only* thing that paid. It had been my attempt to start a legitimate reforestation business that hadn't paid. In the 1980s, Gilded Age II, you didn't feel better for having failed at something honest, you felt worse—not only incompetent, but foolish.

At least I wasn't a real farmer, owing so much that they came and auctioned everything from the front porch. My neighbor,

John Minaric, did me a favor and bought the twenty acres adjoining his place, and I was able to renegotiate the rest with the bank. I got a pretty good price for the mobile home I'd been living in, and lousy returns for everything else I could sell. This left me with one battered pickup, one stripped-down barn, and a front porch that I'd built on to the mobile home in better days. I'd offered to throw the porch in free with the mobile home, but the buyer had declined it as "too rustic."

It's traditional, after going bankrupt in a small rural community, to go somewhere else. But I'd been too busy selling things to think of where to go. I realized that it was later than I'd thought one warm September evening when the mobile home was due to be picked up in a week or two, but the realization didn't galvanize me. The only thing in my head, in fact, was the first phrase of the Andrews Sisters' song, "Enjoy Yourself." The electricity still worked, and the refrigerator contained a large bottle of gin and a small one of vermouth. A few glasses into that, a timeless golden haze settled over the porch, allowing me to enjoy the sunset as the tanagers and grosbeaks stole the last of the Thompson seedless grapes in the arbor.

I wasn't pleased to hear a car coming up the drive, but at least it wasn't the meter reader coming to turn off the electricity. It was a Land Rover. My heart might have skipped a beat if it hadn't been gently bathed in 96 proof grain spirits. I recognized the Land Rover—I'd been extracted from it at gunpoint a year earlier.

Carla Shreve looked better than ever when she got out. She wore shorty shorts and a halter top in the September heat. I just sat in my wicker chair. I did have a chair left. My relationship with Carla had been complicated from the start, and subsequent events hadn't simplified it. A year after they'd occurred, those events were still giving me nightmares.

Carla and I had made headlines. Alec Rice, a fake tree-farmer but an actual rare animal smuggler, drug dealer, and psychotic, had murdered Tom Blackwell, Carla's former lover and my boyhood best friend, in an attempt to cover up a sideline of robbing and murdering illegal aliens along the Arizona border. Then he'd murdered the detective investigating the case, and had tried to murder me and Carla in a chase through the Kalmiopsis Wilderness in Oregon. Alec's own demise, in an earthquake and flood at the bottom of a cave, had been like something in an H. Rider Haggard novel. If I hadn't lived through it myself, I'd say the whole experience was the product of a tabloid-grade imagination.

Unfortunately, some adventures are more terrifying than sensational while they're happening to you. Dragging through the Kalmiopsis with Alec had been like a bad case of intestinal flu, with physical misery intermittently overshadowed by mental anguish. I was still getting night sweats a year later.

The experience might have been expected to create a bond between Carla and me, but being terrified "à deux" doesn't necessarily promote solidarity. I'd pulled Carla into the mess with my amateur investigations of Blackwell's death, so she had reason to resent me. I'd developed an irrational tendency to blame her for the mental turmoil that had loosened my unsteady grip on the tree nursery business. Everybody else I could have blamed was dead.

Carla squinted in the sunset's glare, taken aback by the sparseness of my establishment. Not that she'd seen it in better days. We hadn't met since parting company in the Medford, Oregon, sheriff's office the previous summer.

"George?"

I responded sepulchrally from the shadows. "How are the dragons, Carla?" Carla was a herpetologist, the kind of biologist who studies reptiles and amphibians. She had discovered a species of salamander that turned out to be the only American relatives of a primitive Asian group of salamanders that the Chinese call dragons. "Did you get them on the endangered species list yet?" Carla's dragons lived only in a single swamp in the Kalmiopsis Wilderness.

"It's impossible to get anything on the list now," Carla replied. "Too many other applicants."

"Did you come here to depress me?"

"You already look depressed."

"Want a martini?"

"Alright."

This set me back. Carla liked to keep a clear head and a safe distance. The only time she'd accepted a drink from me, I'd ended up spending the night in her tent. Nevertheless, I invited her in and broke out my other glass. The gin was getting low, but there was enough for two.

"My God, George," Carla said, surveying my empty kitchen, "what is going on?" I explained. "What are you going to do?" I raised my glass.

"Cheers."

Carla seemed affected by my circumstances. I found this a little irritating.

"What can I do for you?" I said brusquely.

"I tried to phone you."

"I still have a mailbox."

"I don't have much time for writing," she said.

"But you do for visits?"

"Actually, I'm on my way to Japan."

"Bon voyage."

She didn't reply, and I began to feel guilty. Conversation with Carla had a way of running off the track, but I couldn't always blame her for that.

"What were you trying to phone me about?" I said.

"Oh, I don't know." She shook her head as though trying to clear it. Carla's hair is the same color as her eyes, a kind of amber. "I felt like talking."

"About the deeply meaningful things we used to talk about?"

"Come on, George. I haven't seen any letters from you in the past year."

"Every time I communicate with you, I get in a life-threatening situation."

"Well, you're not going to insure it with this stuff," Carla said, putting down her glass. "Why don't we go eat something?"

2

Apropos of business failures, the South Fork Restaurant had been the scene of one almost every year since I'd come to Weaverville. One year it was the Trinity Restaurant, the next, The Azteca, the next, The Nugget, then, The Jade Mountain. Cuisines had mostly corresponded to names, except in the case of the Jade Mountain, which had started Hunanese but had limped through its declining months as a pizzeria.

There had been progress. The Trinity Restaurant had been bare-board hippy, with a potbellied stove propped on cinder blocks. By the South Fork era, various renovations had elevated the place to something approximating postmodern, with peach walls and table napkins to match. The California-Basque cuisine wavered according to the chef's feelings about his parole (he'd met with cash flow problems while working at Harrah's Tahoe), but it was upscale by Weaverville scales.

Carla ordered trout, allowing me to observe ingenuously that she'd told me she was a vegetarian the year before.

"I don't mind killing fish," she answered.

"Lower forms of life."

"Easier to kill than a cow."

"So, what's in Japan?"

"I've got a research grant. And I'm giving a paper at a conference."

"All those Asian species of dragons. Don't they eat salamanders there?"

"The Japanese giant salamander. It's a different family than the dragons. More evolved."

"Going to try some salamander sushi?"

"The Japanese giant salamander is endangered, actually."

"How long you going for?"

"Nine months. Then I'll be teaching at Eugene for a semester."

"Ah, success." I sighed.

"For sixteen months."

"What are you doing with your little house?" Carla had a cabin at the edge of the Kalmiopsis Wilderness. I'd spent the most anxious night of my life in it.

"I'm going to rent it. Looking for a place?"

"I can get all the cabin fever I need down here, thanks."

"What *are* you going to do, George?"

I lifted my glass of chardonnay. "Cheers."

"Want a job?"

Carla's trout and my lamb shank arrived at this point, so I had time to think of a witty answer to her question. I gazed into the distance and applied myself to the chardonnay, but none occurred to me.

"Not particularly. Doing what?"

"The Coastal Lands Trust needs a resident manager for their South Coast Preserve. Marshall Mitchell, the director, is a friend. He wanted me to do it, but you'd be better."

"Why?"

"Why what?"

"Why would I be better?"

"Wouldn't you? Forest ranger and all that?"

"Resource officer. Never made it to ranger." I'd already told her that. People never listen to job descriptions.

"But you've had law enforcement experience."

I wondered if she was being ironic. Carla knew about my checkered past.

"Lot of dope-growing around there?" I inquired.

"It's pretty conservative actually. Not too far from San Simeon."

"Reaganista redneck country."

"Well if you look for trouble you can probably find it."

"What does it pay?"

"Not very much. It was just a thought, George. If you want, I'll tell Marshall about you and you can contact him."

I started to tell her not to bother, but then I glanced up from my baby zucchini and saw two of my ex-wife's friends come in and sit on the other side of the room. The breakup of my

marriage had been one of the few immediately negative effects
of my dope-growing venture, and the bad taste had lingered after
the money had been spent, even though my wife and daughter
had long since moved back east. I could tell her friends were
wondering who the mystery woman was, and what she was
doing with the town deadbeat.

"Why not? Thanks, Carla."

"I'll talk to him about it tomorrow."

"You're driving down there tonight?"

"I have to. My plane leaves at eleven in the morning."

"Where will you stay?"

"With a friend."

It was none of my business, of course. The waitress asked if
we wanted dessert. They had mocha torte, peanut butter chocolate pie, raspberry cheesecake, and fresh lemon tart. I couldn't
think of anything witty to say about that, either.

3

I would have preferred to be fashionably late in showing up at
the Coastal Lands Trust's San Francisco office, but I needed a
place to live. The summer weather wouldn't last more than a
few weeks longer. I could have moved into one or two vacant
places in Weaverville, but people who live in hand-me-down
housing up here get this look in their eyes.

I dawdled a few days after Carla's visit, which left me a few
more until they took the mobile home away. One morning
around two A.M., when there was nothing more on TV, I jumped
into the pickup and left the cat in charge. Actually, I hadn't seen
Lewis for a day or so. Since the disappearance of soft furniture
from the mobile home, he had been spending a lot of time on
an old couch on John Minaric's porch. He had cowed John's
nervous retriever bitch, had actually chased her under the porch

on one occasion, and so had carved himself a niche in the Minaric pecking order even though John didn't particularly like cats. But then, Lewis didn't like cats either.

I stopped for breakfast in Corning and watched, or glanced at, the dawn over the rice fields. Smoke from burning stubble combined with haze from a forest fire in the Coast Range to turn the sky brown at the edges, like acid paper left in the sun. The air smelled singed. Downtown, early morning emptiness enhanced the yellowed-paper impression. Except for their formica signs, the brick storefronts looked like a sepia snapshot from the twenties.

The place where I had breakfast had an early 1960s decor. They'd put mirrors all around the walls to counteract the oppressively low acoustical tile ceiling. The restaurant appeared filled with an infinity of rice farmers hunched over the first cup of the day. They turned to stare as I walked in, then lost interest. I didn't look like I worked for a bank.

A stocky individual at the counter eyed me as I walked along the row of booths. He said something as I passed, but I kept on toward an empty booth in the corner. I stuck my nose in a newspaper and ordered ham and eggs. There was plenty of news. The president was optimistic about the Strategic Defense Initiative but pessimistic about the Reykjavic summit. The remains of the Challenger astronauts had finally been officially buried. The U.S. Fish and Wildlife Service had given the order for the last three wild condors in Los Padres National Forest to be trapped and put in southern California zoos with the other twenty or so survivors of Los Angeles's growth. Another federal lands–dwelling endangered species bites the dust. I read the funnies, then glanced toward the counter. The stocky individual had left.

I'd had too much coffee, and felt jumpy and sweaty as I left the restaurant. The stocky individual leaned against a mailbox a half block away, doing something with his fly. I drove away briskly, wondering how greasy spoon coffee can taste so weak but contain so much caffeine.

I got to San Francisco in plenty of time for my nine A.M. appointment with Marshall Mitchell, even after spending an hour at the Bay Bridge toll plaza. As I took the Civic Center exit, a giant plastic fist brandished a wad of greenbacks from a billboard advertising the Montgomery Block Memorial Savings and Loan. It was a clever idea, but the fist didn't seem to have been inflated properly. The fingers looked puffy at the knuckles and withered at the tips, as though the hand suffered from poor circulation.

The Coastal Lands Trust was south of Market, in a building too new to be renovated but too old to be stylish. There were no tree ferns or cacti in the lobby, just a formica directory with one light bulb missing. The Trust's third floor suite was full of people who looked like they came from Walnut Creek, except for the receptionist, who looked like she came from the avenues. She told me Mr. Mitchell was on the phone.

A pile of preserve brochures lay beside the seat she offered me. I picked up one about the South Coast Preserve. It was the southernmost stand of old-growth coast redwood in the state and the northernmost known condor nesting site in the century. The nest, in a broken-off redwood, had been abandoned in 1925, but the redwood was still standing. The eccentric owner had refused to sell the redwoods even after a logger had started cutting them anyway, a hundred feet inside the owner's property line. The owner had lain down in front of the logger's truck, then had thought better of it and jumped out of the way; good judgment, since the logger had shown no intention of braking. Eventually, the law had upheld the sanctity of property, if not of redwoods, and restrained the logger. Sobered by his experience with 1950s-style nonviolent direct action, the owner had willed the place to the Trust, although they hadn't heard about it until fairly soon before his death.

Now the land was not only a Trust preserve and national natural landmark, but the United Nations had designated it a World Heritage Site because it was one of the last complete old-growth-forested watersheds on the coast. The Trust didn't own the whole watershed, but the upper parts were in Forest Service and Bureau of Land Management ownership, and they'd agreed not to log these for the present. This would not have reassured me, but I supposed the Trust had good enough lawyers to keep Smoky, Woodsy, Johnny Horizon, and other backcountry sprites from practicing too much multiple self-abuse in the vicinity.

I looked up and saw what might have been a hard-working junior member of the State Assembly coming toward me, sandy hair tousled, tie askew, sleeves rolled to the elbow. His voice was even more affable and confident in person than it had been on the telephone. I made affable, confident noises in response and followed him to his office, past a knot of congressional aide types who were discussing tennis clubs.

"I was glad when Carla mentioned you," said Marshall, "because we've been looking for somebody . . ." He looked at the ceiling. "Somebody with a little more experience than we usually get for these jobs. Most of our managers are right out of graduate school, which is fine, in most cases. Not that it's ever easy. You take some young person out of Berkeley or Davis and put him . . . or her . . . alone and ask him to finish building a headquarters at the same time he's leading school groups, watching boundaries, doing surveys. But the South Coast is kind of . . ."

"You want me to lie down in front of logging trucks?"

"How about that!" Marshall smiled with white teeth. "That's ancient history up there, though. Well, maybe not ancient. The guy's still alive, but he lives in Monterey now."

"The logger?"

"Yeah, the logger. Boy, you should have heard Hal Roberts go on about him."

"The owner?"

"Hal died the year before last. It's his house you'll be living in. It was originally a whorehouse."

"That's not in the brochure."

"He was an interesting old guy. Most of the whorehouse burned in 1932, actually. He built on the foundations."

"So he didn't run it."

"That's not altogether clear."

"Seems kind of out of the way for a whorehouse."

"There used to be a lot more people up there than there are now," said Marshall. "Homesteading. Marble and granite quarrying. There was still some whaling up until the war. That was one rough area. Still is, in a way."

"Which is why you want somebody . . . experienced?"

"Well, I mean, there isn't any special problem. Just the usual poachers, wild pigs, pyromaniacs. But it's our biggest property, and one of our newest, and with the Forest Service and BLM as neighbors we wanted somebody with more public land background than we usually get."

I didn't know how much Carla had told Marshall about my public land background, and I didn't ask. She evidently hadn't told him *too* much.

"Actually," Marshall continued, standing up, "why don't we go take a look, if you can spare the time?"

"A look at the preserve?"

"Yeah, I feel like getting out today. I've got a plane down in Burlingame. We can be there before lunch." Carla knew the right people.

4

Flying over Big Sur was a little disappointing. The canyons and headlands that loom majestically from sea level looked like part of a model train set from three thousand feet. Everything seemed artificially smooth, tidy, and curiously static, the surf little more than ripples at a goldfish pond's rim. It made me ponder the outlook of land managers who fly in light planes a lot. Land as toy.

Marshall waved at a cleared space on a ridgetop to the east. "There's a Forest Service airstrip over there. I've asked Jerry Lester to meet us. He's the district forest ranger for the Bureau of Land Management. He's kind of keeping an eye on the place."

It seemed a little odd that we were dealing with a BLM forester when most of the surrounding land was in Los Padres National Forest, but I didn't mention it. I was just as glad not to rub elbows with too many Forest Service types. "How many foresters do you need to see?" to paraphrase California's most famous governor, Ronald MacDonald.

"Let's take a swing over the preserve first," Marshall said, as though proposing a drive through Golden Gate Park. Being in a light plane is not unlike being a thousand feet up in a Volkswagen beetle, at least, it is when you're the passenger and it's a perfect September day.

A few minutes farther south, Marshall banked over a canyon that was noticeably deeper and longer than the others. Its mouth was so wide that U.S. 1 had to cross it on the bottom instead of on a bridge as with the canyons farther north. I'd have expected to see pasture or artichoke fields on such big flats, but I saw only green scrub of alder and cottonwood, with thin white lines of sycamore along the creek banks.

"Looks pretty wild," I said.

"Macho Creek goes through there like a house on fire in winter storms," Marshall said. "It's over four thousand feet from the top of the watershed to the bottom, and it's steep. Whatever's not bound to tree roots goes right out to sea. That flat down there is nothing but granite mulch. If they'd logged here, the whole canyon would be out in the Channel Islands. I don't really know why it isn't, anyway. It's like these redwoods know something we don't about soil conservation."

"They've had time to learn."

Marshall seemed embarrassed by our plunge into anthropomorphism, and pulled the plane around to the east, giving me a fleeting sensation that the ridgetops were moving instead of us. The canyon narrowed quickly, and the bright green of deciduous trees narrowed too. A belt of green so dark it had a bluish cast spread out on each side of the creekside vegetation. It extended about a mile up the canyon slopes, ending in the gray-green of mixed oak and chaparral that continued to the ridgetops.

"There they are," cried Marshall, with an impolitic note of enthusiasm, "the southernmost stand of *Sequoia sempervirens* on the planet. It's ten miles north to the next one. These guys have probably been isolated down here since the Pleistocene

THE VERMILION PARROT

glaciers melted on the Sierra. They don't get as tall as the ones in Del Norte County, but they get wide. Some of them look almost like *Sequoiadendron* up in Yosemite or Giant Forest." He banked the plane and pointed. "See that gray spar down there? That's the condor nest tree. It's probably over three thousand years old. Lost its top around the time of the Norman conquest, maybe eleventh century. Condors may have started nesting in it then, although they must have had some competition from bald eagles. It seems to have been unusual for condors to nest on the coast, although it made sense, since they got a lot of their food from dead whales and seals."

"When was the nest discovered?"

"The year it was abandoned, 1925. That's condors for you. They don't like voyeurs, but don't quote me on that." Like every other conservation organization in California, the Coastal Lands Trust had been involved in the ill-fated Condor Recovery Plan that had tried to increase the wild population of California condors by captive breeding in the early 1980s. After biologists started robbing nests to get eggs for captive rearing, four of the five adult breeding pairs had disappeared mysteriously. That was why the U.S. Fish and Wildlife Service had ordered the remnant taken into captivity—so they wouldn't *all* disappear mysteriously.

The canyon twisted back and forth a few times, then branched into tributaries that led toward the ridgetops with varying degrees of abruptness. Looking up the one farthest to the south, I glimpsed a high valley rimmed with cliffs and floored with meadows and groves.

"That looks like a nice spot," I said.

"That's the center of the BLM's Robles Negros Wilderness Study Area. Twenty thousand acres. We'd like to see it designated. There are enough roaded tributaries for the stream-flow monitoring program. But the BLM is being stuffy about it. They say they're afraid the Indian caves and petroglyphs up there will be adversely impacted if backpackers get in. They've got a helipad up there they say they need for fire crews, and there used to be a Nike base in the valley, but the road to it is all slid away and overgrown. Roads last about a year here if they aren't bulldozed out every spring. I don't know why they're being so particular about that place. There isn't even a trail up there. If they put logging roads in, that sure would be the end of the petroglyphs."

I didn't share Marshall's puzzlement about the BLM's reluctance to designate Robles Negros. I'd seen the BLM's recommendations for designating wilderness areas in central California. Out of seven areas, they'd recommended designating parts of two. It would be hard to imagine a conservation agency more grudging toward wilderness and wildlife than the Forest Service, but the BLM probably is. My deceased friend Tom Blackwell had told me about going on a field trip on some BLM land where an endangered species called the blunt-nosed leopard lizard lived. The first blunt-nosed leopard lizard he'd seen had just been run over by a truck full of BLM surveyors, who'd waved cheerfully to him as they sped past.

"Ever been up there?" I asked.

"There's no place to land a plane. From the ground, I don't know if I could even find that valley. I haven't seen all *our* land yet."

Jerry Lester was waiting by the Forest Service runway. He looked like a BLM forest ranger, a little leaner and more rugged in his tan uniform than his green-shirted Forest Service counterparts, like a cowboy who'd come in from the sun. His handshake was like emery board: maybe he roped steers as a hobby. He winked at me.

"Marshall give you a smooth ride down here?"

"Like velvet," Marshall said, defensively. Jerry looked at me inquiringly.

"No complaints," I said.

"You're either lucky or brave."

"Coastal air turbulence is a fact of life," said Marshall.

"So are cancer and heart disease."

Jerry's driving didn't confirm his self-avowed cowardice. He had us bouncing in the high-cabbed BLM pickup as he roared over fords. There didn't seem to be any bridges, and I asked why.

"Creeks stay pretty low except in winter storms," Jerry said, "then you don't use the road much."

"What do you do?"

"Stay home."

We drove to U.S. 1, then south on it for a dozen miles before we reached the road leading up Macho Creek Canyon. Crossing the rocky flats of the canyon mouth was like crossing a trampoline, but it got smoother as the road passed into the redwoods. Except for the occasional pothole, the tires whispered over a pad of roots and fallen needles. I could see what Marshall meant about the trees. They were different from the pillar-like redwoods of the north coast, squatter and shaggier. There was something almost comic about them: they reminded me of the knobby-nosed trees in the Arthur Rackham illustrations to *The Wind and the Willows.*

We drove a mile or two through the redwoods, which is a long time to drive through virgin redwoods, then emerged into a clearing I hadn't seen from the air. A little meadow dotted with fruit trees extended to the creek. At the upstream edge, a white gabled house shaded by a couple of bigleaf maples stood in a cluster of barns and sheds. Jerry pulled up in front.

"Weird place for a whorehouse, isn't it?" he said.

"How'd they get in here?" I asked.

"That was before they built U.S. 1, so they had to come from the south, or by boat. San Luis Obispo, Santa Barbara, even L.A. It was a popular resort. It was supposed to be a hunting lodge: That was what they could tell their wives. They'd spend the days after blacktails and the nights after whitetails, so to speak. There's still a bunch of antlers in the barn."

"You must be from around here."

Jerry shook his head. "I'm from Nevada, but it's good to catch up on local history when you get transferred someplace. Usually it's still going on, in one way or another."

"Let's hope not," Marshall said. "Doesn't seem to have been anybody around since Phil left."

"Who's Phil?" I asked.

"Phil's the kid we had managing the place," Marshall explained.

"I keep my eagle eye on things," said Jerry.

Marshall opened a padlock on the front door. It was about as I'd expected inside, maybe a little worse. Plywood floors showed traces of ancient carpets or linoleum; figured wallpaper had been painted over first green, then white. The pipe of an old Franklin stove ran into the wallboard ceiling without benefit of sleeve, and the stove stood on a piece of sheet metal. Yet there wasn't too much mildew or water damage, and there was electricity.

"I'm afraid Phil wasn't too handy," Marshall said. "You know how it can be after an old person has lived alone in a place for a long time. Newspapers piled in the kitchen. Junk in all the bedrooms. The kid had to spend weeks hauling to the dump. There was a whole shed piled to the ceiling with broken furniture."

"Was that why he quit?"

"Like I said, it's a lot to ask of somebody just out of school. Actually, he was married, but that didn't help. In fact, it made it worse."

"How long were they here?"

"Until June. About eight months. He has a teaching job now."

"You want me to do renovation?"

"It's kind of up to you. We'd like to have a visitor center on the first floor, and the kitchen and upstairs would be for your use. Not that there'll be that many visitors, but we'd like to have a volunteer program. They can help with the building stuff as well as the outdoors. We can't provide much of an operations budget. You'll have to depend a lot on donations and scrounging."

"Self-reliance is the name of the game out here," said Jerry heartily, if absentmindedly. He was looking out the window, although not at anything I could see.

"We got the septic tank pumped out, anyway," said Marshall.

The kitchen was a little better than the front room, with glassed cupboards, fir flooring, and a counter made from a single hardwood slab. The floor was still covered with black linoleum glue, but could be sanded and varathaned. Upstairs, the linoleum was still on the floors, but the rooms were light, with big windows. Probably chilly in winter.

I stood in a dusty shaft of sunlight and tried to get a feeling for the place. It seemed a little pinched and sour, but not ominous. I wouldn't have bought it: the walls shook every time

Marshall and Jerry moved downstairs, but that was Marshall's problem. I'd even get paid for living there, although probably not much, judging from Marshall's reticence on the subject so far.

I wondered what they were talking about downstairs. Jerry sounded more serious than he had earlier, and seemed to be telling a long story. Things tend to sound more interesting when they're just out of earshot, but if I'd eavesdropped, Jerry probably would have been talking about his firewood supply.

5

I was back in Weaverville by midnight. When you move in today's world, you really move (and when you don't move, you go backward). Marshall and I had been back inside his airplane by two P.M. We'd grabbed a bite at a McDonald's after landing in Burlingame.

"I really shouldn't be in this place," said Marshall.

"Do they get their hamburgers from the rainforest?"

"I don't think so. It's hard to keep track." We ordered chicken. "Of course, they feed this factory chicken on fishmeal that depletes the food supply of seabirds like puffins."

"Same chicken everywhere."

"In Sweden, they've outlawed factory livestock."

It was the kind of conversation that one can have a dozen times a day—if not about factory chicken, then about freeways, styrofoam, population growth, acid rain—but that soon dribbles away into weariness. We started talking about money instead. Marshall offered me the predicted small salary, but there were some benefits. At least, I wouldn't have to withhold my own taxes anymore. Pre-paying tax on money I wasn't even sure I was going to make had always been tiresome. Anyway, I think I would have taken the job without the benefits. The idea of living in a two-story house, even a moribund one, was attractive after many years in a mobile home. I was used to isolation, and if I got shack simple, there were always redwoods to talk to. (Somehow, I knew that Lewis would never talk to me, no matter how crazy I became.)

Marshall had seemed a little surprised at how readily I'd accepted his slightly apologetic offer. He didn't know that my current residence was scheduled to be towed away. Back at his office, he'd given me an application form, but evidently it was just a formality because we'd arranged for me to move onto the preserve in a week.

As I pulled into my drive, I was feeling a little more secure than I had in a year. Then my headlights reflected on something. A Honda station wagon was parked in front of my front porch. I didn't recognize it. I stopped the pickup, flicked on my high beams, and waited. The wagon appeared empty, and there was no movement in the surrounding shadows.

I suppressed an urge to turn around and drive back to San Francisco, and got the flashlight out of the glove compartment. I turned off the motor and listened, but heard only the creek. It was probably just some campers who thought they were on public land, I told myself.

I climbed out of the pickup and stepped on Lewis, who'd been waiting for me to emerge and feed him. He squawked and ran for the porch, and I dropped the flashlight, which went out. Somebody was walking up the driveway, fast. I crawled under the pickup. Perhaps the flashlight had rolled there.

"Who's there?" said a man's voice with a funny accent. It rang a bell.

"I might ask the same of you, Ricky," I replied. Ricky Karhu was the only redhead I knew with a Tagalog accent.

"George. Why are you under your truck?"

"Answer me first."

"What are you asking?" He had me there. My hand encountered the flashlight, and I turned it on the voice. Ricky had shorter hair than the last time I'd seen him, and grayer. It had been, what, eight years? We'd been at forestry school together.

Ricky had been one of a few environmental activists, and eventually had dropped out, to the mild regret of the profession, since he was a computer whiz.

The last I'd heard, Ricky was running some kind of data center at UCLA and chairing a Sierra Club committee. It was a long way from Luzon. Ricky's Filipino mother had met his Finnish father when they were working for an insurance company in San Francisco. The father had died when Ricky was four, and the mother had taken him home to the family, where he'd lived until he came to college in California. I'd never quite understood how this background had produced an obsession with conservation, but it had. While the rest of us Ranger Ricks were aspiring to bureaucracy, Ricky was getting arrested for standing in front of logging trucks.

"Are you by yourself?"

"Only me. What's the matter, George?"

I climbed out from under the pickup. I didn't feel like explaining my neuroses to Ricky just then, so I changed the subject.

"How'd you find me?"

"I remembered you were working for the Service up here. They gave me your address. How come you quit?"

"Come in and have a drink." I climbed the porch steps behind Lewis's frantic form. When I opened the door, he sped inside, and could be heard demanding food in the kitchen.

"Whoo, not much furniture," said Ricky when I turned on the lights. I was glad there was still electricity.

"I'm in the process of moving."

"Oh? Where?" Lewis came out of the kitchen and started to sharpen his claws on my leg, so I went and put some mackerel in his bowl (whose food supply did *that* deplete?) while I brought Ricky up to date.

"Coastal Lands Trust, eh?" said Ricky. "It's better than the Forest Service."

"Nice of you to say so."

"Still sarcastic all the time, George."

"What's wrong with the Coastal Lands Trust?"

"Nothing. It's a good organization, as far as it goes."

"What eight-thousand-acre stand of virgin redwoods have you saved lately, Ricky?"

"They should have saved it in 1925, when condors still nested there."

"The Coastal Lands Trust didn't exist in 1925."

"They exist now, but condors are still disappearing."

"You want them to buy southern California?"

"They could buy more of it if they weren't riding around in airplanes, George."

"Or hiring mercenaries like me, right? Anyway, you didn't hitchhike up here. Honda looks pretty new. Did you come up just to guilt-trip me some more?"

Ricky sat down on the floor and leaned against the wall. He had wrinkles that I didn't remember. He looked tired.

"No. I came to get away from condors for a little while. Do a little hiking. Relax."

"It sounds like there won't be any condors to get away from pretty soon, except in zoos."

"Those are the ones I need to get away from, George, the ones in zoos."

"You've been working in a zoo?"

"I've been trying to get your friends from putting all the condors in zoos."

"*My* friends?"

"Forest Service, Fish and Wildlife Service, National Audubon Society . . ."

"*Those* friends."

"Why'd you quit the Forest Service, anyway?"

"Didn't pay enough."

"Ha ha, George." Ricky looked at me. "I thought you used to have blond hair?"

"I do."

"Looks kind of brownish gray now."

"Silver threads among the gold, Ricky."

I looked in the refrigerator and found some eggs and bread. I'd picked up milk, butter, and a bottle of Zinfandel on the drive up. I'd decided not to buy gin for a while. Ricky brought some artichokes and potatoes from his car, and we had a potato omelette and steamed artichokes.

Afterward, we sat on the porch and looked at the night sky. There were a lot of falling stars. Lewis had taken a liking to Ricky, and sprawled on his lap while Ricky flattered him in Tagalog.

"What are you telling him?" I asked.

"That he's an old tiger."

"Anyway," I said, getting in a parting shot, "they didn't put all the condors in zoos. Eight of them just disappeared, right? Just flew away and never came back."

"How do you know they aren't in zoos?" Ricky scratched Lewis so hard the cat opened his eyes and grunted.

"What zoos?"

Ricky opened his mouth, then closed it. "Who knows, George."

I went to bed and dreamed I was in the basement of drug dealer Alec Rice's warehouse again. Alec had taken me there once to show me his contraband collection of rare and endangered animals and to generally confuse and intimidate me. This time, Alec wasn't there, and the cages were empty.

I saw a closed door, and realized that there was a part of the basement I hadn't entered before. I knew I should go tell the police about it, and let them open it, but I moved toward it anyway. The door opened into a stone vault that I realized was Alec's tomb: A sarcophagus stood in the corner. I approached, feeling an irrational desire to open it, but before I reached the sarcophagus I heard a sound behind me.

I awoke to the rattle of rain on the mobile home's aluminum windows. I felt relief, then alarm as someone walked across the kitchen. I remembered Ricky. There was a knock on the bedroom door.

"George? I've got to take off."

"Already? Wait a minute." I got out of bed and started to get dressed.

"I've got to get home tonight," Ricky said when I emerged from the bedroom. "I've got a family now."

"Kids?"

"Two. Didn't you get married?"

"Yeah. She's back east now."

"Thanks for the hospitality."

"Such as it was. You get rained on?"

"I slept on your porch."

"Summer's over."

"Keep in touch, George. You'll almost be a southern California now."

"Geez."

After Ricky drove away, I ate some cereal and sat on the porch. Towhees and sparrows scratched for weed seeds in the remains of the garden. I felt like the day, overcast. It didn't look as though a big storm was coming, but it didn't promise to clear up right away. A week seemed a long time to hang around. I felt like getting on a plane to someplace. I took a walk up the creek instead.

6

Lewis didn't make moving any easier. I had to hide my suitcases until the last moment so he wouldn't disappear. Lewis dislikes moving so much that he disappears not only on departure but on arrival. When my wife and I had first brought him to Weaverville, he ran away for two months. He finally showed up the day the fall rains started, with a tapeworm as big as the Ritz. Giving Lewis tapeworm pills had been like going nine rounds on the mat with the Masked Avenger.

I have to sympathize with Lewis because he does get carsick on winding mountain roads. I'd sympathize more if he didn't make such a ruckus in the process that I can't go over thirty miles an hour. If I go faster for more than a few minutes, Lewis whines, moans, and gives an impression of having swallowed a live bullfrog. This is unnerving when a fully loaded logging truck going sixty-five is passing me on a curve. *Then* he throws up.

You'd have thought he'd jump for joy out of the pickup cab when we finally pulled up in front of old Mr. Roberts's house, but as usual he had to be coaxed out, wide-eyed, ever distrustful of mobility. He headed for the gloomiest shed to have a sulk, a luxury I envied. I'd forgotten, as one always does after living in the same place a few years, how insanely complicated it was going to be to equip a new home with toilet paper, onions, picture hangers, candles, soap, matches, aspirin . . .

I moved in my one armchair and my boxes of kitchen paraphernalia, fixed a cup of tea, and sat down. It was midafternoon: I'd gotten an early start. The weather had turned warm again, and the sunny living room had a drowsy smell. Yellowjackets buzzed and banged their heads against the windows.

I was getting ready to fall asleep when I heard a car. I wondered where the road went after it passed the house, if anywhere. I hadn't thought to ask Marshall Mitchell. The car didn't go past: it pulled up in front of the house. I went to the door, thinking it might be Jerry Lester. A couple of young men I'd never seen were getting out of a white van. They wore polo shirts and jeans, but somehow the effect wasn't casual. I wondered if they were going to try to sell me insurance.

"Hi," said the driver, who was blond and tallish. He had a slight Australian accent. "Looks like you've only just arrived." I didn't know what to say. He saw my hesitation, and smoothly changed from breezy-familiar to serious-polite. "I'm being forward, aren't I? I'm Peter Eliott, and this is Henry Green." He indicated his companion, who was short and looked Mediterranean despite the Anglo name.

I introduced myself and shook their hands. I asked Peter what I could do for him.

"I was going to ask the same of you," he replied. "Didn't Phil mention us?"

"Phil?"

"Phil Tefler. Your predecessor."

"My predecessor?" Peter wagged his head slightly at my obtuseness, but didn't stop smiling. "Oh, that Phil . . . They didn't tell me his last name."

"You never talked to him?"

"No."

"Well, we told him to let whoever was coming along after him know that we're here to help. We're probably some of your nearest neighbors, down south along the highway. We'll be glad to supply some muscle when you need it. We know how you depend on volunteer help."

"Well, gee, thanks."

"We think it's great what you're doing here. Henry and I were on our way to Monterey, and we thought we'd just stop in and introduce ourselves, see if you wanted help moving in or anything."

I was wondering who "we" were, but I couldn't think how to ask without seeming rude. I didn't much want loquacious Peter and silent Henry moving my household effects even if they were my neighbors. I made affable noises, but didn't invite them in. Peter quickly picked up on this.

"You don't want strangers bothering you at a time like this," he said.

"No bother."

"But seriously, we would like to help. I know you're going to do wonderful things here. Just give a ring and my buddies and I will shoulder pick and shovel and march right over."

I took the business card he proferred. It said simply "Aliso House" with Peter's name and a phone number. The talk of buddies and marching rang a bell. It sounded like one of those cult houses in the woods you hear about, where they take college kids off the streets and brainwash them. But I'd never heard of them doing volunteer work.

"And drop in when you get a chance," Peter continued. "We'll give you a good dinner. We're three miles south on the highway, you can't miss us."

I didn't miss them when they left. Still, I thought it might be nice to have my volunteer needs taken care of so conveniently, even if by slave labor. If problems developed, I could always pass the buck on to Marshall Mitchell. It wouldn't be like when I was hiring backwoods hippies to plant trees for me.

It was only four P.M. but the sun was at the redwood tops. I could see the winter nights would be long. I moved the rest of the stuff out of the pickup, almost wishing I'd accepted Peter's help, at least in getting my monastic single bed up the stairs. The box springs weren't a problem, but the mattress clung to every step going up the stairs, as though it had heard about the house's unchaste history.

I turned on the water heater and took my first bath and ate my first meal. The only noise I didn't make was the wasps banging on the windows, and even they stopped after sunset. I sat looking out the kitchen window as bats replaced robins over the meadow. When it was almost dark, a scratching at the door made me jump. I'd expected Lewis to spend the first night out, but he'd decided I was the only game in town.

I paused to look out the door for a moment after I let Lewis in. I could hear the creek. Abruptly, there was a thumping roar, and a big military helicopter passed over the house, heading southeast. It was lit up like a Christmas tree, but it moved too fast for me to see much except flash and glare.

It was startling, but not surprising considering the proximity of Fort Ord and Hunter-Ligget. I've heard they've designed helicopters so you can't hear them until they're right on top of you.

7

Marshall Mitchell had never heard of Aliso House, but he thought a built-in volunteer supply for the preserve might be nice. He was diplomatically vague on the subject of cults, as long as they didn't proselytize on the preserve. If I wanted, I could check up on them. Then he asked me when I thought a visitor center might be ready. The Trust wanted to dedicate the preserve formally by the end of the decade. I became diplomatically vague, and the phone conversation trailed off into mutual optimism.

Jerry Lester was more talkative about my unexpected visitors. He'd met them.

"They're not so bad," he said, "not as bad as some people think."

"Some people?"

"Mm."

"Are there stories about them?"

"Oh, sure. There's always stories about a bunch like that. You know, brainwashing, mind control. Hell, they never bothered me. Gave me a hand with my truck once."

"Why do they want to volunteer? I thought groups like that just wanted to get people to work for *them,* sell flowers on the street and all."

"I don't know, George. Maybe they want to bring you into the fold. Marry you off to a nice cult gal."

"Did whatsisname say anything about them?"

"Phil Tefler? He was happy for all the help he could get."

"What'd they do?" I asked. Jerry pointed at the roof, which had new asphalt shingles on it. "They put that on?"

"Most of it."

Jerry himself didn't show much eagerness to donate labor. He visited with the casual, frank nosiness of the true countryman, and probably would have hung around as long as he wanted even if I'd rudely ignored him. I asked him in for coffee, of course.

"You've got your work cut out for you here," he said, nodding at the living room. "They'll come in handy."

"Not if I have to join up."

"Oh, hell, you're old enough to think for yourself."

I got off the subject, and asked Jerry how long he'd been in the area. He thought a moment.

"Must be five years now. Time flies."

"You were in Nevada before?"

"Yep. Down by the Pahrump Valley." He pronounced it "pay rump."

"Must have been a change."

"You can say that. You never know what's gonna come out of the woodwork around here."

"California flakes."

"There's plenty nuts in Nevada too, but the landscape spreads 'em out, like. At least you can see them coming through the creosote bush. All these big trees keep you guessing."

"Like what?"

"It makes the people down at the house seem pretty normal, I'll tell you. Day before yesterday there was a guy riding one of those big grown-up tricycles around the creekbed, ass over elbow, naked as a jaybird. Flipped his wick about three feet in the air ever'time he hit a rock. Couple of little kids sitting on a boulder watching him."

"This was on the preserve?"

"It was down toward the highway. I don't know if your line is down that far."

"What did you do?"

"I waved," Jerry said. "Might be his property for all I know. I can only boss people on BLM land."

"What about the kids?"

"Probably his kids. I phoned Bill Kouts, the deputy, about it, but by the time he got by there, they were gone."

"What does BLM do around here, anyway?" I asked.

"You're looking at it. Got a few mining claims, grazing allotments."

"Logging?"

"There's some good pine and cedar along the crest, but it's isolated. It's just watershed for now."

"Marshall Mitchell doesn't think there should be *any* logging in the watershed." Marshall hadn't actually said that, but I figured I might as well use the authority I'd been granted.

"Well, there probably won't be, for now. Those trees up there'd make some awful nice houses, though."

"So would these trees down here."

"As long as Marshall owns them, he can do what he wants with them. We've got to do what the public wants, and they want to live in nice houses."

"How about that roadless area up there, that valley?"

"What about it? Robles Negros?"

"Think they should designate it?"

"Hell, that place. What they ought to do with that place is get the pigs out of it. Looks like somebody took a roto-tiller to it. Might as well pitch your tent in a barnyard. Grunt and squeal all night long. I've seen tuskers up there must weigh a quarter ton. Don't even back up when you yell at them, just bat those long eyelashes at you. I'd hate to think what might happen if some young couple with a child or a dog backpacked in there. I carry a sidearm when I go up there, which isn't often."

"Are they bad down here too?"

"They're bad everywhere. But they like those high valleys best. It's the acorns. There's not much for them to eat in the redwoods, except the odd fawn or quail brood. Or cat."

Lewis, who had just come down from a nap on my bed, sniffed Jerry's pant leg politely, then went and ate some dry food. I thought of asking Jerry why BLM had put a forester in charge of a place where they had no plans to log, or what kind of forestry he'd been practicing in the Nevada creosote bush flats. But I was afraid of being rude, and reluctant to lead the conversation around to my own forestry background.

"Looks pretty from the air, anyway," I said, continuing my Robles Negros probe.

"In the daytime."

"Don't suppose I'll ever have time to get up there," I sighed, but Jerry wasn't offering any sympathy.

"If you're going to get any projects going on this place," he said, "you better do it before the storms start."

8

I thought Jerry was being alarmist about the weather. It was early October: the big storms wouldn't come until November, maybe January. I pottered for a few weeks, furnishing my rooms, walking the preserve boundaries, cleaning up trash that had accumulated along the road during the summer, and politely banishing deer hunters and unauthorized campers.

A bobcat appeared in the meadow by the house one day, to Lewis's alarm, and I saw mink and otter farther up the creek. I spent a lot of time gawking at the trees. Some of the bays, tanoaks, golden chinquapins, and live oaks were nearly as big around as redwoods. There was a species I hadn't encountered before, California torreya, which resembles a miniature redwood except that it has giant needles and plum-sized green fruitlike coverings on its seeds. An ancient, almost extinct species, it gave the redwood forest an even hoarier aspect than usual.

I was beginning to have as good a time as I'd once thought I'd have as a forester. I was actually getting paid for protecting trees. I dug a little garden in some neglected beds by the house, and put in radishes, lettuces, and brassicas. I found a box of bulbs in a shed, and divided and planted them. I had no idea what they were, but I looked forward to finding out. When a Berkeley graduate student doing a thesis on tree-fungus interactions showed up, I took him around in a comfortably proprietary way.

Reality intruded soon enough. The editor of the Trust newsletter phoned to find out my planned activities for the fall issue. I couldn't tell her there weren't any, so I improvised. I'd been thinking that the downstairs walls could be made presentable if the old paper was scraped off and they were retaped and repainted. It was the kind of labor-intensive, capital-retentive project to convince Marshall he'd hired the right man. I dictated a call for volunteers and tools on a weekend in mid-November.

This satisfied the editor, along with a promise of some nature programs for the winter issue.

Getting the materials for my volunteer painting bee took up the next couple of weeks. I got back from San Jose with a pickup load of off-white latex and taping mud the night before it began. I'd had a half-dozen calls about my newsletter announcement from places like Santa Cruz and Carmel. They sounded like college students and retired people—nice, but not rock-solid dependable. I'd heard nothing from Aliso House, and couldn't decide whether to be relieved.

I needn't have worried. Peter Eliott's white van pulled up in front of the house at eight the next morning, and disgorged not only Peter and Henry but six more well-scrubbed young people equipped with brushes, rollers, scrapers, and paint-spotted clothes that appeared newly washed despite their raggedness. They didn't chant or march in step; they acted normal aside from apparent pleasure at being up early to do a dirty job without pay. They took over scraping and soaking the old paper from the walls so thoroughly that the ordinary volunteers who straggled in had to be given marginal tasks like sweeping and fixing window sashes.

Some of Peter's people surprised me. One man had a gray beard, and the muscles of a 21-year-old surfer. I found myself working next to a woman who could easily have appeared in the pages of *Vogue.*

"Hello," she said, giving me a knee-liquefying smile. "I'm Jill." She had a slight accent that seemed odd with the nursery-rhyme name. I asked about it, enticed to converse even if her heart did belong to the Great Leader. "It's from a Slovakian name," she explained, "hard to pronounce."

"You're from Czechoslovakia?"

"When I was little." That made sense. A refugee from Prague, 1968. Peter's cult was known for its anticommunism. Just the thing for a fanatically religious young immigrant. It seemed pretty deep water, and I edged away from her and took out my energies on a sticky patch of wallpaper. The stout young woman on that side merely nodded at me and kept scraping.

We had the wallpaper off by noon, and the tape and first mud coats on by late afternoon. Peter renewed his invitation to dinner at Aliso House, but I had an excuse. Some of the ordinary volunteers were camping on the preserve so they could help paint the next day.

"Tomorrow night then," Peter insisted. "You really must see our gardens. We grow our own produce. We'll give you some. It's all grown without chemicals."

"An offer I can't refuse." I was feeling cooperative. Merely cleaning off the walls would have taken the weekend if not for Aliso House efficiency. When we stopped work, I supplied beer and coffee while Peter's people drank an herb tea they'd brought. They mingled and chatted with the other volunteers unremarkably except for one thing I noticed. They were never in odd numbers. I never saw a cult person alone, which was to be expected given their reputation for togetherness. What was odd was that I never saw three of them together, or five, or seven. It was always two, four, six, eight—who do we appreciate. Life as a cheerleading squad.

I was still glad when they showed up again at eight sharp Sunday morning. The students were still in their tent, having spent much of the night talking philosophy under my bedroom window, and the retired couple were taking a bird walk. I'd have expected Peter's people to spend the morning praying, but they'd already gotten that out of the way, apparently. We had the rest of the mud and a primer coat on by lunchtime. When the students left in late afternoon, Peter's people were putting on the final touches, doing woodwork, and scraping paint spots off the windows.

"See you at seven, George," Peter reminded me as they trooped out into the sunset. The retired couple were standing by their car as the white van disappeared up the road.

"They're culties, aren't they?" said the man, who'd been a newspaper editor in Bakersfield before retiring to Carmel.

"Something like that."

"Our grandaughter ran off with a bunch like that. My daughter tells me they had her out selling jewelry on the street. Had to bring in a cash quota every day to get her room and board. Kind of odd so see them working for someone other than the Great Leader." He stopped, evidently wanting an explanation.

"It seems strange to me too, but they haven't caused any trouble. Guess they're trying to be good neighbors." It sounded weak, and I shrugged. He looked a little embarrassed.

"They did a lot of work," he said.

"About a month's worth if I was doing it alone."

The man's white-haired wife looked at her watch. She was afraid of missing *Masterpiece Theatre*.

"Do you have a TV here?" she asked.

"No."

"Maybe you should get one of those satellite disks. Don't you think you'll get lonely here?"

"Maybe he likes it without the box," the man said.

"Purify my brain," I said.

"Don't let it get *too* pure," she said. I laughed. The old man started to get in the car, then turned to me and raised his eyebrows.

"Beware of Geeks bearing gifts," he said.

"Ted!" His wife slapped him on the shoulder, then waved at me, and they drove away.

9

Aliso House was a gingerbread Victorian on a headland, with big date palms in front. It was nearly dark when I got there, so I couldn't see much, but I could hear surf pounding on rocks. Not a good spot for car trouble on a stormy night, although the door was answered not by a baleful butler but by Jill, the beauteous Slovakian. She'd put her hair up and changed to a thin, if modest, cotton dress. The stout woman from the painting bee also answered.

"Hey, here's George!" cried the stout woman, with surprising enthusiasm. About a dozen people behind them gave glad cries of welcome. Peter Eliott grabbed me by the shoulder and the stout oak door closed behind me.

"Let's give George a warm welcome," cried Peter. For five minutes, I was barraged with friendliness—glad cries, firm handshakes, happy smiles. It was very strange. Then the crowd disappeared as quickly as it had formed, leaving me with Peter, Henry, Jill, and the stout woman, whose name was Cathy.

"Take your shoes off and get comfortable," said Peter. An alcove off the hall was full of neatly aligned shoes. I did as I was told, and aligned my shoes neatly with the others.

"Come on," said Peter, "let's go hang around until they get dinner ready." They led me into a big room, once a ballroom judging from the high ceiling. Thick carpeting muffled sound, and the room contained two suites of furniture. A group in animated discussion occupied one of the suites. There were seven of them. Six turned and smiled brightly at us, but the seventh, a tall, blunt-featured woman, didn't. I wondered if I looked as uncomfortable as she did.

Peter didn't introduce me to the gang of six, despite the welcoming smiles. He led us to the other suite. He motioned me to the seat of honor on a couch, but I sidestepped and sat in an armchair instead. Peter sat at the end of the couch nearest me. The others arranged themselves tightly around us: Cathy on the floor, Henry on the arm of the couch, Jill on the couch beside Peter.

"We're not afraid of physical closeness here," said Cathy. "Hope that doesn't bother you."

"How long have you been living alone, George?" asked Peter. The way he said it, friendly concern with just a hint of disdain, made we want to justify myself. I fought the urge.

"Quite a while," I said.

"Great," said Peter, "but you never get lonely?"

"The Lord says it's a shame for a man to live alone," said Henry. It was the first thing I'd heard him say. The others ignored him.

"I suppose everyone gets lonely at times," I said.

"I never do, not anymore," said Jill.

"Praise to Him," said Cathy. Peter smiled as parents do when children say cute, slightly naughty things in front of stuffy visitors. "Can I get you a drink?"

"Could I have a martini?" I said.

"We have soft drinks," Cathy replied.

"I used to drink ten martinis a day," said Henry.

"Henry hasn't had a drink in four years," said Jill.

"Praise to Him," said Cathy.

"Is it too late to look at the gardens?" I said.

"Oh, no," said Peter. "Hey, everybody," he cried, "let's go show George the gardens!"

A crowd formed again, a slightly smaller one this time. We swept down a staircase into a large, ground-floor greenhouse with floors swept and scrubbed so obsessively that there was no problem with stocking feet. The night was cool, and there was a hiss of steam heating, and condensation on the windows. The loamy air felt tropical, and I imagined there once had been all manner of exotic greenery, orchids and tree ferns. Now it was severely functional—tomato plants, cucumber vines, brassica seedlings. Some dwarf fruit trees at the far end were the only faintly shaggy note.

"Fresh produce, year-round," said Peter. He flipped a wall switch, flooding a large yard outside with orange fluorescence. Row after row of raised beds marched to a chain link fence topped with stainless steel barbed wire.

"I guess you don't have a deer problem," I said.

"Not any more," said Peter.

"Gophers?"

"No gophers either," said Peter.

"How do you get rid of them?"

"Poisoned peanuts."

"I thought you said this was organic?"

"It is," said Peter. "We don't use chemicals on the food we eat."

"And God said have dominion over every living thing that moveth upon the earth," said Henry.

"All these vegetables are making me hungry," said Cathy. "It's time to eat."

The dining room was almost as large as the ballroom, and arranged like a monastery refectory, with a head table perpendicular to several rows of lower ones. The blunt-featured woman and I got to sit at the head table, though not next to each other. Jill sat between us. The food looked good, roast chicken and lots of vegetables, but first we had to sit through a twenty-minute grace. Peter said some of it, then one of the gang of six said more. They both mentioned me and somebody named Phyllis, evidently the blunt-featured woman, hoping that this sustenance grown with love would bring their guests closer to the community. Everybody kept their heads deeply bowed and eyes tightly shut the whole time, so that nobody noticed when I got tired of bowing and looked around, except the blunt-featured woman. She looked away when our eyes met. After grace, they sang a kind of nursery rhyme that I didn't understand, and finally passed the platters.

Conversation languished while we stuffed our faces. The only people near me who weren't working on seconds within ten minutes were Jill and Phyllis. Given Jill's hearty good looks, this surprised me.

"You on a diet?" I asked.

"We don't do that," Jill answered.

"Do you fast?"

"That's not the same thing."

"I suppose it isn't. Not feeling well?"

"I'm a little tired." She fixed me with another dazzling smile, but I was ready this time. I smiled back, and looked her in the eye. I'd expected a blankness behind the studied warmth, but I thought I saw something else, a hint of irony. She turned away and ate a string bean.

I realized that Peter was talking to me, so I smiled and nodded. He looked a little surprised.

"Wonderful," he said.

"Excuse me?"

"What?"

"I'm sorry, I didn't hear you," I confessed. "What were you saying?"

"I was inviting you to our retreat next weekend."

"Oh, well. Actually, I've got a group coming from San Francisco next weekend." I glanced at Phyllis, who was staring at her plate with an expression of bitter amusement.

"Another time, perhaps," said Peter.

There was to be a community sing after dinner. I pled fatigue, but they assumed I'd participate anyway, so I told them I despised community sings, which was true. Peter, Henry, and I sat in the dining room while heavenly voices drifted in from the ballroom. I told them I had to be going, but they didn't get up to show me the door. Eventually I stood up and started in that direction myself. Peter and Henry followed, one on each side.

As we neared the shoe alcove, I heard a thump, and then an angry voice—Phyllis's.

"Give me my shoes!" Somebody murmured in reply. Another thump ensued. "Give me my goddamn shoes!"

Phyllis stood in the alcove with her back against the wall. Jill and Cathy faced her across a pile of shoes, which Phyllis evidently had been throwing to the floor. None of them looked at us, and Peter ignored them.

"Which ones are yours?" he said to me. I pointed to my shoes, as yet unthrown, and he handed them to me. I put them on.

"Tell them to give me my shoes," said Phyllis, her voice carrying tensely above the singing.

"We'll find your shoes, Phyllis," said Cathy. "Relax. It's too late to go to Monterey now."

"No way!" cried Phyllis, and picked up another shoe. Jill made a stooping gesture, as though to restrain her.

"Maybe I could give her a ride," I said, without much conviction. It was a long way to Monterey, and putting crazed Phyllis up at the preserve for the night wasn't appealing. Nobody responded. We stood until Phyllis cocked her arm for another throw, then Peter gave me a reassuring look and edged me toward the door.

"Is she all right?"

"Oh, sure. She's a good friend. Just a little emotional," Peter replied. We stood under their anti-burglar driveway light. The house looked unreal in its lime-green glare. Peter made affable noises and closed the door. I got into the pickup, but I couldn't bring myself to drive away.

Ten minutes later, the door flew open and Phyllis stumbled out and began hobbling down the drive. She still didn't have her shoes. Peter stood in the doorway a minute, then closed it. I got out of the pickup and walked after Phyllis. She spun around at me, looking frightened.

"Are you alright? Do you need a place to stay?" I said. She just stared at me.

She started away again, teetering on the rough gravel. It was going to be a relatively cold night. I repeated my offer of a ride to Monterey. She began to fade into the shadows.

"Come on, you can't stay out on a night like this." I might have been talking to myself. I got in the pickup and drove after her, but she had disappeared, evidently hiding in the bushes. "Hey, come on, I won't hurt you." I didn't sound convincing. The only reply came from a dying cricket. I called a few more times. Even the cricket shut up. I drove away.

When I got home, I tried calling the sheriff. A woman dispatcher said the deputy would get back to me. When he did, he sounded as though he was in orbit. I wondered if he had a car phone. It was the same Deputy Kouts who'd investigated the case of the nude tricyclist. He took the barefoot cultie in stride.

"I'll drive by there and see if I can find anybody," he said, "but there's not much I can do if she doesn't make a complaint."

"Couldn't you take her in for vagrancy or something?" The Deputy seemed unenthusiastic about the suggestion.

"I'll talk to her if I see her," he said.

"I mean, they stole her shoes."

"Did you see them steal them?"

"She walked away from there without any shoes."

"Are you sure she owned shoes?"

"Come on."

"There are some strange people around here, Mr. Kilgore."

10

I didn't hear from Aliso House for a couple of months. I wondered if Phyllis had embarrassed them. When I asked Deputy Kouts about her, he said he'd been unable to locate anyone of that description. At Aliso House, they'd told him they'd never seen her before she'd shown up at their door that day. They didn't know anything about shoes. I told Kouts that Peter had called her "a good friend."

"Well," Kouts had said. The telephone version of a shrug.

I was too busy to worry about it. Marshall was so pleased with the downstairs that he decided I could have the visitor center open by summer. This involved lots of driving to San Francisco and talking on the telephone. My busyness didn't deter the newsletter from harassing me about a winter nature program. I offered them a late February owl walk, doubting that many people would come to a remote place just to stumble around in the dark. The editor liked it.

"There are spotted owls out there," she said. There probably were, although I hadn't seen one. I told her I'd need a cassette player and tapes to call them, which dampened her enthusiasm. She said she'd get back to me. She listed the walk in the newsletter anyway.

I forgot about it until I started getting calls in mid-February. I got so many calls that I panicked and called the newsletter about the cassette player. They had one, but I had to go get it, and buy a tape of owl calls. Then I had to try the tape on the local owls. I knew they were around because I'd been hearing great horned and screech owls, but I wondered if any self-respecting owl would answer my tape. An adenoidal voice introduced each call at length. The calls sounded like they came from inside a metal garbage can.

The local owls were even less sophisticated than me. A great horned appeared almost immediately after I played the tape, eyes aglow in my flashlight beam. It was a dozen feet away, a huge bird, ready to repel intruders. I hastened to show I wasn't an owl, just kidding. It fluttered away like an enormous moth.

The other calls got no response, not surprisingly, since the "spotted owl" sounded like a Pekingese being tortured in a garbage can and the "long-eared owl" sounded like its mistress being garroted in one. It occurred to me that I might have gotten more response if I'd gone farther from the great horned owl, since the species eats other owls, but it was a wet night. Anyway, I had the great horned.

On the night of the walk, the great horned proved a little too reliable. It showed up within seconds after the walk began. Since some of the group had driven from the Bay Area, I couldn't just send them home after that. I didn't particularly want to anyway. A contingent from Aliso House included Jill, and I'd been thinking about Jill during the past two months as I'd spent my evenings listening to rain rattling the stovepipe flashings. The prim, cultie actuality of her didn't live up to my thoughts, but I still had trouble keeping my eyes off her.

She was standing next to me when the great horned came in. She gasped and grabbed my arm.

"It's like a spirit!" she said. Cathy glanced at us, and Jill withdrew her hand.

"It's just a bird," Cathy said.

"They say owls wait outside where people are dying, waiting to catch their souls," Jill said.

"Superstition," Cathy replied, in a cautionary tone.

"When I was little, our neighbor died, and an owl sat on the electric wires outside his house all night. A white owl with a monkey face."

"A barn owl," I said.

"This isn't the old country," Cathy said.

"There are strange things here, too," said Jill.

"Like what?" I asked.

"I've heard there are giant birds that live in these mountains. Like the ones in the Arabian Nights."

"You mean condors?"

"What are they like?" Jill asked.

Cathy drew a blank too.

"You've never heard of condors?"

"I thought they lived in South America," Cathy said.

"They don't live here anymore, anyway. There's only a few left in the wild, and they're in Ventura County way south of here."

"What do you mean?" said Jill.

"The giant birds couldn't survive near civilization, so most of them have been put in the zoos in San Diego and Los Angeles. They're going to put the others in the zoo pretty soon."

"But I heard people have seen them," said Jill.

"What people?" I asked.

Jill shrugged.

"Probably somebody saw a turkey vulture and thought it was a condor," said a man in rain pants.

"Well, I think there are strange things in these mountains," Jill insisted, with the stubborness of ignorance. "Have you seen every part of them?"

"I bet there aren't many who've seen every part of these mountains, even today," said the man in rain pants.

"I've heard there is a valley that has no bottom, where nobody has ever been," said Jill.

"How can a valley have no bottom?" said Cathy. She was evidently getting tired of the discussion, as were some of the other owl-walkers. I led them down the road to look for spotted owls. I walked about a mile before I played the tape. There wasn't a peep in response. I walked another half mile. Same lack of response. There wasn't even the sound of rain dripping on leaves as there would have been in a deciduous forest. The redwoods seemed disdainful of my ludicrous racket. The night felt like the universe before the Big Bang.

"It's like another world," Jill whispered. Cathy stirred impatiently beside her. I played the tape again. This time, there was a response up canyon with a faint similarity to the tape.

"Spotted owl?" said the man in rain pants.

"Might be a screech," said a woman in a red slicker.

Another call ended the disagreement. We all started, because it came from behind us, and sounded close. Flashlight beams went up and down, around and around, but we saw nothing except redwood branches and a few tiny moths.

"It's too high up to see," said the woman. It did sound high up. My neck was stiff from craning. I looked down, and saw two reddish eyes glowing at me from twenty feet away. The spotted owl had been in a small maple at eye level the whole time. I felt a moment of disorientation—I wasn't shining my flashlight on the owl and eyes don't glow by themselves—then I realized that Jill had her flashlight on the owl. She was standing a dozen feet from it. The round-headed, black-eyed bird didn't look ferocious like the great horned owl, but it did look spooky.

The walkers became aware of the owl, and turned their lights on it, making a pale dome of light. The owl blinked. Jill glanced back at us, and the owl flew away, so swiftly I barely saw it open its wings.

"That's something you won't see in many places anymore," said the man in rain pants.

"Why?" said Cathy.

"They only live in old-growth forest like this, and we've cut most of it down."

"How did you see it?" asked the argumentative woman in red to Jill, who was coming back through the soggy undergrowth. Jill didn't seem to hear, and there was an awkward silence until she realized we were waiting for her to answer. She smiled.

"Yes?"

"You must have a good ear," said the woman.

"Good ear?"

"Owls are ventriloquists. They throw their voices."

"Let's try the long-eared," I said, "then call it a night." I inflicted the dying dowager on the redwoods, but she fooled nobody. We trooped back to headquarters, where I offered hot cocoa and a spiel about the preserve, spiced with a few details about its checkered past. I'd found a broken spitoon and a few fragments of what might have been whalebone corsets and rubber syringes while cleaning out a shed. My visitors seemed amused at these relics, except the culties, who gave each other knowing looks.

Jill approached me afterward, with Cathy in tow. Jill looked nice: she had the kind of translucent skin that goes with chill and damp.

"I like this watching birds," she said.

"Good," I replied. "You must have spent some time in the woods."

"Why?"

"You move very quietly," I said. "You didn't scare the owl away."

"Just lucky." She smiled. "You should have another walk. We can go to this valley nobody has seen." Cathy looked up at the ceiling and shook her head slightly.

"That would be interesting," I said.

"Thank you," Jill said, offering me her hand in a surprisingly enthusiastic shake. Cathy lingered as Jill turned and started for the door, which surprised me.

"So," I said, "you like owls?" Cathy shrugged. "What was Jill doing before she joined you?"

"She was in a halfway house in Santa Cruz."

"Halfway house?"

"Jill was in Napa for awhile." There's a state asylum in Napa. "She lost her family when the Russians went into Czechslovakia."

11

I led another owl walk in March. The spotted owl didn't show, although a pygmy owl did. Jill didn't show either, which was disappointing and a little surprising, given her avowed enthusiasm for birding, but probably just as well. A religious fanatic with mental problems wasn't girlfriend material, even if she was the only material in the vicinity. I should have been frequenting Monterey singles bars on weekends, but there always seemed to be stuff to do in the preserve. Women in bars seemed too young or too old. Women in general were beginning to seem too young or too old.

Marshall decided I was making such good progress on the visitor center that by summer I'd be able to do a trail system too. This seemed easier than house renovation until I started thinking about all the deadfalls, gullies, swamps, and creek crossings. I showed Marshall the problems when he visited at the end of March, but he was his usual optimistic self.

"This is nothing compared to Oxtail Marsh," he said. "We had to build a three-mile boardwalk."

"Hell," said Jerry Lester, "a little flat valley like this. The environmental groups are after us to put in a trail to Robles Negros. Four thousand feet up, riprapped switchbacks through chaparral. No way."

"Why don't you just put it on that old Nike road," I said. I was getting a little tired of Jerry's help. He seemed to appear with questions and advice every time I went anywhere or did anything, except during programs or volunteer work sessions when I could have used him. He was the most ubiquitous ranger type I'd met. This had seemed alright in the beginning, when I'd figured I could use all the help I could get. But Jerry's advice usually left me feeling baffled. It actually took longer for me to accomplish things than if I'd faced them alone. My reduced enthusiasm for the advice didn't seem to discourage him, though. Sometimes I wondered how much Jerry's help had contributed to my predecessor's failure.

"That old road is plumb gone," Jerry replied serenely. "Most of it fell down in the '81 floods, and the rest is brushed in."

"It won't be hard to throw a loop a little way up the side of the canyon, through some of the redwoods, and around to the creek," said Marshall. I realized he was talking about the preserve, not Robles Negros. "Get those Aliso House people to help you. Take a couple of days."

"I don't know about them," I said. I told Marshall about Phyllis. I'd already told Jerry about it, and he'd seemed uninterested. This time he seemed interested.

"Just vanished into thin air," he said. "Weird people around here."

"You think they stole her shoes?" Marshall asked.

"Maybe she didn't have any," said Jerry.

"She looked pretty normal," I said, perhaps exaggerating.

"Well, don't work with them if you don't want to," said Marshall. "We don't want to get mixed up in anything."

"They did get a lot done," I said, looking at Jerry.

"Your call, George," said Marshall.

I actually didn't have that much control over the situation, short of phoning Peter Eliott and telling him to keep away. I put a notice in the spring newsletter for an April trail-building party and waited for people to show up.

When the day came, I got pretty much what I had for the wallboard weekend—college students, retirees, the odd yuppie, and a white van of squeaky-clean culties. Peter and Henry didn't come, but Jill and Cathy did. Jill shook hands again. She'd had a haircut and maybe put on some weight, but she still looked good. She'd evidently been working in their garden; she was tanned. Cathy was too, and slimmer. She gave me a knowing, not unfriendly look.

"See the wildflowers!" Jill cried. There were a lot of trillium, starflower, houndstongue, and milkmaids scattered around. "Won't you destroy too many when we make this trail?"

"I've routed it around the rare ones."

"Only rare flowers have a right to life?" Jill inquired innocently. Cathy made an indulging naughty-child smirk. I put them to work hauling gravel in a wheelbarrow.

I used a chain saw to clear saplings and shrubs from the way I'd laid out with my little plastic ribbons. It was nice to be tying ribbons for a foot trail instead of a logging road or timber sale. I was a little ahead of the rest, making sure some calypso orchids wouldn't get trampled, when one of the college kids came out of the trees to one side.

"Do you do tours for school kids?" he asked.

"When this gets finished."

"Maybe you should do something about this, then. Might upset little kids."

"About what?"

"I'll show you." I followed him into the trees, and after a few yards began to smell something. I supposed I would have smelled it earlier if the wind had been right. A toppled barbed wire fence straggled up the slope. A shaggy pile of dead flesh was draped over it—what had been a wild pig.

"Whew!" Another college kid had followed us. "Didn't you know this was here?" I ignored him, and took a closer look at the pig, holding my breath. There were maggots on it, visible in some holes on the side and back. Caused by bullets, I supposed, although they were bigger than bullets. Exit wounds. Somebody had really shot the pig up. I didn't remember any shots lately, but there's so much shooting in the woods that I wasn't sure. I usually tried to investigate shots; usually didn't find anything.

"Help me get this off the fence," I said, "and we'll bury it." College kids don't like to appear squeamish, so they both grabbed a trotter and pulled. The pig made a snorting sound.

"Ugh!" said one of them.

"Just decomposition gases." The carcass must have weighed several hundred pounds, a big boar with lips curled around white tusks. Eventually we got it into a shallow hole and covered it up, with the rest of the trail workers as audience.

"It was shot," said the college kid.

"Looks like it," I said.

"Didn't you hear it?" another college kid said.

"Must have been away."

"Some nature preserve," somebody said. I might have pointed out that wild pigs were non-native animals that caused considerable destruction of native wildlife and vegetation, but I pretended not to hear.

Work proceeded with a certain lack of enthusiasm after this. The college kids wanted to play with the chain saw too, and weren't impressed when I told them the preserve couldn't risk the liability. They decided they could only stay one day. I was glad at the end of the afternoon, when we all repaired to the visitor center for coffee, beer, and herb tea.

"Missed you at the last owl walk," I said, sidling up to Jill and the omnipresent Cathy.

"I didn't know you had another one," said Jill. "Did you see something wonderful?"

"A pygmy owl."

"Yes?"

"An owl the size of a sparrow. It eats insects."

"It sounds sweet," said Jill. Was there a hint of irony again?

"What's the latest on the giant birds and the unknown valley?" I asked.

"I don't know," said Jill, "do you?" Just to make conversation, I told her about Robles Negros. "But that's not an unknown place if they have guided missiles there," she said.

"They don't have them anymore."

"You have been there?" said Jill.

"No, I haven't."

"I saw some big birds today," Jill said, "flying over the ocean. They looked like dinosaurs."

"Probably pelicans," I said.

"We have to get back," Cathy said.

12

Jerry Lester appeared, predictably, as the last trail workers were leaving on Sunday afternoon. The trail weekend hadn't been as successful as the wallboard weekend. Not only had the college kids left Saturday night, the Aliso House people hadn't come on Sunday, leaving me with five volunteers, three of them a little frail.

"How are the old back muscles, George?" said Jerry heartily.

"Fine," I said, which wasn't true.

"That's one kind of work I never much liked," Jerry continued, "trail-building. Guess I'm the bulldozer type." That I could believe. To change the subject, I told him about the dead pig.

"You never know what you're gonna find, do you?" said Jerry. "I remember I found a mummy in the desert once. It was under a dump we were cleaning up. Amazing how much people can dump out in the middle of nowhere. Don't know how they get it out there. Have to drive a dump truck off-road. Anyway, gave me quite a turn. Looked human as hell, though it was real small. All wrinkled up and black. Thought it was an abducted child, one of those you read about on milk cartons, you know? Got the police out there. Turned out to be a chimpanzee."

"A chimpanzee? In Nevada?"

"This was Utah actually. Never did figure out where it came from. Circuses and carnivals travel through there—might have belonged to one. Thing is, it hardly had any hair on it. I mean, even if it dried up, the hair still wouldn't fall off. Must have been bald before it died."

"Sounds like radiation poisoning."

"Damndest thing."

"Yeah, well, Jerry, do you know anybody who's shooting pigs around here?"

"Probably a lot of people shoot pigs around here."

"On the preserve I mean."

Jerry shrugged. "Can't say I'd mind if they did."

"It was a little close to the house."

"You didn't even hear it."

"How did you know I didn't hear it?" I asked. Jerry shrugged again. "You didn't shoot it, did you?"

"Nope," Jerry said. "Could have been anybody. Pigs are a real popular target. You'd be surprised at some of the things people use on them. I've heard automatic weapons fire up by Robles Negros."

"Guess I'll stay away from that place."

"Like I said, there's nothing up there but pigs."

"You mean there are some left?"

"You should see the sows with their piglets up there in the summer. Looks like the return of the buffalo. Cute little stripy things, but all they do is eat."

Jerry left me with the usual baffled feeling. The place seemed lonelier than it had for awhile. It was cooling after a warm spell. Fog blew in from the ocean, shutting up the birds that had been singing. Even Lewis had gone off somewhere.

I felt like talking to somebody sane. I had Ricky Karhu's phone number written down, and eventually managed to excavate it from a drawer of maps and utility bills. A little girl answered after about a dozen rings. When I asked to speak to her father, she shouted "Ricky!" and dropped the receiver. Ricky came on the line after a lengthy interval.

"Maybe you should get an answering machine, Ricky."

"It's broken. How are you, George?"

"I got through the winter."

"Uh huh."

"How's the condor affair?" I asked.

"You should know. The feds took the last one into custody last week. No more wild condors."

"I don't read the papers."

"You're smart."

"Any news of the missing ones?"

"Nope."

I told Ricky about Robles Negros, Jerry Lester, military helicopters, Aliso House, and the dead pig. He didn't seem very interested. I told him what Jill had said about giant birds.

"A cultie told you this?"

"Yeah."

"You're getting shack simple, George."

"Don't you think it's odd, though?"

"What?"

"All this stuff going on up here."

"There's stuff going on everywhere, George."

"Yeah, but suppose somebody was hiding something up there."

"Hiding what up where?" Ricky asked.

"Suppose they were hiding the missing condors at Robles Negros?"

"George, the government wouldn't hide eight condors in a wilderness study area. They want the condors *out* of the wilderness."

"Maybe you should come up and check it out. Nice weekend backpack."

"I'm kind of busy. Why don't you get the BLM guy to take you up there?"

"I don't think he wants me to go, that's what I've been telling you."

"Well, it doesn't sound like much of a place. Condors haven't lived there for decades."

"Maybe they have, and nobody's seen them."

"Then they must be invisible."

Scraping the bottom of the barrel, I told Ricky about Phyllis's apparent disappearance. "You know any people looking for condors who've disappeared lately?"

"Yeah, but it's a man, and he's in Arizona or Mexico. He hasn't disappeared anyway. We just haven't heard from him for a while."

"Well, there you are. You have to check this place out."

Ricky laughed. "Yeah, sure George, let me get back to you. Don't call us."

To my surprise, Ricky got back to me, a half week later. I was feeling better by then, and actually felt a little put-upon when Ricky said that, on second thought, he would like to take a weekend backpack.

"I'm getting a gut," he said.

"It's pretty rugged," I said, "lots of bushwhacking." I'd decided to devote more time to the singles bar circuit.

"Don't let me impose on you, George."

"No, great, come on up."

"I'm coming because I'm sure there are *no* condors up there. I need to get away from the goddamn condors again."

"You'll never know until you come," I answered blandly.

"Spending my weekends with crazed hermits."

"Better hurry before I go around the bend."

13

Ricky arrived at eleven on Friday night. I'd told him it would take two, maybe three days to hike to Robles Negros and back. I might have underestimated.

"Shit, George, it'll take three days just to get there." He rattled my USGS topo map at me. I'd spent awhile laying out what seemed a direct and accessible route, up Macho Creek's south fork to Five Mile Creek, then up its south fork to the divide with Horse Creek and right down into the valley.

"We better start early," Ricky said.

The going was fairly easy for the first five miles up Macho Creek. At least, it seemed like five miles, around redwood trunks, seeps, and hazel thickets. Then the canyon walls closed in and we had to walk in the creekbed or climb around an endless series of cliffs and landslides. My aged rigid frame pack wasn't entirely suitable for such travel—they work best on terrain where you can stand upright. Ricky had one of the newer frameless ones, so he was more flexible.

"At least you're not getting pulled over backward every time you duck under a branch," I said, when we finally stopped for lunch.

"You're behind the times, George. That's the same down bag you had in 1975, isn't it?"

"It's a perfectly good bag."

"Unless it rains."

"It's too late in the year."

It only rained a little that night, as it happened, although the clouds and wind that came up in the afternoon had threatened a major storm. It probably rained harder higher up, but we hadn't climbed much because we'd been unsure where the mouth of Five Mile Creek was. We'd spent a couple of hours going up one creek, backtracking, then going up another. I was fairly sure we were on Five Mile when we stopped for the night.

Luckily, I'd brought my plastic tube tent, which blunted Ricky's derision of my outdated equipment. With his state-of-the-art fiberfill bag, he hadn't bothered bringing even a tube tent.

"It's the same tube tent I've had since 1975," I said.

"It looks it."

The local deadwood was still dry enough for a campfire of sorts, which was nice, since the night was black and I was too tired to sleep. Ricky objected to the fire at first.

"The forest needs that wood more than we do," he said. "Think of all the carbon dioxide you're releasing."

"Guess I'm behind the times."

"Oh well," Ricky said, "I have children. It's hard not to be self-indulgent." We sat and watched the fire hiss and spatter.

"It doesn't get much wilder than this," I said.

Ricky leaned on an elbow in his bag with his rain parka stretched over his head.

"Hope not."

"I thought you were a wilderness fanatic."

"We ought to leave as much land as we can alone. That doesn't mean I have to personally carry a pack through every acre of it. People shouldn't go in some places."

"Then we would never have seen those lady slippers," I said.

"If there was a trail past those orchids, they wouldn't be there now."

"Are they really there if nobody sees them?"

"Anthropocentric sophistry, George." Ricky turned over and began to breathe regularly. I watched the raindrops in the fire-light for awhile. Something called in the distance, but the crackling of the increasingly damp fire obscured it.

I remembered backpacking near Big Sur a dozen years before in another unexpected spring storm, a serious one that deposited six inches in twenty-four hours. On the evening before the rain drove me out, I'd been sitting beside a creek and had seen a bright pink contrail cross the sky much faster than anything I'd ever seen. Seeing it hadn't really assured me of its existence. The thought made me sleepy, and I crawled into my nylon cocoon.

I awoke from a dream of scrambling over hard surfaces while large objects bore down on me. A large object *was* bearing down on me, judging from the thumps and crashes in surrounding thickets. I fumbled my flashlight on and shone it toward the noise. A wild boar blinked at me from ten feet away. He did have long eyelashes. He actually looked rather shy, but he didn't run away, he merely changed direction as would a pedestrian who encountered a "men working" sign. The boar crashed into the darkness.

"Big-ass pig," Ricky said sleepily. I'd downplayed what Jerry had told me about the pig population, because I wasn't sure I believed him. I heard more pigs trundling about through the night, but none bothered us.

The sky had cleared the next morning, and it was quite cool. I had trouble getting my backpacking stove started. It was only ten years old.

"I bet there's snow on the peaks," I said.

"I don't see any peaks," Ricky replied. All we could see were trees and the sides of Five Mile Canyon, which wasn't really a canyon anymore so much as a slot in the steep slopes. It got steeper and rockier as we climbed. My arms were getting as much exercise as my legs. I was glad I'd brought only three days' worth of food, even after lunch, when half of it was gone and we still hadn't reached the Horse Creek divide. We were still going south, mainly. That was something.

After lunch we broke out of the oak-bay woods into the chaparral belt, which provided a view of the peaks but new restraints on movement in the form of granite boulders and manzanita thickets. Way up ahead, though, I saw big ponderosa pines looming mirage-like at the top of the slope. They meant easy walking, and I scrambled toward them like a thirsty man, which I was. It took several hours to reach them, but it seemed longer.

Finally, under the thin but breezy pine shade, we celebrated with candy bars and the last water in our bottles. I assumed that crossing to Horse Creek would be no problem, so we rested a little too long. The sun sank low as we scrambled up the rockiest gorge yet, its sides hung with blackish-green Santa Lucia firs that had ice on their northern branches.

"Let's just stop here for the night," said Ricky.

"No, it's got to stop going up sometime."

"No it doesn't. It can go up as long as it likes. Fucking Pacific Plate."

"It's only four thousand feet, Ricky."

"Fucking bastards," said Ricky, kicking a rock. I'd probably have felt as cross as Ricky did if I hadn't been able to watch him being cross. I giggled weakly as I struggled ahead of him. I decided it was time for a rest, but I'd take another hundred steps first. When I hit forty-five, I reached the top, so suddenly that Ricky bumped into me. I pointed dramatically.

"Goddamn, George. You're not so dumb after all." It was a picture-book panorama, the kind that makes two-day climbs worthwhile, after they're over. The gorge's rocks and firs framed a gentle slope of black oak and ponderosa that led in a mile or so to a narrow line of meadow and white oak groves. I scanned the meadow with my binoculars, and saw a small deer herd at one end, but no other sign of occupation.

"Looks peaceful," I said.

"Let's camp in the woods for the night."

"Don't you want to see what's down there?"

"We'll see tomorrow."

"I thought you were sure there wasn't anything up here."

"When the government is involved, George, you never know."

14

We found a grove of huge ponderosas to spend the night in. We didn't have a campfire, which was probably paranoid of us, since no unusual sights or sounds came from the valley. We ate and got in our sleeping bags. It was an unusually quiet night. I didn't even dream.

I awoke at sunrise feeling apathetic, and guilty about running off and leaving the preserve without telling anyone. I'd shut Lewis in the house with a food supply so the raccoons wouldn't rob him, but I didn't feel good about that either. I felt that I was chasing shadows, wasting time.

"Do you really think somebody stole those condors, Ricky?"

"Nobody found any condor carcasses, and they're big carcasses."

"Animals disappear all the time, though. Have you got any evidence?" I asked.

"No hard evidence. We've heard that a deal was made between certain developers and underworld figures."

"What could you do with eight stolen condors?"

"Lower the population enough so the feds would have to capture the rest. Then the developers would have a free hand."

"To do what?"

"What do you think, George? Speculate. Subdivide. Put up billboards and banners. Shit, they could pay someone a million to snatch the birds and take care of it out of petty cash, but they can't make more of southern California, and the condors lived on some of the best parts."

"So why not just shoot the birds?"

"Maybe they did. But that might have gotten messy. My guess is they hired people who wouldn't have wanted to kill the birds, people who know how to handle them. Rare things are valuable, and condors live a long time. In ten years, maybe they could even be sold back to the government or to conservation groups. Eco-hostages. Some biologists advocate reestablishing the condors in the Grand Canyon instead of southern California."

"Sick."

"Whoever stole them might want to try to breed them, too."

"Even the feds can't do that yet," I said. I sounded more skeptical than I felt. It was exactly the kind of deal that Alec Rice would have liked. He'd bragged to me about breeding endangered species. Of course, Alec Rice was dead, drowned in a cave in the wilderness after trying for three straight days to kill me.

And here I was in the wilderness again, blundering ignorantly toward the unknown. I hadn't actually been backpacking since my death trek with Alec. My breakfast tea and oatmeal suddenly tasted like horse urine and sand.

"You feeling okay, George?"

"Nothing a couple of Valium wouldn't fix."

"You take Valium? That's a dangerous drug."

"Must be the water. You feeling a little queasy?"

"No, I feel pretty good."

"Well, let's go see what we got here." I rattled my pots, stowed my stove, bagged my bag, packed my pack, and twiddled my thumbs while Ricky finished his breakfast. "You always were a cool son of a bitch, Ricky."

"Whatever's here's not going away, George."

"That's what *bothers* me. I thought you were in a rush to get back to L.A.?"

"I'm having kind of a good time."

We left our packs in camp, a precaution that seemed excessive as we strolled through woods full of sunshine-yellow hermit warblers and western tanagers. When we got to the meadow, we tried sneaking along the edges at first, but soon tired of it and started walking through the middle. Nobody seemed to mind. I saw deer, pig, and coyote tracks in muddy spots, but no human ones.

Ricky pointed to a tracked place, at what might have been part of a large bird footprint. We looked up. A couple of turkey vultures and a red-tailed hawk circled in the early updrafts, no condors. It only vaguely resembled a bird track anyway. A deer slipping in the mud could have made it.

We walked farther, and saw rusty metal sticking up where the meadow ran below sandstone cliffs. It was an ancient radar scope, fallen on its side and partly buried. The Nike site.

"Those things were new when I was a little kid," I said.

"Looks like a relic of an ancient civilization." There wasn't anything else to see except scraps of metal and cable, but the ground still had the scarified, compacted aspect of a bulldozed site. The hard soil gave little sign of what had passed there. I imagined this was the BLM's helicopter pad, but the place seemed quite empty and abandoned.

"Guess that's it," I said, looking forward to starting home.

"There must be a bunker here," said Ricky.

"Why?"

"Missile sites always have bunkers."

"Maybe they sealed it off."

"Come on, George, it'll only take a few minutes to look." A grove of young oaks screened the cliff from the open meadow. They cast a dense shade in the mid-morning sun. Once our eyes adjusted to it, we saw that there were a number of openings in the sandstone. The first three we looked into were shallow. The back of one was blackened by fire, and had some petroglyphs of deer, stick people, and other things chipped in it.

The fourth opening narrowed at the back, then opened into an area of darkness high enough for a man to stand in. The sandy clay floor was as hard as adobe.

"Did you bring your flashlight, George?"

"Nope."

"Me neither. How about a match?"

I felt my pockets. I always stuff matches about my person when I go camping. There was a crushed, linty pack in my back pocket, from the Mission Bell Motel in Daly City. I didn't remember putting it there. I crept into the cavity after Ricky and scratched a match. It sputtered out, as did the next two.

"How old are those matches?"

"Got me."

The fourth match flared up, illuminating a bare sandstone cavity, without even petroglyphs. The match went out, and I tried to light three more unsuccessfully.

"Must be a draft in here."

"Funny that there's no petroglyphs," said Ricky. "You'd think this would be the place for them—dark and mysterious."

I turned and started back toward the outside. The sunlight dazzled me, and I stumbled on a piece of sandstone. I put a hand on the smooth rock wall at the entrance to steady myself.

"Did you do that?" said Ricky from the darkness.

"What?"

"There was a clunking noise."

"I tripped."

Ricky came out. "It sounded like it came from inside the rock."

"I didn't hear anything," I said.

"Do what you did again while I listen in there." Ricky went back into the cavity, and I tripped on the piece of sandstone again, feeling foolish. "Did you do it.?"

"Yeah."

"I didn't hear anything this time." Ricky emerged again. "You tripped just like you did before?"

"Well, I put my hand on this wall too."

"Do it again." I did, and we both listened. Silence. Ricky put his hand on the wall too, but nothing happened.

"This is stupid."

"Let's just take one more look in there," said Ricky. There was no arguing with Ricky when he made up his mind. We went back in and I scratched some more damp matches. "You'd think there'd be bat shit in here or something."

"Ow!" I dropped a match I'd held too long and tried to light the last one in the pack, unsuccessfully.

"This place doesn't feel right."

"Write your congressperson."

There was a whining sound, and a piece of the wall slid upward, filling the cavity with light. It was like something out of a movie, but it was terrifying in real life. Ricky and I didn't stop running until we were in the trees on the other side of the meadow. We looked back at the cliff, but nothing came out of it.

"How do you feel, George?"

"Scared."

"Me too. But we haven't done anything wrong. What are we scared for?"

"Who knows if you've done something wrong."

"That's what I mean. I'm going back in there."

"Let's think about this a little."

"If we're in trouble for coming up here, then we're already in trouble."

I doubted the logic of this, and Ricky was already halfway across the meadow. I caught up with him at the cavity entrance. Seen twice, the light coming out of the opening didn't have the science-fiction brilliance it had seemed to have. It looked like ordinary fluorescent light. Ricky looked at me, and started into the opening. A corridor led at a slight downhill angle. We crept along it until we came to a metal staircase winding downward out of sight.

"Must be the bunker," I whispered. Ricky didn't reply. There was still no sound. We started down the stairs. It was just like a bad dream. Down, down, down.

The stairs made a final twist and ended at a metal landing above a large, brightly lit room. It had the look of a mission control center, but appeared to have been converted into an office and living space, with bookcases and cabinets stacked to the ceiling. I could see what looked like a tiled kitchenette off to one side. A large table covered with books, papers, and plants stood in the room's center.

I thought the room was empty at first. Nothing was moving. But it wasn't empty, it just took my eyes a few scans before they registered what they were seeing on my brain.

At the far end of the table was a microscope. Seated behind it was what appeared to be a large parrot, with red and beige plumage. When I say large, I mean about five feet tall. The parrot looked at us with eyes the color of some semi-precious stone I can never remember the name of—chalcedony or garnet.

"Good morning," it said.

15

The parrot put down a wildflower it had been holding, and I saw it wasn't really a giant parrot. It had short arms ending in three scaly fingers with an opposable thumb. Short, downy feathers covered the arms and the backs of the hands. What had first appeared to be a beak turned out to be a naked, bony bulge that extended from the top of its head to its mouth, which contained small, even, pointed teeth. It did have long, birdlike feathers on top of its head and down its back. It still looked enough like a parrot that I kept thinking of it as one. I couldn't think of anything else to call it.

"They didn't tell me you were coming," it said, without much enthusiasm. Its voice was a little high-pitched, in fact, parrot-like, but perfectly understandable.

"Excuse me?" said Ricky.

"Are you from NASA?" it asked.

"NASA?"

It began to show more interest in us. Its pupils dilated and it stood up. The stool it had been sitting on turned out to be a stiff tail several feet long and also covered with short feathers.

"Your prints aren't in the computer. What's your clearance?"

"Clearance?"

"You're beginning to sound like a parrot."

"Excuse me," said Ricky, "but you look like one." Ricky was indomitable.

"What did you expect?" the parrot asked.

"We didn't expect *you.*"

"Then what *did* you expect?"

"We're backpackers," I said. The parrot looked at me. It seemed about to say something, then stopped.

"Would you like something to drink?" it said.

"Something to drink?"

"Coffee?"

"Alright," said Ricky. The parrot went into the kitchenette. Its feet were like a bird's, with three forward toes and one backward one. It held its tail straight out behind it as it walked.

"Come and sit down," it said, as it put a kettle on a gas stove. We obeyed. Armchairs were ranged against the wall outside the kitchenette. "This isn't very fresh," it said, spooning coffee into a filter. "I don't get many visitors."

"Don't drink it yourself?" said Ricky.

"Doesn't really agree with me."

"I suppose it wouldn't."

"I'm more of a tea drinker."

"So you can eat Earth foods?"

"Oh yes."

"Where is it you come from?"

The parrot glanced at us, but answered readily enough. "The planet gurgle in the Galaxy trill." The sounds it made couldn't be easily transcribed into human language. It was like trying to transcribe birdsong, except that the parrot's utterances included sounds made by all the birds I'd heard along with many sounds I hadn't. Imagine a raven simultaneously imitating a hermit thrush, a mockingbird, a hummingbird, and a warbler.

"What are you doing here?" I asked, not wanting to seem altogether mute and stupid.

"On Earth?"

"Well, yeah, but I meant this place right here."

"Cream or sugar? Creamer, that is." It didn't return to my question after we'd voiced our preferences. It gave us the coffee in the heavy china mugs they use in the armed forces, but drank its tea from an expensive looking China cup and saucer.

"Tea tastes best when I drink it out of one of these," it said, "but the rest of the set is broken."

"This is *really weird,*" said Ricky.

"Yes," said the parrot, "and what do *you* do?"

16

"Would you answer just one question?" said Ricky.

"I've answered a lot of questions," replied the parrot-like creature. We were following it through the woods. It said it wanted to look for fungi that had come up after the rain. It carried a sack into which it put various mushrooms.

The coffee hour had been frustrating. The parrot creature had questioned us at length, but had seemed unconvinced of everything we said, including our interest in missing condors. It knew about condors, but wouldn't explain how. It answered our questions ironically if at all. What was it doing at Robles Negros? Botanical studies. Why? It was a botanist. How did it get to Robles

Negros? As a guest of the U.S. government. How did it get to the U.S.? In a spaceship.

"Just explain why you speak such good English," Ricky now persisted. Ricky never ceased to amaze me. Flattering an extraterrestrial.

"I'm good at languages."

"Yours is so different from ours."

"Whit, swit, sees a pic terlarooyxz."

"What does that mean?" Ricky asked.

"The forest is the mother of tongues."

"There are forests on your planet?"

"Would I be a botanist?"

"You were the expedition botanist, like?" I asked.

"Biologist, actually. We're not as specialization-minded as you," the parrot explained.

"Where's the rest of the expedition?"

"I suppose they're in Florida."

Flattery seemed to work. Ricky tried some more. "How many earth languages do you speak?"

"A dozen or so."

"You've learned them all since you got here?" I asked, admiringly. The parrot looked at me. Ricky rolled his eyes.

"So, how long have you been here?" he asked.

The parrot leaned over and picked up a morel, an edible mushroom with a wrinkled, conical cap. "Amazing," it said. It sounded sincere, for once. "What do you call these?"

"Morels."

"You eat them?"

"Yeah."

"We'll have some for lunch," it said, picking more. "Do you know if they're mycorrhizal?"

"If they grow on tree roots? No."

"They have mushrooms on your planet?" Ricky asked. The parrot sighed and looked away.

"I've been here since July 9, 1969," it said.

"That's almost the same date as the moon landing," I observed.

"Odd, isn't it?"

Ricky showed impatience for the first time since his out-burst over coffee. His democratic feelings were offended. "You mean this country has been in contact with an extraterrestrial civilization for twenty years and the public hasn't been informed?"

"What would you do," the parrot asked, "if you were the Joint Chiefs of Staff and you fished a load of space parrots out of the Sargasso Sea?"

"Tell the U.N."

"No you wouldn't."

"You couldn't keep it secret," Ricky insisted.

"I'm here to tell you you could," the parrot said, "as you are perfectly well aware. And I'm getting tired of these tricks. I've got work to do here."

"What do you mean?"

"It's time for lunch. I don't suppose you brought anything?" the creature said. It led us back to the cliff and opened the back of the cave by placing a hand on the same part of the wall I'd leaned on.

"Aha," I said.

"Oho," the parrot replied.

"It reads your hand print. I've heard about those. How come it opened for us?"

"I didn't want to be inhospitable," it replied.

"You knew we were out here?" The parrot didn't answer. It led us back to its kitchen and gave us each a glass of Italian white wine.

"California wines give me a headache," it said, as it sipped from its own glass, fried morels in butter, and boiled fettucine. When it set the food before us, I was surprised to find that I was hungry. The creature didn't eat much.

"I'd get too fat if I ate as much as you do," it said. "Different metabolism."

"I still don't understand how you can eat Earth food," said Ricky.

"I'd be in trouble if I couldn't."

"After twenty years, yes. Don't you get homesick?" The parrot didn't answer. "Won't they let you go home?"

"You're breaking my heart."

"Do you have one?"

The parrot opened its arms. Its breast feathers were pale vermilion, a very pretty color. Ricky fearlessly leaned across the table and put his ear against it.

"It's pretty fast."

"How's this," the parrot said. Ricky looked astonished.

"You can control the rate?"

"It goes down to ten beats a minute when we sleep."

"But you can do it deliberately?"

"So can you, up to a point. We have a wider thermal range. More efficient in some ways." Its eyes were sparkling. If it had such a different metabolism, I wondered what alcohol did to it. For nearly the first time since the creature had spoken, I felt a hint of fear. Until now I'd been too dazed to feel much of anything.

Its feet were really talons, as sharp as a hawk's. If the public didn't know about it, perhaps it was because it didn't want to be known about. I glanced at Ricky, who appeared thoughtful. The parrot stood up suddenly. Instead of leaping the table to grab me by the throat, it began picking up dishes.

"Can we help with those?" Ricky asked.

"Sure can," replied the parrot. We helped it stack the dishes in the sink.

"You have hot water up here?"

"I'm well taken care of. No complaints."

We stood by uncertainly as the parrot washed and stacked the dishes. There wasn't room at the sink for us to do anything else.

"Can we help dry?" I asked. I didn't see a dishtowel.

"They'll drip," the creature said. "Now, if you'll excuse me, I have some notes to write up."

"You want us to leave?"

"There's really not room for more than me here." The creature edged us toward the door.

"Thanks for the lunch."

"Say hello to Crix opsixyz swit peryoo for me."

"What?" But the parrot had turned back to the table and was sorting through papers. Ricky and I climbed the stairs and walked out through the opening, which closed after us.

"Bon voyage," said the creature's voice, which seemed to come from about two feet away. Its French accent really was excellent.

"Let's get the hell out of here," said Ricky.

17

Since the return trip was mainly downhill, we got back to the preserve Tuesday morning. We'd left Ricky's car on the road, where Macho Creek's south fork entered the main canyon. It was a relief to drive the last few miles, but not to get back to the house. Jerry's pickup and the Aliso House white van were parked in front.

"You've got visitors." said Ricky. "Maybe I'll leave right now."

"Oh no you don't."

Ricky sighed. "I'm missing work, George."

"We just talked to an extraterrestrial, for Chrissake."

"You know what Thoreau said: 'One world at a time.'"

"He said that on his deathbed. Maybe those creatures can show us how to save the planet."

"That creature?"

Jerry Lester came out of the front door. I supposed he still had the key Marshall had given him. He walked toward us, and I got out of Ricky's car.

"Ho, George."

"Hi, Jerry."

"You've been gone awhile. Your cat was hungry."

"You fed him? Thanks."

"Who's your buddy?"

"A friend of mine from L.A." Ricky got out of the car and I introduced them.

"Been doing a little hiking?" Jerry could see the backpacks in the back of Ricky's station wagon. "Go up to Ventana, check out the hot springs?"

"Little backpacking," I said, noncommitally.

"See anything interesting?"

"What's up with you, Jerry?"

"Well, we may have a slight problem here, George."

"Something to do with Aliso House?" I indicated the white van, but Jerry didn't answer. He climbed on the porch and opened the front door. Ricky and I exchanged a glance, then followed him inside.

The hall seemed very small and dark after four days outside. Jerry proceeded toward the kitchen. As we followed him, I saw Peter Eliott and his sidekick Henry leaning against the counter. Jerry stepped aside as we entered the room. Jill sat behind the kitchen table.

Jerry nodded to Peter, who picked a metal box off the table. It looked like a geiger counter.

"Let's get a reading," said Jerry. Peter pointed a microphone-like object at me, and the box began to crackle.

"Been up to Robles Negros, huh?" said Jerry.

"What is this?"

"Guess I misjudged you, George. Thought you were more the responsible, stay-at-home type. Should have checked your background sooner."

"What do you mean?"

"The reason we're trying to keep people out of Robles Negros is there was a minor nuclear incident up there about twenty years ago. Levels are still kind of iffy."

"It's over nine," said Peter.

"Uh oh," said Jerry. "You're going to have to come with us, George. We can get you to the detox center in Salt Lake City within twelve hours, there shouldn't be irreversible damage."

"This is stupid," said Jill.

"Shut up," Henry said. He turned to me. "You know Ms. Nitra, don't you?" It didn't sound like the name she'd given me when I met her. "Or Lieutenant Nitra. Her government is interested in our problem here. It's not much compared to Chernobyl, but it's something. Of course, twenty years ago her government had its own problem nobody heard about."

"We know about your nuclear accidents," said Jill.

"It sure is stupid," said Ricky. "What is that up there?"

"What do you mean?" said Jerry.

"That purple people-eater up there." Peter turned the box off and put it down. Jerry shook his head.

"Goddamn Coastal Lands Trust," he said.

"You should have condemned the property," said Peter.

"Purple people-eater?" said Jill.

"What *is* it?" I said, curiosity overcoming discretion.

"It's classified, George. And you are in deep shit."

"I didn't see any signs saying it was classified," said Ricky. "What law did we break?"

"Democracy," said Jill.

"Put a gag on her," said Jerry. Peter took a roll of duct tape out of his attaché case and stuck a piece over Jill's mouth as Henry held her down on the seat. I realized that her hands were cuffed to the table leg in front of her. Jill was an eastern bloc agent? Jerry, Henry, and Peter were CIA or FBI? I felt I had chopped liver in my skull.

"It's out of my hands now," said Jerry. "You guys going to cooperate or am I going to have to be mean to you too?"

"Who are these people?" Ricky said. "Where's your authority?"

"You're going to have to go somewhere and talk to some people," said Jerry.

"I'm going to Los Angeles," said Ricky. "I have to get back to work."

"Should have thought of that before you got into this," said Jerry.

"We were looking for condors," I said, trying to postpone confrontation.

"Condors?" Jerry was amused.

"Ricky's with the Condor Preservation Committee in Los Angeles. They're looking for eight wild condors that disappeared."

"Don't know about that," said Jerry.

"I thought you worked for the BLM."

"We're asking the questions, George."

"I'm going home," said Ricky.

"Sit down," said Jerry.

"You want to come, George?" said Ricky. It sounded attractive. Ricky lunged toward the back door. Jerry stepped in front of me and punched me in the stomach so hard the lights went out.

18

I returned to consciousness with a startling inability to breathe. I was dimly aware of some commotion at the front of the house. When I got a lungful of air, I opened my eyes. Jerry stood above me, looking surprised. Then he was gone, and something heavy and sharp landed on my chest, knocking the wind out again. There were thumps, crashes, shouts, then silence.

I opened my eyes again, and saw nothing but the ceiling. I turned my head and saw a pair of unshaven, feminine legs in Nike running shoes. I sat up and peered over the table edge. Jill looked back at me. We were alone in the room. I opened my mouth, but nothing came out but grunting noises.

I stood up and noticed that the kitchen screen door had been torn off its hinges and thrown onto the back porch. Jerry lay flat on his back in the grass below the porch. Ricky crouched over him.

"His heart's beating," Ricky said.

The parrot-like creature from Robles Negros came around the house. The feathers on its head were standing up: It looked like a demented cockatoo. It approached Jerry. Ricky jumped back, but it did nothing more violent than remove a pair of handcuffs from Jerry's pocket and snap his wrists together behind his back.

"I'm really getting tired of him," it said.

I sat down on the porch. I could think of nothing to say. A robin began singing in idiot composure from the maple tree above us. The parrot cocked an eye at it.

"How come you have feathers?" said Ricky.

"It's an efficient form of insulation," the parrot replied.

"So you evolved from scaly creatures, like birds did?"

"Yes." The parrot didn't seem interested in the matter. It nodded toward the kitchen door.

"Who's she?"

"Her name's Jill," I said.

"What's she doing here?"

"Why don't you ask her. What did you do to him?" I nodded at Jerry.

"It kicked him through the door," said Ricky. The parrot went into the kitchen.

"What happened to Peter and Henry?"

"They ran in their van."

We followed the parrot back into the kitchen, where it regarded Jill. It had taken the tape off her mouth, but Jill was silent.

"She won't tell me what she's doing here, Mr. . ."

"George Kilgore."

"*Who* are you with?" it asked.

"I'm with the Coastal Lands Trust, like I told you. I manage this nature preserve."

"You don't work for Jerry?"

"Did it look like it?"

"What did Jerry say about her?"

"That she's a Soviet agent, I think."

"Excuse me," the parrot said. It dashed out the back door. I followed and saw it gaining rapidly on a fleeing Jerry. It ran with its neck stretched out, grabbed the seat of Jerry's pants in its mouth, and lifted him off his feet. It carried him back, kicking and twisting.

"He's a tough old bird," it said out of the corner of its mouth as it hauled Jerry into the kitchen. It took a key out of Jerry's pocket, undid Jill's handcuffs, and put them on Jerry's ankles.

"Goddamn traitor," Jerry said.

"Be quiet, Jerry, I'm not defecting to Moscow," said the parrot

"Liar."

"Use your brains."

"I never trusted you things." Jerry sounded bitter.

"Where's your bedroom?" the parrot asked. I pointed upstairs. It grabbed Jerry by his chained ankles and dragged him down the passageway. I heard his head going bump, bump, bump on the stairs, then a squeaking of bedsprings.

"What's it doing, raping him?" said Ricky. But the parrot quickly reappeared in the kitchen.

"Whose Honda is that in front?" it asked. Ricky didn't answer. "Come on, I'm not going to steal it. I just want a ride."

"Where?" asked Ricky.

"Los Angeles."

"Why do you want to go to Los Angeles?"

"Where would you want to go," the parrot asked, "if you looked like me?"

19

An hour later, I was driving my pickup down U.S. 1 with a disgruntled cat and nervous spy. I didn't feel any better about it than Lewis did, but there seemed to be more of a future for me in Los Angeles than in Jerry Lester's vicinity, at least temporarily. Maybe not much more. I felt little confidence in the parrot's motives, on which it had not elaborated.

I could see its head in the passenger seat of Ricky's Honda ahead of me. It had put on a scarf, a raincoat, and a pair of sunglasses, and rode with one elbow jauntily out the window.

"You can't stay with me," Ricky had said, "I have a family."

"Just until I find a place of my own," the parrot had replied soothingly.

"How are you going to do that?"

"Through the classifieds."

Jill had been persistent about coming along, for which I couldn't blame her. The parrot had told her she could come along if she told who she really was, which had seemed sensible, if high-handed. Jill had given this some thought.

"Well, I'm a Czechoslovakian agent." The creature seemed satisfied with this, although Ricky and I were not. Jill came aboard and quickly feel asleep. I supposed she'd had a rough night.

I was getting sleepy myself after an hour's driving, so I turned on the radio. Jill awoke with a start.

"Where are we?" she said.

"Near Lompoc. Did you know about this thing?"

"This creature? No."

"What were you doing here?"

Jill made a disgusted gesture. "You have no idea what it's like in that place. Talk about spying. They watch you every minute.

"Aliso House?"

"At least in Napa there's some privacy."

"Yeah, but what were you doing in Aliso House?"

"They have munitions factories and paramilitary groups all over Asia and the Middle East. They have to be watched."

"You were just . . . watching?"

"My last contact told me something odd was going on."

"Phyllis?" Jill didn't answer. "What happened to her?"

"I don't know. I think Peter and Henry were already suspicious of me by then. I've been incommunicado ever since Phyllis left. I've never been so frightened in my life."

"Why did they send volunteers to the preserve?"

"It was supposed to be part of a good-neighbor policy. But I could see Peter was nervous about having a nature preserve around, with people hiking."

"Did you know Peter worked for the CIA? For Jerry?"

"Jerry's not CIA," Jill said. "I don't know what Jerry is."

"How do you know?"

"I'd have heard about him if he was."

"Really? Everybody watches everybody, eh?" Jill didn't answer. "Cathy said you lost your parents when the Russians invaded Czechoslovakia. That true?"

"The Nazis killed my grandparents."

"Why don't you answer the question?"

"I came here alone in 1968," Jill said.

"To be a spy?"

"I was ten years old."

"They indoctrinate them young in Stalinist countries."

"Not just Stalinist countries. My parents were divorced. I went to live with my aunt in Spokane."

"How old were you when you started spying?"

"I haven't started spying," Jill said."I'm not breaking any laws. I just keep in touch with some friends."

"A child spy. That's a new one."

"I was *not* a child spy."

"So you've been living here eighteen years waiting for your first assignment? What's that, a mole?"

"I'm an American citizen."

"No, I think the word is 'sleeper.' "

"You read too many spy novels."

"Hell of a life."

"I like California. Czechoslovakia's depressing."

"So why are you spying for its government? I thought you Czechs all hated Soviet domination and all that."

"I'm not Czech. I'm Slovak."

"What's the difference?"

"It's a different country! Oh, the wonderful, poor freedom-loving Czechs. Phooey. Slovakia's much nicer."

"You go back to visit, eh?"

"I'm tired of this interrogation." Jill yawned and scratched her arm through a rip in her sleeve. It looked as though she hadn't changed clothes in a few days.

"You a communist?"

"You a capitalist?"

I didn't have an answer to that. We rode in silence for a while. My mind was beginning to work a little more clearly now that the adrenaline level was down. I wondered why we hadn't been arrested already. Jerry and Peter would have taken down our license numbers, I felt certain of that. Maybe it meant they didn't want the law involved, which was a relaxing thought, until it occurred to me that it would mean that Jerry and his boys didn't want to be restrained by the law. There didn't seem to be much to do about it, except to drive down U.S. 1 at a sedate 55MPH.

"At least we're both human beings," Jill said.

"Huh?"

"We should work together on this, George. Find out what that creature is up to."

"Jerry wanted me to work with him."

"No he didn't. He was going to lock you up."

"An option you don't have."

"There are more of these creatures, aren't there? Who knows what they're up to?"

"Who says there's more? Thought you didn't know anything about them."

"Do you know what's in that bundle?" Jill asked.

"No."

The parrot had run into the woods just before we left and returned carrying a bundle that it had insisted on stowing in the Ricky's Honda even though there was more room in the back of my pickup.

"Well, don't you think we better find out? It might be a new kind of plague."

"Gimme a break." I felt a sinking sensation. She might be right. "They've been here almost twenty years. Why would they . . . wait a minute . . . you're pumping me."

"You want money?"

"I don't want to spend the rest of my life in Leavenworth."

Conversation languished. Los Angeles started about a mile south of where Santa Barbara ended. The green folds of the Ventura County hills sprouted plywood, formica, and pre-weathered softwood in a thousand minor variations of mineshaft modern. If it hadn't been for the billboards and banners, I might have thought we were in the Welsh coal measures. Soon the Quail Hills Estates and Ventura Oaks Ranchettes oozed together to form Buena Vista Technology Parks, Millennium Insurance complexes, and Malpaiso malls. The developers hadn't exploited one element of local color, however. I saw no billboards for Condor Condominiums.

The malls and complexes had metastasized into high-rises by the time we fronted the Pepto Bismol haze of the Los Angeles Basin.

"You don't call *this* depressing?" I asked.

"It's more on the manic side."

"The depression comes later."

Jill didn't reply. I supposed environmental issues were foreign to the world of international intrigue.

Ricky lived in Santa Monica, on a tree-lined street of 1920s bungalows that seemed out of place in freewayland. Even the air seemed anachronistic. It had a kind of chlorophyll sparkle, as though it were piped in from a fossil deposit of unpolluted atmosphere. In a way it was: Santa Monica is on the Pacific.

Ricky pulled into a garage, and an automatic door closed on him and his mysterious passenger. Jill and I sat in the truck for a few minutes before going in. Introductions would take awhile. I tried once more to get a straight story out of her.

"So what are you doing down here?"

"What are *you* doing down here?" she replied.

"I asked you first."

"I'm doing my job."

"You're a sleeper planted here by the Czech government to watch an extraterrestrial being kept in a BLM Wilderness Study Area by an unknown agency of the U.S. government? A sleeper placed here, by the way, a year *before* the extraterrestrial landed on earth?"

"What is BLM?"

"Bureau of Logging and Mining. Very high-security."

"The creature was in a mine?" Jill asked.

"Stop changing the subject."

"We thought it was some kind of new weapons system.
"The Russians kept picking up these transmissions about big birds. They thought it was part of SDI."

"So you do work for the Russians."

"I work for socialism." Jill tossed her head.

"So that's what all that stuff about giant birds was. You thought Aliso House was involved in that?"

"We thought we should know if they were. Fanatics. Also connected to certain right-wing Asian governments."

"But what made you think so?"

"Transmissions started coming from Aliso House," Jill said.

"Did you know Peter and Henry worked for Jerry?"

"No. Did *you?*"

"What are you insinuating?" I asked.

"What are you doing down here?"

"Following the crowd."

"You seem to be a passive personality," Jill said.

"Well, shit, how many times do you get to go to Los Angeles with an extraterrestrial?"

"You sound so bourgeois alienated I almost believe you."

Jill got out of the car and started up the walk. I followed her past pieces of a Darth Vader doll.

Inside the door, things were quieter than expected. Ricky's wife, who was black, evidently had a more flexible world view than many Santa Monica housewives. She regarded the parrot warily but matter-of-factly. Her children seemed quite comfortable about it, perhaps as a live manifestation of morning television. They were mildly annoyed when Ricky's wife, Mona, packed them off for a "visit" to her mother from which they did not return.

"Sensible, your wife," said the parrot after they had left.

"She says she wants you out in five days," said Ricky.

"No problem."

One member of the household was upset, but that was more because of Lewis than the parrot. A half-grown ginger kitten spat and arched his back as Lewis slunk out of his carrying cage. The kitten climbed the curtains, something Lewis had not accomplished in years. Lewis was unimpressed, and glided through the cellar door to sulk in the heating ducts. The creature picked up the kitten, which seemed fascinated by its feathers.

"Mammals really have improved enormously," it said. "We used to regard them rather as you regard snakes: nefarious, slithering things. Some of them were quite venomous." It looked up and saw the confused looks on our faces.

"You have mammals on your planet?" said Ricky. The parrot sat back on its tail, looking fatigued.

"Look," it said, "I know this is difficult, but I'm not an extraterrestrial. I'm more of a time traveler than a space traveler. I lived on this planet seventy million years ago."

"What do you mean? You're a dinosaur or something?" I said.

"I dislike that word. Would you like to be called a 'terrible monkey'?"

"There never was a dinosaur civilization."

"How do you know?"

"There aren't any fossils."

"How many fossils of your civilization will exist in seventy million years? We had lower population densities than you. We didn't have to eat so much to maintain our metabolisms, so our infrastructure was simpler."

"What is this time machine crap?" said Ricky.

"Just a metaphor," the parrot said.

"So how did you get here?"

"As I told you, I was the biologist on an interstellar expedition. Unfortunately, we never found any interstellar biology."

"In seventy million years? How could you live seventy million years?"

"Space is a big place, and nothing decays in it if properly insulated."

"So how did you get back here?"

"The ship was designed to track radio waves. When you began broadcasting it homed in. Unfortunately, the rehydration system was running down, and the pilots didn't regain consciousness in time to monitor the landing. We crashed."

"Into the Sargasso Sea." I remembered that part.

"Three of us drowned."

"How many are left?"

"Five, including me."

"Look," said Jill, "there's no evidence that dinosaurs could have evolved intelligence."

"You've found a little over three hundred species of ... archosaurs, that's the name I prefer, for the two hundred million years we existed," said the parrot disdainfully.

"Then how *did* you evolve intelligence?" Jill persisted.

"From the few fossils we found, rather as you seem to have. Our ancestors lived in trees, got driven to the ground, possibly by drought, and began flinging sticks and stones about with their former tree-climbing apparatus. Cultural evolution. Only seems to take a few million years once it gets going, which is one reason fossils are rare. Our civilization had been going much longer than yours when we left, about fifty thousand years. I'd like to know how long it lasted afterward, but I suppose I never will."

"How can you be sure this is your planet?" Jill said, still not convinced.

"Because there were oaks and redwoods and birds and mammals on my planet."

"Then what happened to your civilization?"

"Your guess is as good as mine."

"A comet?" asked Ricky, who began to seem more impressed with the parrot now that it said it came from Earth.

"If the comet that Prof. Alvarez says struck the earth sixty-five million years ago destroyed my civilization, it would have had to have lasted five million years," the parrot said, "which seems unlikely."

"Why?"

"Civilization has discontents."

"Wars and pollution?"

"We were a fairly aggressive lot."

"So your space travel was grasping at straws, just like with us!"

"Somewhat more successfully," the parrot said. "May I see the newspaper?"

"What for?" said Jill.

"I need to look for a house." Ricky brought the parrot a copy of the *Los Angeles Times,* and it did in fact turn to the classifieds. We sat around it for a few minutes, scratching our heads.

"What have you been doing here for twenty years?" Jill asked finally.

"I've been catching up on the last seventy million years."

"What? How?"

"I'm a biologist."

"But . . . your shipmates?"

The parrot rattled the paper, then made a movement that might have been a shrug.

"If a Concorde crashed in the Amazon," it said, "would the crew be able to build a supersonic jetliner for the local Indian tribe?"

"So that's why it's been kept secret," said Ricky.

"A jetliner," Jill asked, "or a jet bomber?"

"The fact is," the parrot said, "that they haven't been able to build much of anything. The engineer was one of the ones that drowned."

"But why would your shipmates spend twenty years to build a spaceship if they know there's nothing out there?" Ricky asked.

"They *like* doing it. How do you think the Reagan administration came up with SDI? But I shouldn't be talking in front of our friend here." It nodded at Jill. "Anyway, just because we didn't find anything in seventy million years doesn't mean there's nothing out there."

"Yeah, but," said Ricky, "why are they still pouring billions into space research if they know they may not find anything in seventy million years of looking?"

"Why do you think we're such a big secret?" the creature asked.

"Why are you running around loose, then?"

The parrot put the newspaper down. "It's a long story," it said. It handed me the classified section. It had circled some properties, pricey items in Malibu and Topanga Canyon, estates with grounds. "Would you mind looking at these for me, George?"

"Wow. How are you going to pay?"

"Cash," the parrot replied. We knew one thing it had in its bundle.

20

I spent the next two days looking at private Xanadus, of which there are an amazing number and variety in Los Angeles. The parrot had me buy a Polaroid and photograph everything (it also had me buy a new BMW to drive around in, which I didn't object to) and we spent the evenings looking at them. They made Jill indignant. She was in a bad mood anyway because the parrot wouldn't let her out of Ricky's house unaccompanied (which seemed a sensible precaution to me).

"It's unbelieveable that you have people living on your streets. Look at this porch, you could house a family in it. Two families."

"Soviet families," I jeered.

"You afraid the FBI is listening, George?"

I *was* feeling furtive. I'd snuck off and phoned Marshall Mitchell from a booth and told him I'd left the preserve temporarily because of a death in the family. He hadn't seemed concerned, and had said he'd have Jerry look in while I was gone. Marshall's normality seemed reassuring at first, then increasingly ominous. I had no idea what Jerry would do.

The parrot didn't seem worried about it. When I wondered aloud why we hadn't been arrested, it said Jerry would hardly be expected to go through normal channels. When I asked what channels he'd go through, it said he'd have to improvise some, which would take time.

The parrot decided it wanted a personal look at a half dozen of the places I'd photographed. This seemed an unnecessary risk, but it was adamant. Jill was glad to get out of the house. We bought a wheelchair and a bunch of shawls and bandages. The stiff tail posed a problem, but the creature was short enough that it was able to balance with its tail on the seat and not look too gigantesque when shawled and bandaged. Jill and I introduced it as our aged, convalescent mother, or father. Its high, gravelly voice could have been male or female. The parrot was in fact evasive about its gender, which fed Jill's suspicions. (Ricky, whom it seemed to trust, was allowed to go to work and avoid these circuses.)

"Maybe it reproduces by budding," Jill said. "Like in that horrible body-snatcher film."

"You'd make a good red-baiter," I said.

"What?"

"That's what *Invasion of the Body Snatchers* was about. Anti-communist hysteria. Anyway, dinosaurs laid eggs."

"Dinosaurs didn't have feathers, George."

"They may have, actually. Some of them."

Jill was more interested in the creature's bundle than she was in its reproductive arrangements. The parrot took it everywhere, however, and even slept with it. It didn't require a bedroom, but slept sitting on its tail in the living room. It even took the bundle into the bathroom with it (it had a fondness for showers). Jill and I got to sleep in the children's rooms.

The parrot finally decided to make an offer on a five-acre property in Topanga. It was in a steep gully, surrounded by live oaks and chaparral, the only access from the driveway. Like most of the places we saw, it had an expensive security system.

"What are you going to do there?" Jill asked, as we drove home.

"Live quietly and studiously," the parrot replied.

"Why do you want to be so secluded?"

"Don't be obtuse."

"When you move in, can I go?" Jill asked.

"We'll see."

"You can't keep me a prisoner."

"You wanted to come along," the parrot said.

"We could help you," Jill said.

"I've had twenty years of that kind of help."

Ricky was on the telephone when we got back to his house. He seemed elated when he hung up.

"We may have found them!"

"What?"

"The condors. They heard from the guy I told you about, Terry Phelan, the guy who was missing in Arizona. He's in Mexico, in the Sierra Madre in Sinaloa, near some big canyon."

"He's seen condors?"

"No, but he says there are rich Americans there who have big cages with big birds in them."

"Could be a lot of big birds."

"Fifty miles into the Sierra Madre?"

"Maybe they're smuggling parrots," I said. Again, just the kind of thing Alec Rice would have done. I was glad I wasn't Terry Phelan.

"We're going to find out," Ricky said.

"What are you going to do?"

"Find out if it's true and get the law in there."

"That could be tricky in Mexico," I said.

"Then we'll get them back ourselves." I admired Ricky's dedication, but the whole thing seemed remote under the present circumstances. The parrot was interested, though.

"You thought they were hiding condors at Robles Negros," it said. "Why would the government do that?"

"To please developer friends of President Reagan's maybe," I suggested.

"You trust your government even less than I do."

"We have to pay taxes," I said. "Where *did* you get all that money, anyway? Is it a piece of the SDI budget?"

"We had endangered species in the Cretaceous. The giant pterodactyls were getting quite rare. They were carrion eaters too."

"The ones with the forty-foot wingspans?" Ricky was entranced.

"They could swoop down and rob a tyrannosaur without moving a wing." The parrot made a very convincing roaring sound that seemed to come from above the ceiling. It was an excellent ventriloquist, and sometimes amused itself by calling us from rooms it wasn't in, a primitive sense of humor for an interstellar explorer.

"What did you do about tyrannosaurs?" I asked.

"Killed the ones that got in our way. Set aside preserves for the others."

"Did it work?"

"It's hard to say, They seem to have outlived us."

"God," said Ricky, "I'd have liked to see a *Quetzalcoatlus.*"

"A what?" said Jill.

"That's the pterodactyl with the forty-foot wingspan. Lived in Texas."

"I'd like to see a condor," said the parrot.

"I thought you knew about condors," I said.

"I've read about them, I haven't seen one."

"You'd have to go to the zoo now," Ricky said.

"I don't think I'll go to a zoo again. Not after the past twenty years."

"They kept you in cages?"

"Let's say we had to earn our status."

"Did you earn that money?" I asked.

"I had information to sell," it answered.

"Like what? Genetic engineering?" I could hear Jill's ears growing across the room.

"Nothing that wouldn't have been discovered anyway in a couple of years."

"Why didn't you have an auction? Or are you planning one?"

"I've got enough to last me awhile," it said primly.

"You still haven't explained why you were stuck up there by yourself. Or anything else."

"It was part of the exchange," the parrot said. "I was tired of all the muddling. Look what they just did to that schoolteacher."

"You mean on the shuttle *Challenger?*"

"They were tired of my complaints. So we made a deal."

"Who was tired?"

"Everybody."

"Your shipmates?"

"I'm beginning to think," the parrot said, eyeing me balefully, "that you're with some agency after all. You have so many."

"You thought we were spying on you when we came to Robles Negros?"

"I overestimated Jerry's competence."

"Anyway," I said, "you seem to have reneged on your deal with them. You think you're going to get away with it?"

"I feel all ruffled in these bandages," the parrot said. "I'm going to take a shower." Evidently it was ruffled, because it left its bundle in the living room when it went into the bathroom. Jill made a beeline for it.

"Wait a minute," I whispered. "Let's think about this."

"We may not get another chance."

"Shhh!" Ricky said. He was looking out the window. He closed the blinds. "There's a van out there."

I peeked through the blinds. It was a black, customized van with one-way bubble windows on the side. It nuzzled the back of my pickup as though sniffing it.

"Was it there when you pulled in?" Ricky asked. Mona had taken Ricky's Honda, and we were keeping the parrot's BMW in his garage. Long-suffering Ricky was taking my pickup to work.

"I don't think so," I said. "You've never seen it before?"

"No."

"Maybe somebody visiting the neighbors."

"The people across the street are in their seventies."

"Seems a little early to jump the gun."

Jill looked out, having let go reluctantly of the creature's bundle.

"You have to act fast in these situations," she said.

"I thought you were a sleeper."

"I've had some training."

"She may be right, George," said Ricky. "Maybe you should go."

"*I* should go?"

"I've got to think of my family," Ricky said, reasonably.

"Where?"

"I've been thinking. You could go to Mexico. I'll tell you how to find Terry Phelan, the guy I was just telling you about. You could stay with him. It's real remote. In the mountains east of Los Mochis."

"Maybe he's right, George. Maybe we'd be safer," Jill said.

"Safe? Mexico?"

The parrot suddenly appeared in the living room, headed for its bundle. I gave Jill a look, but she ignored me. Informed of the van, the creature peeked out, thought a minute, and nodded.

"That's the kind of thing Jerry would do. I'll have to go."

"What about your estate?" I asked.

"It's too crowded around here anyway."

Ricky told it about his Mexico idea. The parrot seemed to like it.

"Do you know this man in Mexico?" it asked.

"I've met him a few times. Nice guy. Knows a lot about condors."

"Can you contact him?"

"That's the problem," Ricky said. "But I can tell you where he is and you can probably find him. There won't be too many six-foot-two blond, bearded gringos around there."

"Well, George?" the parrot said.

"Well what?"

"I could use some help."

"I'll come with you," said Jill.

"I thought you wanted to leave us?" the parrot said.

"I don't want Peter and Henry to get me."

"Is that so?" the parrot said. "What is it that you dislike about them?"

"They're crazy."

"Takes one to know one," I muttered.

"Jerry never told me about them," the parrot said. "Do you know why he has them working for him?"

"Maybe because he thinks they'll do anything he tells them," said Jill. "They're brainwashed."

"Chickens coming home to roost," I said.

"What do you mean?" the parrot said, a little impatiently.

"The communists started using brainwashing in the Korean War. Then their enemies started imitating them."

"This isn't really the time for ideological argument," the parrot said.

"They're still violent fanatics."

Jill had a point. I still felt argumentative about going to Mexico, though. "You want Peter and Henry to get you in Mexico?" I asked.

"Don't come if you're too scared," Jill said.

"I'm not too scared. I'm just scared enough." I would have loved to stay in Santa Monica, but I knew I wouldn't like myself if I did. I tried one last argument anyway. "If we go," I said, "they'll just follow us."

"Let's stop wasting time," the parrot said. "Go out and talk to them George."

"Me? What for?"

"Go on," said the parrot. "Trust me."

"Yeah, okay." I went anyway. The suburban afternoon seemed surreal, a man mowing a lawn, children riding big-wheels. I pounded on the driver's seat window of the van, although there was nobody in sight. The back was screened off. I kept pounding, and finally a surfer type appeared through the screen, and rolled down the window. I asked what he was doing."

"Sleeping," he said. "That a problem?" A red claw shot past my ear, grabbed the surfer by the neck, and plucked him out of the window. It reminded me of a description I'd read of a screech-owl picking baby birds out of a nesting box. The surfer evidently hadn't been told what he was watching for. He lay on the street in paralysis. I heard a lawnmower race and stall down the street. The parrot opened the door and disappeared inside. I heard thumps, then its voice telling me to drag the surfer inside.

Two more surfers lay handcuffed under a pile of spotting scopes, tape decks, cameras, radios and other gear. A radio squawked inquiringly.

"Tie him," said the parrot, offering me some extension cord. It pulled off the engine cover and began ripping out the soft parts with its talons. It had put on the raincoat and scarf, but it still must have looked very odd to the small crowd that had gathered down the street by the time we got out of the van. I half-expected them to applaud as the creature streaked toward the house door with ten-foot leaps.

When I got back inside, it was handing a wad of bills to Ricky.

"This will help with any legal expenses," it said. "Thanks for your help. Do you know where Los Mochis is, George?"

"More or less."

"Good. Let's go." Jill started to pick up the bundle, but it grabbed it from her and headed for the garage.

"We'll take care of Lewis," Ricky said.

"Sorry about this."

"They probably won't do anything once they know she's gone. Anyway, I can get a good lawyer."

"How much did it give you?" I asked.

"George!"

I followed Jill to the BMW. The parrot sat in the back seat with its hands folded. It looked like a grandmother from hell.

Ricky opened the garage door and we shot out like a rocket. There didn't seem to be any immediate need for blast-off. The black van stood quiet, and the crowd down the street had dispersed. A normal day in La-La land.

21

Los Angeles finally ended at Camp Pendleton Marine Base, but San Diego began on the other side. It was past rush hour, fortunately. Cape Cod Barrack was the reigning style of the new apartment complexes, which marched along headlands and ridges like tank traps escaped from the Marines.

The freeway exit we pulled into to seek our foregone dinner promised all kinds of gaudy services, but proved to contain only one food outlet. Middle-aged women in uniforms fit for Rommel's Afrika Corps—tan forage caps and frilly Germanic aprons—dispensed deep-fried patties on microwaved buns. The only other people in the place were two tiny, barely pubescent girls at a table with a large, fat baby between them and a mound of styrofoam, paper, and half-eaten food in front of them.

"What a dirty baby you are," said one girl.

"Yes, a dirty, dirty baby," said the other. The baby, which seemed no dirtier than any baby, ignored them.

"What is this?" said the parrot, when we brought the food to it in the car.

"Chicken."

"Extraordinary."

"They didn't have morels."

"What?" said Jill.

"Private joke."

The parrot had been studying maps. "I think we'll cross at this place called Lukeville in Arizona," it said. "Looks like a quiet spot."

"Shouldn't we get across as soon as possible?" I said.

"I think it would be best for me to bypass the border station. I'll go cross country," it said.

"It's desert."

"Yes, I've been wanting to get a good look at it. The Sonoran desert hadn't evolved in my time, you know. The cactus family were still all rainforest trees. Living on the California coast was a little frustrating because everything was so familiar. Washington and Cape Canaveral were the same—magnolias and palmettos. Of course, it was homey, but I've wanted to get a look at the new things—the Arctic, African savannas, the Galapagos. It's not enough to see them in books and television programs."

Jill rolled her eyes at me, still unreconciled to a dinosaur in the back seat.

"There must have been deserts in the Cretaceous," I said.

"Small ones, but they weren't as interesting because the angiosperms hadn't really adapted to them yet. There was a lot of ephedra and some specialized cycads and other gymnosperms, but there was simply a lot of bare rock and sand."

"There still is."

"Yes, but you have these marvelous giant cacti and elephant trees and ephemeral wildflowers. And sand food. I must see sand food."

"Sand food?"

"It lives in the dunes and parasitizes the roots of shrubs. When it comes up, the flower looks like a clot of sand, but the stem is edible. It's supposed to taste like sweet potato."

It was dark by the time we climbed the mountains east of San Diego. Jill fell asleep, and I thought the parrot had too until I glanced in the rear view mirror and saw it peering over my shoulder, its eyes glittering in the light of approaching cars.

"Nervous, George?" It sounded like a gnat was talking about an inch from my ear. Jill didn't stir.

"You startled me."

"Not getting sleepy?"

"Not yet."

"Have you wondered why the van appeared?"

"Uh, yeah," I said uncomfortably.

"Jill is of course not to be trusted."

"Why would she tell the feds?"

"How do you know they were the feds?" the parrot asked.

"Weren't they?"

"I don't know. Anyway," the parrot said, "I haven't let Jill out of my sight."

"Ricky wouldn't inform."

"I think Ricky has principles. I don't know about you."

"I didn't tell them."

"What *did* you do?"

"I called my boss from a phone booth. I told him there'd been a death in the family."

"Why?"

"I felt bad about abandoning the preserve."

"Afraid of losing your job?"

"It's a good job."

"How did he seem, your boss?"

"Normal. He said he'd have Jerry check on the place."

"Jerry can be a charmer when he wants." The creature was silent a moment. "Talk to me before you do something like that again."

"Yessir."

"I do appreciate your help. Do you want money?"

"I'd like to know what you're doing."

"It isn't harmful."

"Why don't you say what it is, then?"

"It's private," the parrot said.

We got to Lukeville at dawn. Jill had taken the wheel at midnight, so I'd gotten a little sleep, although not enough. I've passed the age of all-night drives. Jill also looked wilted in the gray light. The parrot appeared bright-eyed, but it hadn't driven.

"Did you have cars seventy million years ago?"

"Something like that. My, look at these things." We approached Lukeville through Organ Pipe Cactus National Monument. The cacti were blooming, and there were a lot of other flowers. The parrot was glued to the window. "That's mesquite and acacia in the washes, isn't it?"

"I suppose."

"They covered half the southern continent in my time. Now here they are with these bizarre organ pipe objects. It makes me half-believe I was really in space for seventy million years."

Jill rolled her eyes again, but I ignored her. The parrot consulted the map again, then peered at the dashboard.

"Pull over at the next big clump of cacti," it said.

"There'll be lots of cactus to look at across the border."

"That's what I mean to do."

"Come on," I said, "you're not really going to walk across the border. It'll take hours. Why don't you just bandage up again?"

"I want to get out."

"You think they'll be waiting for us in Lukeville? They'll get you pretty fast anyway, if they are. You'll probably get lost, too."

"Just pull over." I did. The creature stripped off glasses, scarf, and raincoat, and opened the door. Jill glanced hungrily at the bundle, but the parrot lifted it out.

"You're going to walk across the desert with *that?*" I exclaimed.

"Give me until midmorning," it said, "about three miles south of Lukeville."

"Midmorning? What time?" But the creature had vanished into the cactus, bundle on its head. Jill looked at me reproachfully.

"What's the matter?"

"You shouldn't have let it go, George. What if it has a rendezvous here?"

"With what? A spaceship? I didn't see you ordering it back into the car."

"What are we going to do?"

"Cross the border and wait for it. You got a better idea?"

"I want to take a bath," Jill said, rubbing her face.

"Be my guest."

"Isn't there a river here?"

"Here?"

"The Rio Grande?"

"Don't they teach geography in KGB school?"

"I'm not KGB. Stop being tiresome. Can we at least get something to eat?"

"The restaurants in Lukeville probably won't be open yet, if there are any. Maybe we can find some sand food."

"What?"

"I'm going for a walk. Come on."

"I'm too tired."

"I'm not leaving you with the car."

"Why not? You're taking the keys."

I marched the protesting Jill into the desert. It wasn't hot yet; in fact, it was chilly, the sky overcast. The desert birds didn't seem to mind. Black-throated sparrows tinkled sweetly from ocotillo tops, cactus wrens cackled in chollas, white-winged doves moaned erotically.

Fatigue affects the pituitary. I cast covetous glances on tight spots in Jill's jeans and jersey as she flounced through the sand. The parrot had bought them for her: she'd had nothing but a shirt and a skirt when we'd fled the preserve. My romantic interest in Jill had flagged under the stress of events, and I knew this wasn't the time to revive it. But glands have their own ideas.

We found a shady spot, a sandbar under a dry wash cutbank overhung with paloverde bushes. Jill lay down and closed her eyes. I wondered if my eyes looked as puffy as hers.

"Were you really in Napa?" I asked.

"Yes."

"Why?"

"I committed myself. Temporarily."

"As part of your cover before infiltrating Aliso House?"

"I was having a breakdown."

"Spies have breakdowns?"

"Hah!" Jill scratched her knee impatiently.

"What were you doing before your breakdown?" I persisted.

"Getting a Ph.D. in economics and political science."

"No wonder you had a breakdown."

"And working as a welfare case worker," Jill continued.

"At the same time?"

"And doing some union organizing."

"Um. What happened when you had your breakdown?"

"I couldn't stop crying. It began in a movie. *Out of Africa.* I shouldn't have gone to it. Terribly incorrect politically."

"You do look a little like Meryl Streep," I said. "Wait a minute. *Out of Africa* came out last year, in 1986. I thought you were already in Aliso House?"

"Some other movie," Jill said, scratching her knee again. "I don't have time to remember movies." I stared at her. "America is such a lonely place. I wanted to jump off the Golden Gate Bridge. Or turn myself in to the FBI just so I could talk to somebody that would understand me."

"Did they understand you at Napa?"

"No. They don't have time."

"How about Aliso House?"

"That was better for me than Napa, actually. More restful. I didn't have to be myself at all. I could just hang myself in the corner and not worry about it."

"Why didn't you stay?"

"I'm not stupid."

"Are you okay now?"

"As long as I keep busy," Jill said. I couldn't think of a response to that. She began to snore daintily.

I awoke covered with sweat. The sun had burned off the overcast; it blazed into the cutbank, roasting me. Jill was gone. I slapped my pocket in panic. The car keys were still there. I jumped up and began to run back to the road, then saw Jill sitting in a mesquite's shade, smirking.

"You looked like a bee stung you," she said.

"I'll sting *you*." I grabbed her by the ribs. She jumped and shrieked. "Ow, my head," I cried.

"You startled me." She smiled, suddenly coquettish, but my erotic vapors had dissipated in the heat. My mouth felt like a hospice for desert termites. I struggled back to the car, which was already hot enough to scorch my hands when I laid them on the doorhandles and steering wheel.

We found no restaurant in Lukeville, but got some bottled orange juice, sour coffee, and stale pastries at a gas station. I approached the border crossing with a pounding heart. The American side almost pointedly ignored us, as though it was our problem if we chose to enter the Third World at this savage spot. The Mexican side showed more concern, although not in an encouraging way. A tall, hawk-faced young man pressed Mexican auto insurance on us as though it were our only chance of survival. The immigration official, who had a startling resemblance to W. C. Fields except that his skin was a deep copper color, considered me incompetent to choose a destination.

"Where are you going?"

I tried to answer in my rudimentary Spanish, but he would have none of it, shaking his head until I confessed in English that I meant to go to Los Mochis. He shook his head again.

"No," he said, "you are going to Mazatlan." Mazatlan is a beach resort for gringo tourists. Los Mochis is on the way there, so I didn't argue. He took his fee, handed me my turista card and sticker, and dismissed me.

"It's like going back fifty years," said Jill as we drove south through Lukeville's Mexican counterpart, which was largely bare or whitewashed adobe. The place was too isolated for Tijuana-style sprawl and sleaze.

"Yeah. What a relief."

"No, George, this country needs development."

"If they want development, all they have to do is come north. At least they have a choice."

"Don't be a bourgeois romantic. You can't keep a country primitive just so Americans can come and visit national parks."

"Why not? You can keep the United States overdeveloped so Europeans and Japanese can come and visit Disney World."

"What's wrong with Disney World? I suppose you hate circuses too?"

"Who said anything about circuses? Anyway, I do. Degrading, gladitorial displays."

"You're against people amusing themselves. Like a puritan. Capitalism is basically puritanical."

"So's communism. You won't even let people into your national parks."

"What?"

"I read that Soviet nature reserves are closed to the public. They're afraid people won't meet their quotas if they let them loose in the woods."

"I'm not Soviet, I told you. At least they don't have animals going extinct, like your condors."

"That's because they're not as overdeveloped as us. And they wouldn't admit it if they did. And they do anyway. The Siberian tiger. So just shut up and look for the creature, okay?"

"Don't tell me to shut up so rudely, please."

We drove on, sullenly, through a cactus desert like its northern counterpart except for increased numbers of goats. We drove ten miles, but saw no giant parrot.

"See, George? It tricked us."

"Cool it, okay?"

"What are we going to do now?"

I pulled off the narrow highway to consider the possibilities. It was 10:30, still within the parrot's timetable. I supposed it had gotten lost in contemplation of a prickly pear. I made a U-turn. When we'd gone nine and a half miles back toward Lukeville, again without sightings, I pulled off again.

"We can't just drive back and forth all day," said Jill.

"I'm aware of that."

"Every time a car passes, I'm afraid they're after us."

"Did you ever wonder if you were too neurotic to be a spy?"

"You're not so normal either. Afraid of women, I think. So you live in the woods."

"Beats the nuthouse."

"That was mean."

"Sorry."

Intersexual arguments are a lot like driving back and forth on a Mexican desert highway—hell on wheels. I made another U-turn. This time, I drove at twenty miles an hour, which enraged the driver of a bus that came up behind us. He blasted us with his horn and almost blew us off the road as he slammed past, leaving faint strains of the Viennese waltz he was playing on his tape deck.

"This is like electroshock therapy."

"Stop exaggerating."

"At least electroshock has a purpose."

I didn't really want to hear more about electroshock therapy. I held my tongue and proceeded at my sedate pace. The car had air conditioning, fortunately, although the engine heat gauge was edging to the right. It takes a surprisingly long time to go ten miles at twenty miles an hour. I gave up at seven, did another U-turn, and roared back toward Lukeville at full throttle.

"What a foolish way to die," said Jill.

"Why don't you say something positive for a change? You Slavs are really downers, you know?"

"Wait until you've been overrun by armies for a few centuries. Then see how you feel."

It took no time at all to get back near Lukeville at ninety miles an hour. When I began to slow down, Jill spoke up again.

"I think I saw something."

"Where?"

"About three miles back."

"Why didn't you say so?"

"I was too frightened." I turned again and sped back southward with a satisfying shriek of rubber. After a couple of miles, I slowed down and began to peer into the cactus. Suddenly, Jill recoiled against my shoulder, making me swerve to the other side of the road. When I got control of the car again I looked out her window and saw the parrot running alongside. The speedometer read thirty-two.

22

"That was a bit much," said the parrot, after downing a quart of orange juice. "We're not built for long-distance running like you grassland mammals." Having retrieved its bundle from the cactus, it put on scarf, raincoat, and dark glasses again, and also a colorful, flounced skirt. Now it looked like a Mexican grandmother from hell.

"Where'd you get the skirt?"

"It was hanging on a bush. It'll cover my feet and tail quite nicely."

"You stole it."

"There was nobody around."

"They were probably hiding, doubting their sanity."

"Then they'll keep quiet about it."

As we resumed southward progress, the parrot became silent and immobile, possibly asleep, although it was impossible to tell. The gray and tan state of Sonora unreeled past the windshield: mountain rocks, valley sands, unexpected bits of range and farmland.

In late afternoon we reached Hermosillo, which looked more like a new Italian suburb than traditional notions of adobe Mexico. We pulled into a sparely elegant Pemex station with trepidation. It was the first time we'd stopped for gas in broad daylight with the parrot in the car. Nobody seemed much interested. Even the small boy who washed the windows gave the creature only a covert glance, perhaps finding red, beaklike faces typical of Norteamericanas.

We drove on into a smoky orange sunset, largely alone with the slope-shouldered road and the piles of concrete slabs and steel tie rods left by bridge repair crews beside arroyos. I was glad the rainy season hadn't started in the mountains, sending flash floods across the highway. Once we passed a family walking beside the road: two grown men and a little boy in straw Stetsons, two adolescent girls and an older woman in scarves. One of the girls had blonde braids. They ignored us the way the Amish ignore passing cars along midwestern highways. They may have been Mennonites.

The desert got drier as we moved southwest toward the Sea of Cortez. Some valleys contained nothing but burrowweed and creosote bush; others held black lava flows that might have been deposited the year before.

"There's so much of it," the parrot said.

"Try the Great Basin," I said. "The Sonoran seems small and friendly in comparison."

"You're so adapted to adversity. All these thorny little shrubs with tiny leaves and flowers. There's a kind of meanness to the Cenozoic. I'm surprised it evolved intelligence."

"Intelligence is how we survive. And what was so intelligence-making about Cretaceous swamps?"

"It was a generous world, then," the parrot said. "Warm, plenty of water almost everywhere, giant flowering trees. There was time for things to grow. Your deserts didn't produce your intelligence, anyway. They produced your religions."

Jill regarded the parrot with near appreciation for a moment, as though she expected it to start spouting dialectical materialism. Instead, it launched into an exposition of the role of forest in brain evolution that soon had our eyes glazed with incomprehension. I began to feel drowsy. It was getting dark. I gave Jill the wheel and fell into a dream about a border station between two ancient jungle civilizations. Animated Olmec idols served as immigration officers and ate travelers unable to state a proper destination. They had small, pointed teeth.

When I awoke, we were rolling along the waterfront in Guaymas. The night air was soft and moist. I felt rested for the first time since we'd left Los Angeles.

"I have to eat," said Jill. She parked across from a brightly lit seafood place that appeared empty inside, although a group of men stood against the outside wall. Jill and I had fresh shrimp with lime juice and Dos Equis beer at a table in front while the parrot remained restively in the car.

"My tail's getting tired," it had said. "If we sit away from the light, they won't notice me."

"You see all the loiterers? You'd make their night."

"Maybe I'll take a stroll on the beach."

"Come on. You can stroll all you like once we get to the mountains."

"You're getting to be like Jerry," the parrot had said ominously, but it subsided into the back seat, and now appeared safely grandmother-like in silhouette from across the street.

"Why didn't you let it go for a walk?" Jill said. "Maybe it would have left the bundle."

"No way, José."

"How much is it paying you?"

"Paying me?"

"That's why you're doing this, isn't it?"

"I don't know why I'm doing this," I said, truthfully. "You're the one who's getting paid."

"Well, you should think about the meaning of this," Jill replied. "Whatever this creature is, it's not human."

"It's rational, though."

"We have no way of knowing its intentions."

"It told me last night they aren't harmful."

"And you believe it?"

"Hasn't done me any harm."

"You're being irresponsible, George."

"You want me to turn us all in to Jerry? That's what I should do as a good American citizen."

"The United States has been irresponsible to keep these creatures hidden away for twenty years."

"It apparently hasn't done us any good."

"If you won't help me look in the bundle, at least help me get in touch with my contacts down here so we can start negotiations with the creature."

"Oh, yeah, so I can start getting chased by Soviet thugs as well as American thugs."

"They're not Soviet thugs. I'll contact them eventually. You can't stop me."

"You can do what you like after I've gone home. Which I'm doing as soon as we get the creature to this hideaway."

"You think it will let you? What if it kills you?"

"Probably eat me too," I said.

Jill got up and stalked back to the car, leaving me to pay the bill. When I got to the car, she was arguing with the creature about whether to get hotel rooms and spend the night in Guaymas. Since I didn't want to spend the night keeping her away from telephones, I voted with the parrot against it. While we were debating, a man in a soiled guayabara approached the car. He was swaying a bit, and leaned against the window for support.

"A donde va?" he said.

"Los Mochis," I said, then regretted it.

"Bueno," the man replied, "Voy contigo."

"What's he saying?" Jill asked.

"He wants to go with us." The man reached back and tried to open the back door. Finding it locked, he put his hand firmly on the front window so I couldn't close it. With his other hand, he took out his wallet and showed me family pictures. He appeared to be a bigamist as well as a sot. I took out my wallet and showed him some money, but he threw up his hands at my crassness before grabbing the window again.

I tried to think of a way to say sorry, no room. I got as far as "lo siento," but the man had dismissed me. He looked past me, first at Jill, to whom he nodded respectfully, conveying disbelief that such a gentle lady was traveling with such a dolt, then at the back seat.

"Buenas tardes, Señora," he said.

"Chinga tu madre, hijo de puta," the parrot replied. It whipped off its sunglasses and lunged open-mouthed at the man, hissing. He took a step backward and sat down in the street. Faces began turning in our direction. The creature leaned back in the seat, making a simmering noise. I headed for Los Mochis.

"Was that your idea of a joke?" I asked, when we got outside the city limits.

"It got rid of him," the parrot replied.

"I mean, did you think it was funny? Is that dinosaur humor?"

"Humor is the hardest thing to translate," the parrot replied. "Don't be supercilious."

"By the way, do you have a name?"

"Yes."

"What is it?"

"Sibsxy Seet Popleopits Zxyva."

"I can't pronounce that."

"You probably could if you tried. It took me awhile to pick up your languages."

"I didn't know you spoke Spanish."

"Everyone in the Western Hemisphere should be able to speak Spanish," the parrot replied, superciliously.

"Americans should know more languages," Jill agreed.

"Do you speak Spanish?"

"No, but I Speak Czech and German."

"And Russian," I said.

"A little," Jill replied.

We got to Los Mochis at dawn, after spending some time sleeping beside the road because I'd been unable to rouse Jill to take over the wheel. I wondered if catatonia was in her behavioral repertoire. She finally stirred when the sky lightened.

"It's getting tropical," she said, stretching prettily. This was an overstatement, but there was a tinge of green to the landscape, and some real trees among the cactus and brush, although most were leafless. The air had the spicy, garbagey, wood-smoke smell that pervades slash-and-burn Latin America. We started seeing more people along the road, small, slim, dark people, the women in colorful shawls, the men in blue denims.

If Hermosillo was like a new Italian suburb, Los Mochis was like a middle-aged one. Rows of low cinder block buildings stood around a largely treeless "zócalo" with stucco benches painted blue and white. As a destination, it could have been depressing. We weren't to seek Ricky's condor detective Terry

Phelan here, however, but in a village in the mountains along the railroad to Chihuahua. There was some confusion about the village's name, Los Toris or Los Pozos, or possibly Los Tozis, but it was near where the railroad crossed the Rio Fuerte. We were then to ask around for the "rancho" of Don Emilio, or possibly Don Ramilio, where Terry was staying. As Ricky had said, there wasn't a telephone book for the area.

The immediate problem was getting on the railroad. When we finally found the station, a brown shed on the edge of town, we found that the train had left. The next train would leave at 4 A.M. the day after tomorrow, and we'd have to go back downtown to buy tickets.

"Now we *have* to get hotel rooms," said Jill. We found a small stucco place, also painted blue and white, at the edge of town. Jill wanted a room of her own, but the parrot vetoed that. It thought we could all stay in one room, but I explained the problems with that.

"You're supposed to be my mother, and it would look normal if Jill was my wife. Mothers don't sleep with married children."

"Why not?" There were gaps in the parrot's education, evidently. I explained incest and other anxieties. "I forgot that you copulate all the time," it said.

"Not all the time."

"You seem to think about it all the time."

"When do *you* copulate?" Jill asked.

"Not very often. But we live longer than you."

"How often?"

"I haven't since ten years before I left, actually."

"Before you left?" I asked.

"On the expedition."

"Wow. Seventy million years of celibacy."

"This is grotesque," said Jill. She jumped out of the car and marched into the hotel.

"We better go in. No jokes, okay?"

"Yes dear." The creature suddenly produced an eerily perfect little old lady's voice. It climbed slowly and feebly from the back seat and tottered toward the hotel bent-over, clutching my arm (there was nothing feeble about its clutch—I had to stifle a gasp).

The three women at the hotel desk seemed convinced when they looked up from a halting conversation with Jill. They smiled indulgently at the creature, and didn't seem surprised when it (we still didn't know its gender) produced a Mexican little old lady's greeting, although they should have been, considering my doltish Spanish. I suddenly remembered its tail, but a glance behind it revealed nothing shocking. The skirt was a good idea.

I had a tense moment when one of the women (with a reproachful glance at me) tried to relieve the little old lady of her bundle. I was afraid it would kick her across the room, but it stayed in character and merely clutched the bundle, squeaking in protest.

"Las Joyas de la Reina," I said, trying to make a joke of it. The queen's jewels. They looked at me blankly a moment, then one of them got the idea and explained it to the others. They laughed dutifully and allowed the parrot to carry the bundle upstairs to its room, which shared a bathroom with ours. I tipped the two women who had accompanied us upstairs lavishly to dispel any lingering doubts about our correctness.

When I looked in on the parrot, it was taking off the raincoat, preparatory to a shower, I supposed. I heard the water start in the bathroom. Jill had gotten there first.

"Tell her not to take all afternoon," it said. "And keep her away from the telephone downstairs."

I went next door and found lumpy-looking twin beds. They'd given the parrot a room with a spacious double bed, so the poor old thing would be comfy. I lay down on the lumps, curious to see in what state of undress Jill would emerge from the shower, and dozed off.

This time I had a nice dream. I was swimming in the ocean, but the water was so clear that it was like flying. I could see the bottom far below, a mile maybe, and I felt a *National Geographic* sense of discovery. "First man to fly over ocean bottom." I saw mountains, plains, and canyons, and this marine landscape didn't have the drabness of terrestrial landscapes seen from a mile up.

It sparkled with coral reef colors. As I glided along, the landscape sloped toward me, and I saw in more detail. I realized that what I'd once taken for a rocky ridge was actually a stone city.

Somehow, I knew the city was long-abandoned, so I felt no shyness, only an archaeologist's lust to explore and collect. I kicked out happily and dove toward it. But then I heard noises, a reverberating boom and a series of thuds. I began to feel anxious: maybe the city was occupied after all.

I heard a scream, and felt out of breath, which made sense, I realized, since humans can't breathe under water. I sat up in panic, knocking aside the pillow that had been on my face.

"Geeeoooorge!"

There was a door beside the bed: the scream had come from there. I opened it into a steaming wet bathroom with soggy towels on the floor. There was another door. I pushed that open, and finally remembered where I was.

Jill was lying on the floor in a contorted position. The parrot was standing on her, like a hawk on a rabbit. One of its claws had punctured the soft flesh of Jill's upper arm, making a small trickle of blood. The creature looked at me with the blank, dispassionate fury of a raptor. Jill's head was twisted toward the opposite wall, so I couldn't see her face.

"Ow, it hurts," she said in a small voice.

The thudding started again. Someone was pounding on the door to the corridor. There was an indistinct exchange in Spanish, then a shocked voice.

"Que pasa? Señora! Abra la puerta!"

The parrot didn't move, except to clamp Jill to the floor when she stirred. I went to the door and spoke through it.

"Esta bien. Solamente un, er, little accident. Accidente. No hay problema."

"Pero su madre, señor. Esta herida? Necessita un Doctor?"

"No, no. Está bien, gracias."

"Pero hay demasiado ruido."

"No mas. No mas."

"Ai!" There were more sceptical sounds, but, eventually, receding footsteps. I turned back to the room. The parrot stared at me. I could see Jill's face now. She looked at me, then glanced over by the bed.

The parrot's bundle lay on the floor. It had been opened, and various objects scattered about, packets of dollars, botanical books, what looked like a plant press, other things I didn't recognize. Most prominent was a suitcase-like box of some kind of shiny metal, which also had been opened. Inside one half was some intricate-looking machinery. Inside the other half were six elongated, pale green eggs set in a soft, foam-rubber-like matrix.

23

"I thought you hadn't copulated in seventy million years?" I said, in as calm a tone as I could manage. The parrot shifted its grip on Jill slightly.

"I haven't."

"Whose eggs are these, then?"

"Mine."

"You're incubating them?"

"Yes."

"Excuse me, but don't eggs usually have to be fertilized to develop?"

"Usually. Close the case for me, will you? Carefully." I hastened to comply. The parrot relaxed visibly as the eggs disappeared from sight.

"You're a parthenogenetic species?"

"Would we copulate, in that case?"

"Guess not."

"It must have been all the time in space. We usually ovulate every few years, but neither of us ever did after the landing."

"Neither of you?"

"There's another female. The pilot."

"And three males?"

"George." Jill seemed to have her breath back. The creature glared down at her. I gave her a look, Jill, that is, and she subsided.

"Then at Robles Negros, I suddenly did. Maybe it was the change in diet, or spending so much time outside. It's still triggered by day length. But I didn't want to go back east, so I missed the lek."

"Lek?"

"Our males have leks in March. They come into breeding plumage and dance and sing and carry on."

"Like prairie chickens?"

"It's a lot more elaborate. And colorful. Of course, there were always some females ovulating in any given year, so an interval of a few years didn't matter, until now. But they've been doing a lek every year anyway. I think they'd do one even if we were both dead. It's their form of football, although they say they're doing it to stimulate us."

"You, like, choose the dancer you prefer and go off and mate with him?"

"There's a great deal of cultural overlay now, but that's the general idea." It, or she, was beginning to look less ferocious.

"I'm very uncomfortable," said Jill.

"You should be, sneaking little bitch."

"Ow! I'm sorry."

"Why didn't you go to the lek?" I asked.

"I told you. I was fed up."

"But you need to reproduce. You'll become extinct." This seemed to weary the parrot. She got off Jill and began replacing the scattered objects in the bundle, after first fiddling with some dials on the egg box. Jill lay there a minute—it looked like a very uncomfortable position—then sat up.

"I feel like I've been torn limb from limb."

"You should have been," said the parrot out of the side of her mouth.

Jill was resilient, however, and answered the creature less apologetically this time. "You should have told us what was in it. It might have been some terrible weapon."

"It's my private affair."

"You want to sleep in the same room with us and you talk about privacy?"

Jill's question struck me as confusing. I tried to move to firmer ground. "But the eggs began to develop anyway?" I prompted.

The parrot stopped glaring at Jill and carefully placed the egg box in a special compartment of the bundle. "It happens sometimes with us. Very rarely. The problem is, I'm going to have to bring them up. I don't want them to be lab specimens or zoo exhibits. I want them brought up properly."

"You're running into the mountains for that? Does Jerry know about this?"

"You two are the only ones that know," the parrot said. She gave me a blood-curdling look. "Regrettably."

"Why? Maybe we could help."

"Help to raise little monsters?" Jill muttered.

"Jill thinks you want to conquer the world," I said. Neither was amused. "So you . . . just laid the eggs and they began to develop?"

"I could tell before. We have tests."

"They'll all be females? Clones?"

"Females?" said Jill.

"Parthenogenesis is when an egg begins to develop without being fertilized by a sperm. The egg grows into a female that's genetically identical to its mother," I explained.

"There'll be six *more* of it?"

I was almost relieved when somebody began pounding on the door again. This time the voice was older and more authoritative, and demanded the door be opened. I virtually got on my knees and convinced the parrot to don scarf, glasses, and a shawl we'd bought in the market, and to get into bed. Jill dusted herself off, and I opened the door. The landlady marched into the room, while the two maids hung back as though ready to flee.

"Esta es casa decente, Señor."

"Claro."

"Lo siento," piped the creature, "pero estoy muy cansado. Tuve una pesadilla." A nightmare. True enough.

"Pobrecita," whispered one of the maids. The landlady eyed Jill's disheveled clothes and bloody arm.

"Exijemos buen comportamento aqui. Entiende? No queremos ni ruido, ni violencia."

"Si. Entendemos. Está bien. Okay." I bowed and scraped and crept and crawled until they left. I was getting tired of mollifying female bipeds.

24

There was embarrassed silence the next morning as we walked out past the hotel desk. The parrot still insisted on carrying her bundle, which must have looked odd, but the proprietress didn't remark on it. We'd managed to spend the rest of the previous night quietly. Jill had gone to bed complaining of nervous prostration. I complained of hunger, and the parrot allowed me to go out to the zócalo for some tacos, but insisted on staying in the room with Jill until I came back. But Jill remained in apparent unconsciousness until 7 A.M., when I awakened to find her eyeing me.

"Are you satisfied now?" I said.

"Why?"

"She doesn't have a new kind of plague in the bundle."

"We don't know what's in those eggs. They might be full of viruses," Jill said.

Now she blinked grumpily as we trailed out into the bright Sinaloan sunlight. The creature wanted to drive out to Topolobampo on the Sea of Cortez to botanize.

"I want some breakfast," Jill said. I had to agree with her, although the creature didn't seem very interested, so we went back to the zócalo, and Jill and I had some huevos rancheros while the creature waited in the car. Then Jill had to go to the bathroom, and I had to lurk around to make sure she didn't use the telephone or sneak out of a window. We got back into the car in vile moods.

We drove westward past large fields on which nothing was growing, then into a desert that seemed to get drier the nearer we got to the coast. A coyote ran across the road.

"That's a species that's going to last awhile," the parrot said.

"Now that you mention it," I said, "what are your plans for species survival?"

"My species?"

"Were you just sitting up there at Robles Negros waiting for somebody to come along and drive you to Los Angeles?"

"I was going to walk."

"To Los Angeles?"

"Farther south in the Coast Range. There are a lot of deep canyons, the kind where the condors nested. They're so isolated, I thought they would be good places for me to hide for a while. But when you and Ricky came, I thought I'd been found out. That's why I followed you, to see what Jerry was up to. I didn't want to be caught by surprise."

"What made you decide we didn't work for him?"

"I didn't think even Jerry would beat up his help."

"But what are you going to do?" Jill said impatiently. The creature looked out the window a minute before she answered.

"What I've told you," she said.

"Sit in the mountains, when you could be increasing our knowledge of genetic engineering?"

"Who said I could do that?"

"You said you sold information for that money," Jill said.

"Yeah," I said, "how did you work that?"

"That's my business," the parrot said, "I'm under no obligation to serve humanity."

"You see, George."

"That's not a very progressive attitude," I said.

"I have an unusual perspective on progress."

"She's so conceited," said Jill. At least she had started using the feminine article for the creature.

"Pull over here for a minute," said the parrot. "I want to look at these plants." I had to sit in the car with Jill while the creature wandered through the brush with her plant press and botany books. She left the bundle with me this time, with injunctions not to let it stay in full sunlight.

"She's turned you into her slave, George."

"She needs help."

"You think she would do this for us?"

"If you arrived in the Cretaceous Period eight months pregnant? I think she might."

"Why should she?"

"What are you, a sociobiologist?"

"She's violent."

"Good reason to keep her happy."

To my unease, the parrot eventually emerged from the bush with two other small figures in shawls, old Indian women. She stood with them for several minutes before getting in the car, evidently having a conversation. The women seemed bemused by her, fascinated and puzzled, which wasn't surprising considering the dark glasses, bandages, and gloves. But they also seemed friendly, and they laughed several times.

"Do you think that was wise?" I asked, as I drove away, watching the two old women standing beside the road as they dwindled in the rear-view mirror.

"Those ladies know a lot of botany," the creature said, scribbling in her notebook. "Just sharing collector's experiences with them."

"You think they meet up with bandaged old ladies in BMWs every day of the week? They're going to talk about you."

"They probably meet with strange gringos fairly frequently," the creature replied. She had a point.

"Gringos who speak good Spanish?" I persisted.

"What good is it knowing languages if you don't get to speak them?"

The Sea of Cortez at Topolobampo wasn't too impressive, silty water roiling against a rocky shore littered with the detritus of a fishing village. A crowd of children observed us as older people carried on their everyday seaside pursuits.

"I was hoping to do a little marine collecting," the parrot said.

"Oh no, you're not going wading around in that getup."

"Why not let her do what she wants, George," said Jill.

"You'd like us to get picked up by the police."

"The authorities should know about this. It's their country."

"Maybe I should tie you up again."

"Let her alone, George," the parrot said. "She has more sense than that."

I bought some beer and roasted fish at a little stand and we ate it in the car. The parrot liked the fish. Then we started back to Los Mochis. On the way, we passed a swampy looking area, and the parrot again wanted to look around. The area seemed deserted. Jill and I went with her. The swamp was mostly bare mud with bits of mesquite-like brush sticking out here and there, but there were a few stagnant pools. A roseate spoonbill poked about in one.

"My," the parrot said, "that looks like one of the lesser hadrosaurs."

"What a beautiful color," said Jill.

"Did, uh, hadrosaurs have colors like that?"

"Oh, yes, in the breeding season it was quite spectacular," the parrot said.

"There were already plenty of birds when you . . . lived," I said. "What were they like?"

"There weren't so many little ones. And there were some really big ones. But rather similar."

"Condors?"

"No, they came with the big mammals. The pterodactyls were still the best fliers back then."

Some caracaras flew over, then a little flock of tree ducks. Jill and I sat and watched birds while the parrot fussed in the underbrush, occasionally making "sipoxzypliop" sounds to herself. It was a pleasant, if bizarre, way to spend an afternoon.

Back in Los Mochis, the creature retired to her room with her trophies. It was hot. I wanted to take a shower, but I was afraid to let Jill out of my sight.

"Oh, stop worrying, George," she said. "I got to a phone yesterday afternoon while you were sleeping."

"Bullshit."

"Ask the creature. She probably knows. You're such an amateur at this."

"How would she know?"

"By asking the woman at the desk."

"Alright, what if you did? Are they going to have the Cossacks here by tomorrow morning?"

"I couldn't reach my contact, actually."

"You expect me to believe that?"

"The phones were down or something."

"I think I will ask the creature. I don't know what to make of you."

"Or, if it would make you feel better, we could take a shower together." I decided I might as well ask the parrot later.

25

There was a man at the hotel desk when we checked out at 3 A.M. to get the train for Chihuahua. Despite the early hour, he got excited about our trip.

"Ah, los montañas! Hay muchos Indios, quien tienen de oro. Muchissimo oro, y hace muy frio." (I assumed that he meant the mountains were cold, not the gold.) "Brrrr, helado. Y mira!" He took what appeared to be a large gold nugget from behind the desk and brandished it. "Puro *oro!*" He put the nugget back, spent by this enthusiasm, but then, as we were walking out the door, he revived and cried, "Hay plata tambien!"

We'd arranged to store the car at the hotel. If they could keep gold nuggets under the front desk, they could keep BMWs in their yard, I hoped. We walked to the train station through black, empty streets, which was just as well. The spectacle of a little bandaged old lady carrying a large bundle while the young couple with her bore only airline bags (which we'd bought to carry our meager possessions) might have caused comment.

Footsteps echoed around a corner, and a squad of soldiers marched into view, square copper men in steel helmets and thick brown uniforms. Despite the modern gear, they looked like something carved on a wall at Teotihuacán. They clattered past us and receded down the street. When we got to the station, they stood together beside the train like a block of chocolate soldiers melted together.

"To protect us from bandits," Jill said. "Romantic."

"More likely leftist insurgents," I said.

"You're the romantic," Jill replied.

"You wouldn't need much protection, anyway."

"That's not very nice, George."

The parrot looked at us from the shadows of its bandages and shawl.

"Have you copulated?" it asked.

"What?"

"That's *our* private affair," said Jill.

"Just trying to keep up to date," the parrot said.

"Weren't you listening at the door?"

"It's easier to ask questions."

"Like at the hotel desk?" I asked. The parrot didn't answer, because a dozen more travelers came on to the platform, big, fleshy men and women in vacation clothes. From their booming conversation, we learned that they were Texans returning from deep-sea fishing. Pretty soon, they disappeared into a gleaming Pullman car. The rest of the train looked like something out of a western movie. The ordinary passengers, which included us, a crowd of Mexicans, and the soldiers, had to wait on the platform for another half hour.

"I'm just trying to make sure where loyalties lie," the parrot said.

"George's loyalties lie where they always have, with himself," said Jill.

"I thought copulation formed a pair bond in your species."

"Yeah, well, I don't think Jill's loyalties lie with me."

"Seems dreadfully complicated," the parrot said. She was right about that: the night before had been dreadfully complicated. Not the shower and bed part, but the aftermath, in which I had asked Jill idly how long it had been since she'd slept with someone, assuming that it must have been a long time, as she'd been in Aliso House for a year or so. She told me that she'd been sleeping with Peter Eliott. I had become consumed with what I first thought was moral indignation, but which I later realized was simple jealousy, as I tossed and turned through the rest of the night. I eventually decided she was probably right when she said there wasn't much she could do to not sleep with him, under the circumstances. But by that time, our relations had returned to their usual querulous state.

The conductor, an austere, bespectacled man, finally let us board. Like the immigration official in Lukeville, he had an authoritarian bent. He pointed us to three seats and firmly stuck our ticket stubs on their backs to make sure we stayed in them. When I asked if the train stopped at Los Toris (or Pozos or Tozis), he shook his head and said we'd have to get off at someplace I didn't catch.

The seats were wooden. I was glad we weren't going all the way to Chihuahua. Jill and the parrot sat together (or rather, Jill sat and the parrot crouched on the seat and balanced on her tail) and I took the seat across the aisle. The car filled up with families and groups of old or young men. As the only gringos, we were the center of attention, although the sole overt signs of this were smiles from Mexican matrons toward our "mother." We were still too close to the U.S. border for friendly curiosity. A pair of young men with a guitar sat behind me, and promptly fell asleep.

The sky was gray when the train left the station and moved across irrigated farmland and scrub. Ahead, the Sierra Madre looked unimpressive, a line of flat-topped ridges. The train bumped along hesitatingly for an hour, until sunrise, then stopped at a station crowded with food vendors. We'd stocked up in Los Mochis, but I bought some tortas, oranges, and hard-boiled eggs while the lads behind me listened critically to my Spanish and then imitated it. The creature accepted a torta and an orange, but rejected an egg.

After the stop, the country became more interesting: foothills dotted with exotic trees upon which perched the long-legged, black and white crested caracaras that eternally kill rattlesnakes in Mexican national iconography. The Sierra remained flat-topped, more a range of buttes than peaks, but it got bigger. I began to wonder just how the train would climb it. After a few more bends in the track, deep gaps in the mountain wall appeared, and children in the car began calling "barrancas, barrancas!" The train soon plunged into a barranca, past an aquamarine river bordered with sycamore, fig, and red-barked Indio desnudo trees.

Unfortunately, my seat was on the side facing the road cut. After ten minutes of canyon rocks close up, I walked out to stand between the cars. This proved breathtaking, especially when the train slammed into a tunnel, filling it with diesel fumes. A middle-aged man in a yellow polo shirt was already out there.

"It sure is beautiful, isn't it?" he said.

"Sure is."

"Where in the States you from?"

"California. You've been in the States?"

"Many times. I worked there. Ah, that water sure looks clean." He looked down at the river, almost directly below. We could see its bottom.

"Do you know the name of it?" I asked. The man asked an old Mexican standing nearby.

"He says it's el Rio de Plata. Silver." My map said it was the Rio Fuerte, but I didn't argue. "I'm coming from Hermosillo," the man continued, "it's very nice and quiet there."

I noticed that he had red-stained teeth. I'd heard that this meant he came from Chihuahua, because the water there is full of iron oxide.

"You live in Chihuahua?"

"Yes, I work there in the biggest hotel. I've worked in Texas too. San Antonio . . . See there on the side of that mountain?" He gestured toward a burned patch in the low forest. "That's where an Indian is trying to grow corn. There are very many Indians here."

It was getting chilly between the cars. The man in the polo shirt went back in. I stayed out until the train went into a particularly long and sooty tunnel. When I got back to my seat, I found that the two young men behind me had reversed theirs so that they now sat with their backs to me, facing a man and woman who evidently were their friends. Unfortunately, the seats didn't reverse very well. As the two men reclined in theirs, their weight gradually forced my seat back forward. I found myself sitting first in an austerely upright position, then in an uncomfortably hunched-over one. To their amusement, I pointed this out to them. I got them to pull theirs forward, but the downward creep began again, and in ten minutes I had to crane my neck tortoise-fashion to look out the window.

The young men were engrossed in music. They tried to sing "Guantanamera," but didn't know the words. They sang ranchero songs, crying "Ai! Chihuahua!" and stamping their feet. I slipped out of my tortoise shell and leaned on Jill's and the parrot's seat.

"Having a nice trip?"

Jill looked at me strangely. The parrot peered at her bundle, in the luggage rack above.

"We heard a noise in it," Jill said. A woman in the seat in front glanced back sympathetically at the bandaged creature, then looked away shyly when I smiled at her.

"In the bundle?"

"Like a squeak."

"You mean they're *hatching?*"

"She says it should be too early. There hasn't been any noise for an hour. She says they may start making little noises a few days before they actually begin to hatch."

"Phew."

"She also says they sometimes hatch early if they get disturbed."

"How long before we get to this place?" the parrot asked.

"I don't know."

"It better be soon."

I decided to stroll through the train. The "Caballeros" promised temporary refuge, but was "ocupado." I continued through a car consisting of a big yellow metal box with a corridor on one side, then stumbled through a glass door into a dining car such as I hadn't seen since I was seven years old. There were thick white tablecloths, shining silver place settings, waiters in white tunics. It contained the officer in charge of the soldiers, three middle-aged Mexican men, including the man in the polo shirt, and the half-dozen Texan couples from the Pullman car.

"I wonder why they use cabbage instead of lettuce?" a woman was saying.

"It's because they don't have the lettuce," a man replied.

Another Texan was trying to get the waiter's attention. The waiter, zipping up and down the aisle like a hummingbird in a penstemon patch, seemed unaware of his ponderous gestures.

"I guess they work pretty hard," said the woman across the table from him.

"Yes," the man replied, "they do."

I would have liked to summon the waiter, but the atmosphere in the car somehow implied that a lone, youngish gringo might be pushing it simply by sitting at one of the immaculate tables. I contented myself with the view through the plate glass windows. We passed more corn patches, freshly burned for spring planting, but no other signs of humanity, no houses or roads. It was very different from the California mountains. The vegetation was comparatively sparse, but at the same time showy, even in the brown dry season.

Suddenly, the waiter hovered over me. I ordered only coffee, which I was afraid might elicit angry hummingbird squeaks, but he simply zipped away so abruptly he might have walked away backwards. The coffee arrived posthaste, silver pot, creamer, sugar jar, spoon, and china cup and saucer seeming to place themselves on the table as the waiter sped past, eyes on the horizon.

I returned to the coach with a caffeine-induced sense of reassurance that was quickly shattered. Even before entering, I could see something was wrong through the glass of the door. Instead of dozing or looking out the window, many of the passengers were turned toward the center of the car, where our seats were. When I took a deep breath and entered the car, many turned their eyes toward me. So did Jill, whose eyes were the widest in the car. I acted preoccupied, and strolled to my seat, which was now completely horizontal, the two young men asleep on it.

There was a peculiar noise, muffled but unmistakable, a kind of raucous gasp. The other passengers stopped staring at me and looked back toward the parrot's bundle. Mexican trains have a reputation for accommodating livestock, but that wasn't true of this one. Anyway, the sound from the bundle didn't resemble that of any common livestock.

"We have to get off!" said Jill in a loud whisper. "Stop the train!"

"Stop the train?"

The car door opened and the conductor came in. He seemed to think I was the cause of the disturbance.

"Donde es su asiento?" he asked reprovingly, as though I'd concealed it. I pointed at the sleeping musicians, but I'd lost his attention. The parrot had stood up, lifted Jill out of the way, and reached for her bundle. Her skirt got hiked up in the process, and her tail whipped past the eyes of a family across the aisle. They crossed themselves. The tail remained visible as the creature headed for the caboose, bundle on head.

"Pull the emergency brake, George!" Jill pointed to a red handle at the rear of the car, and I headed for it on impulse. The conductor came after me, shifting from reproof to agitation.

"Cuidado! Peligro!"

I pulled the thing anyway, and the train, which had been climbing a grade, came to a shrieking, lurching halt. It flung me, Jill, and the conductor to the floor of the aisle. Picking myself up, I saw two pairs of black-trousered legs waving at the ceiling. The musicians now had their heads wedged in the front of my seat, but I didn't have time to gloat. People who had remained upright now looked wonderingly out the window.

The parrot receded across a corn patch with bounding leaps which soon took her out of sight, apparently over a cliff. I heard doors slamming and feet pounding from the caboose, where the soldiers were. I grabbed the flight bags, grabbed Jill, left the train and took off across the corn patch. Somebody shouted "Alto!" but I didn't look back.

26

The cliff at the edge of the corn patch wasn't high or steep, fortunately. I slipped and slid out of sight of the train. There was no sign of the parrot.

"Let me go, George." I was still clutching Jill's arm, already black and blue from the parrot's grip. She rubbed it and winced.

"We've got to get away from the trucks." I was afraid the soldiers were pursuing, although I couldn't think of any particular reason why they should. We hadn't robbed anybody, and as far as I knew it wasn't illegal to stop a train and get off. I hobbled down the tricky rhyolite slope, wondering what kinds of poisonous snakes lived hereabouts.

"We only have food for a couple of days," said Jill, following me without confidence. I wished I'd brought camping gear, but it hadn't seemed necessary for a trip to Los Angeles.

"We'll stay here a couple of days," I said, "then walk the tracks into town. It can't be much farther."

It was an interesting situation, in a frightful sort of way. I'd never been so completely without equipment, orientation, and plans.

At least there wasn't much doubt about what direction to take. The cliff ended in a talus slope that led down to a steep, tree-filled gully with brushy sides. It was simply a question of up or down. The railroad was up, so we went down. When we got well into the trees, I listened, but heard neither pursuing soldiers nor retreating train.

"I have to go to the bathroom," said Jill.

"Watch out for snakes." I tried to see back along our path as Jill disappeared into the trees, but the only movement was a pair of fast-flying birds, possibly parrots—real parrots. Jill took a while. A fine time to come down with turistas. When she finally appeared, though, she looked as though more than her stomach was bothering her.

"My God," she said, "she's killing them!"

"What?"

"That . . . monster. She's wringing their necks!"

"What? Where?" I started in the direction Jill had come from.

"Don't go down there. It's horrible."

I stumbled down to a place where the trees thinned and the ground leveled to a little rocky meadow over a breathtaking drop into the canyon. I stopped at the edge. The dinosaur parrot sat in the shade of an oak tree. She'd taken her disguise off. I could see the top of the bundle beside her, but rocks and grass concealed everything else.

Things didn't seem particularly horrible. I spied awhile, but she didn't move. I finally walked toward her. She didn't seem surprised. Her eyesight was very good. She didn't say anything, just watched me approach.

The egg box stood open, with three eggs in it. Two were whole, the other was cracked in half. A small, wet head protruded from it, mouth open and eyes closed. From faint movements of its neck, I could see that it was breathing. The dappled shade of the oak made it hard at first to see what was on the ground around the box. I made out some pale shards of eggshell, then, startlingly, two miniatures of the parrot, sitting on their tails. Their pale, buff-colored down was still wet, but their eyes were open and apparently focused. The parrot spoke, startling me.

"You probably shouldn't be here. They might imprint on you."

"Jill thought you were killing them."

"One was badly damaged. The others would have killed it if I hadn't."

"The others?"

"They aren't very nice at this stage. It's different from mammalian development. They're physically precocial for the early months, but the brain isn't developed, so there's not much we can do with them. They can take care of themselves, but they're aggressive to one another, so crippled ones don't survive."

"They just run wild?"

"They aren't completely independent. They'll follow me. And you, if you stay around much longer. But maybe it's a good idea to get them used to humans."

"You seem so calm."

"Try threatening them." I didn't take her up on this. It was odd how she could combine rational detachment with strong instinctual aggressiveness. Or maybe it wasn't so odd.

The head protruding from the egg gave a shake, and got its arms free. A hole had appeared in one of the remaining eggs. The little creatures had beaklike egg teeth that made them look even more parrots than their mother. They were about parrot-sized.

"You don't help them hatch.?"

"No, it's an important experience for them."

A snout protruded from the new hole and made the same raucous gasp we'd heard on the train. This stimulated the half-hatched one. It shook itself again, and flopped over with only its feet still in the egg. It looked pathetic, its feathers slick with albumen, but its eyes were already open a crack.

"They hatch fast."

"They'll be speed demons for a while."

"What happens then?"

"When?"

"When the brain starts to grow, like you said?"

"They get confused, lose coordination, become less aggressive, less independent."

"Strange." The parrot didn't answer. "I mean, animals usually get more self-sufficient as they get older."

"Like human infants, which can swim and hang on to branches right after birth?"

A grasshopper landed on a stem near one of the fully hatched baby parrots. She (I assumed) looked at it, then made an instinctive dash at the insect. It was a clumsy movement, and the grasshopper shot away. Its sudden flight disconcerted the little creature. She scurried to her mother, and actually climbed on her foot. She made a little, gasping sound, and the parrot blinked down at her. I thought of female alligators.

"They eat insects?"

"Insects, lizards, fruit ... anything they can catch, really. I'm glad we came here. It's a lot like the Gwawactxtlopxt in Sceexxchyzzziou. Surprising how little things have changed— sycamores, figs, cypresses, oaks, palms. Good climate for us."

27

I was in water again, but it wasn't clear. It was greasy gray-brown, like some kind of effluent. I looked for someplace to swim to, but there were only some steep rocks, and after I'd looked at the rocks a minute, I realized they were covered with pterodactyls, or some other kind of flying reptile. They were the same color as the water, and had big ochre eyes with vertical pupils. They were all staring at me.

I thrashed around anxiously, and touched bottom. It didn't seem any more promising than the water. It felt slimy, with sharp objects in it. I stepped on something that moved, and felt a pain in my toe.

"Agh!" I struggled awake, but the pain persisted. I moved my foot: there *was* something attached to the toe. It squeaked and thrashed around as I shook it off. I opened my eyes and saw one of the parrot's hatchlings teetering beside my foot. Evidently, she had seen soft, pink objects protruding from her mother's skirt and shawl (with which Jill and I had covered ourselves for the night) and had given one an exploratory bite. Seeing me look at her, she cocked her head, interested and unintimidated.

I looked across the canyon. The sun hadn't risen yet, but the sky above the rim was pink, what I could see of it. The roof of the rock shelter we were in cut off most of it. The shelter was a recess in the rhyolite canyon wall, about ten feet deep and eight feet high. I'd spent a relatively comfortable night in it, two nights actually, since we'd left the train. Evidently other people had too. It contained a stone hearth, sleeping platforms, and various rocked-in pits and compartments that probably served for storage. Whoever lived there wasn't around—there were no personal belongings except some corn husks and broken plates—but they had been. Fresh ashes lay in the hearth, and the floor had been swept recently. I'd read that Tarahumara Indian families use canyon rock shelters in winter, then move to the high plateaus in spring.

Jill made a protesting sound at my movement, but didn't awaken. The creature seemed asleep too, crouched in the corner with her other four offspring clustered around her like baby quail. But they were awake, and watching my interaction with their sibling.

I put my shoes on and went outside. The sun came up, and it felt good, making me shiver slightly. I heard a galloping sound and looked behind me. All five young parrots (I didn't know what to call them. Parrotlets? Parrotlings?) had emerged from the shelter. They paused in a patch of sunlight and blinked, obviously enjoying the warmth. Their down had fluffed out and gotten paler, making the naked skin around their eyes and snouts seem dark. Despite the down, they looked more lizard-like than their mother, lacking her domed cranium.

But they were by no means lizards, although I'd begun to wish they were. Lizards spend most of their time sitting inoffensively in the sun. These little creatures already were more like a troop of fledgling jays, swarming around with inquisitive and exclamatory cries. They were still weak and clumsy, but considering that they'd been hatched three days before, the prospects for peace of mind weren't promising. The parrot hadn't been fooling about their imprinting on me. They liked to swarm around me almost as much as around her, and they liked biting my toes even better than her scaly claws.

I desperately wanted a cup of coffee. A piece of toast and a fried egg would have been heaven. I had to content myself with three crackers and some icy water from the spring that rose in a little gully near the shelter. The hatchlings followed me there, and almost caught the resident frog this time, splashing water on my leg in the process. I felt sorry for the frog.

There was a throaty sound from the shelter, and the horde returned in that direction. Their mother was calling them for the morning head count. The frog stuck its head back out of the spring pool, and I found myself eyeing it speculatively. I supposed frog legs could be roasted over an open fire, although it wasn't a very substantial frog. Still, it seemed increasingly possible after three days of stretching a two-days' supply of oranges, hard-boiled eggs, crackers, and sardines, although if the hatchlings couldn't catch it, I probably couldn't either. They'd already put a dent in the local insect population.

When I went back to the shelter, the parrot was holding up one of her offspring by the leg and inspecting her critically.

"What are you looking for?"

"Fleas, ticks, funguses."

"Do you think there are dinosaur parasites left after seventy million years?"

"Microorganisms are very resourceful." She put the small creature down and hastily grabbed another. They were getting harder to grab.

"What will you do when they get too fast to catch?"

"Stop catching them."

"Seems kind of undisciplined." The parrot didn't answer. One of her offspring was trying to bite her hand. "How did you raise them in cities?"

"We didn't raise them in cities. Might as well raise cows and pigs. It's one of the sillier things you do." She put the hatchling down, and the horde dashed back into the sunlight. They looked pretty much alike, but behavioral differences were beginning to appear. The one that had bitten my toe seemed an emerging dominant.

"Human children don't eat grasshoppers."

"You'd be better off if they did."

"Be quiet, will you?" said Jill, turning over on the sleeping platform and pulling the parrot's shawl over her head. Then she threw off the shawl and sat up. "I can't stand this anymore."

"Have some crackers."

"We've got to get some decent food, George. You've got to go to town."

"I will."

"If you don't, I will."

"We've been through that," I said.

"Why don't you trust me?" I didn't bother answering this. Jill had indeed made a phone call from Los Mochis, although the parrot and I had no way of knowing if her story about not making contact was true. "Where would I go if I ran away?" she continued. "I have no money and I don't speak the language."

"We need a woman's hand with the young'uns."

"Ha. It's you who they think is their mother."

"I'll go today."

"You should have gone yesterday. You're just afraid to." Jill had a point. The idea of strolling into town after having participated conspicuously in the great train escape wasn't appealing. The prospects of finding Terry Phelan seemed slim. "How do we know *you* won't just run away?"

"Gimme a break."

"I haven't been this hungry since I was in Czechoslovakia."

"Are you going to eat those crackers?"

"Days with nothing but lousy black bread in the stores."

"Because if you aren't, I could use some extra energy for the walk into town."

"I feel light-headed."

"So eat the goddamn crackers."

"Split them," the parrot said. She hadn't complained of hunger at all. I suspected her of snapping up the odd grasshopper.

I departed with two extra crackers under my belt. At least I didn't have to carry a pack. The small parrots began to follow me, probably hoping I'd lead them to more insects. I tried to shoo them away, but that didn't work for long. I went back to the shelter and complained.

"Such a good mother," said Jill.

"They'll get tired pretty soon," said the parrot.

"Come on. Control the damn things."

The parrot made her throaty call sound, and I fled up the gully.

The town was four hours' walk up the tracks from where we'd left the train. It was a fairly steep climb, and by the time I got there, the country was different, the air colder even in the bright spring weather. It was pine and madrone forest, like California, except that the pines were small and the madrones lacked the colorful garnet and beryl bark of the California species. Although it was forest, it looked heavily populated. The grass in meadows was cropped to the ground. Yet I didn't pass a soul on the walk—at least, I didn't see anybody.

There wasn't any sign, so I didn't learn the town's name. Boxcars stood on a siding, and buildings straggled up a steep, unpaved street. Some of the buildings were derelict, but the boxcars looked lived-in, with flowerpots on windowsills and hanging wash.

An adolescent boy in a ragged sweater stood beside the tracks as though waiting for the train. He greeted me effusively, and launched into a speech that seemed to be about progress, brotherhood, and world peace. His eyes had a faraway look. I gave him some pesos, and he went back to waiting for the train.

I started up the street, looking for someplace to buy food. Three tiny men in jeans, T-shirts, and Stetsons watched me.

"Buenos dias," I said.

"Yos," they replied, virtually in unison, and glanced away shyly. I wondered what "yos" meant. Short for "adios"? I passed a group of children, who said "gootbye."

I came to a pair of swinging doors painted the toxic turquoise beloved of Mexican publicans. I could see a man behind a bar inside, but no food. I would have liked to have kept looking, but I saw nothing resembling a food store farther up the street. I pushed through the doors.

The bartender nodded at me. A pair of men in blue work clothes talked earnestly but almost inaudibly in a corner. They ignored my entrance, but two others standing at the far end of the bar looked up with interest. One had bright greenish-blue eyes and honey-colored hair and skin. The other was the Olmec type, squat and powerful, with kinky black hair.

I asked for coffee, but the bartender shook his head, so I ordered a beer. Then I asked, not very hopefully, about food. Some eggs and tortillas, maybe. The bartender seemed to have a brainstorm, and went through a back door to talk to somebody. Some minutes later, as my undernourished system was starting to fly from the beer, a little girl came in with a plate of beans and eggs and a basket of tortillas. Nothing had tasted so good in years. The two men down the bar looked on with amusement as I stuffed my face.

"Hongry," said the green-eyed man. At least, that's what I thought he said.

"Si, tengo hambre."

"Where you coming from?"

"California." That seemed a sufficiently vague response, but it didn't seem to bore them as I'd hoped it would. I should have said I was from Nebraska. The two men drifted along the bar toward me, and the bartender drifted away.

"Ah, California. You come on the train?"

"I've been hiking. Vacation."

"Kiking?"

"Caminar." I wriggled my fingers.

"Ah, you walking. You look for gold?"

"No, looking at birds. Mira pajaros. Birdwatching." The green-eyed man discussed this with his companion, who evidently had no English. The green-eyed man smiled a lot, but the other didn't.

The talkative one pointed to himself and said, "I am Carlos. My friend here," he pointed to the black-haired man, "Tito."

I introduced myself. "Pleased to meet you."

"You Americans like look at birds. We have many Americans coming here. They go into the barrancas, look at birds. Don't you have birds in California?"

"Different kinds."

"Why you like look birds so much?"

"It's kind of a hobby."

"Kobby?"

"For fun."

"Ah, fun. You want some fun? You want some drogs?" Carlos asked. Tito snapped his fingers to get my attention, then waggled them in front of his eyes and said "flores, flores." He had a tenor voice. He reminded me a little of Oliver Hardy.

"No. No me gusta," I said, trying to look "correcto y decente." "Muy malo." Tito finished his beer, and I offered to buy another round. They agreed, and invited me to join them at a table. I'd been hoping to bring the bartender into the conversation, but I couldn't see any way to refuse the invitation.

Tito repeated his "flores, flores" routine as we sat down, but I scowled righteously, so they gave up on that. Carlos invited me to admire his partner's gun, hidden under the tail of his guayabara. Tito also showed me a laminated Policia Judicial badge, with his picture in color. I was appreciative.

The two men in the corner had vanished, I noticed. The bartender seemed to be having an out-of-body experience. But my brain cells were so pleased with the food and alcohol I'd just given them that they couldn't seem to concentrate on the situation.

"There were some Americans that hold up a train," said Carlos. "You know these people?"

"Held up a train?"

"To rob the passengers."

"Mm?"

"Drog addicts."

"No, I don't know any people like that."

"You watch birds? Where your . . . ?" He imitated somebody holding binoculars to their eyes. "Eh?"

"Binoculars."

"Where your binoculars?"

"I left them in my camp."

"Ah, you komping here?"

"Near here."

"You should be careful to komp here. Some bad people." Tito nudged Carlos and asked a question, and they talked awhile. Carlos smiled at me.

"Where your komp?"

"In the barranca."

"We go there with you. To make sure is safe."

"Thanks but . . . it's very far. Muy lejos caminar mucho. Appreciate it, but really . . ." Tito shook his head.

"No, no. We go with you," said Carlos.

"Okay. But first let's have another beer. Tres cervezas mas, por favor." The bartender roused himself from his trance and brought beers, which my new friends accepted. I'd thought this might give me time to think, but I began to wonder if I'd made a mistake. The two men began to seem a lot drunker than they had at first.

"Yes," said Carlos "there are some bad people here, who like to kill. Last year they have found a man who was torture."

Tito sat slumped, with a sullen look. Carlos seemed to be working himself up to something.

"Listen!" he said. "This man was my friend! Terrible things they did to him. They cut off his . . ."

The swing doors opened on a blond, bearded Anglo so tall his head almost touched the doorframe. His backlit hair formed a sort of halo. He was dressed Mexican style, in a Stetson, blue work clothes, even rubber sandals. He peered at us, eyes not yet adjusted to the barroom gloom.

"Terry!" I cried, hopefully. He hesitated, obviously surprised.

"Who's that?" he said. He had a deep voice, with a nasal, southwestern edge.

"Ricky Karhu said to look you up. Terry Phelan? I'm George Kilgore." I got up from the table, walked toward him, and held out my hand. He hesitated again, then shook it. He looked past me at Carlos and Tito, then at the bartender, who looked back impassively.

"How'd you get up here?" he said.

"On the train."

Terry went to the bar, bought a beer, and took a long swallow. He belched, and looked at Carlos, then said something in Spanish so good I couldn't understand it. Carlos laughed, a little reluctantly. Tito looked straight ahead.

"On the train, eh?" he said.

"Ricky thought we could stay with you a while. Get a look at the mountains. Birdwatch."

"I wish Ricky had told me about it."

"He would have . . . but . . ."

Terry took another long drink from the bottle and put it down. He put some money on the bar, and nodded toward the two men. The bartender opened two more bottles, and Terry placed them on the table.

"Salud, hermanos," he said. Carlos lifted his bottle and drank. Tito waited a moment, then drank.

THE VERMILION PARROT

Terry asked a question, again in Spanish too good for me to understand. Carlos answered him, and they got into a heated discussion. Tito shook his head and said something a few times. Then Terry turned around and looked at me.

"Come on," he said, and started toward the door. I followed very readily. I glanced back when I got to the door. The two men sat staring into space as though I'd never existed.

The sun hurt my eyes. I had the beginnings of a headache from the beer. Terry got into a Land Rover parked in the street, and started the engine. I got in too. He put it in gear, backed out, and drove away.

A few minutes later, we were jouncing along a rutted track through the pine forest. Terry hadn't said a word, and I couldn't think of anything that didn't sound foolish.

"You said 'we,'" Terry finally said.

"Excuse me?"

"You said 'we.' Who are *we?*"

"Two other ... ah ... people." Terry glanced at me in a not particularly friendly way.

"So what's going on? Ricky send you to check up on me?"

"No. He thinks you're doing fine here. We, uh, had some trouble with the government?"

"What government?"

"The U.S. government."

"Well, you just about had some trouble with the Mexican government back there."

"Uh huh."

"Something about some gringos tried to hold up a train?"

"We just stopped the train and got off a little early."

"Why?"

"Thanks for getting me out of that, by the way. You know those men?"

"Yeah, I know them, Why'd you stop the train?"

"We felt like camping out for a while."

Terry gave me another unfriendly look, and stopped talking. The road started to descend into a large arroyo.

"Where are we going?" I asked. "Ricky said you were staying at a ranch around here?"

"That's right."

"Do you think we could stay there awhile?" Terry didn't answer. "I know it's an imposition."

"Doesn't look like I've got another option. Carlos and Tito up there were thinking about arresting you."

"I was afraid they were thinking of throwing me in the barranca."

"Not unless you gave them a real hard time."

"How did you talk them out of it?"

"I traded on some goodwill."

"Maybe we could help find the condors." Terry gave me a third unfriendly look, like he didn't need help from tourist amateurs. I saw his point.

"What did Ricky tell you?" he said, sharply.

"That there were some rich Americans with big birds in cages around here, and you were investigating it."

"Does Ricky go around telling everybody this?"

"He'd just found out. No, I'm sure he doesn't. We were in some trouble."

"What trouble?"

"You should . . . ask my friends about that."

"Where are they?"

"About four hours' walk down the tracks from town." Terry gave me the silent treatment again for a while. The road got steeper and rockier. Finally he spoke again.

"There's a trail that goes by the tracks near there. We can take some horses tomorrow and get them."

"That's really generous of you."

"Are either of them women?"

"Yes."

"Shit."

"What's the matter?"

"This isn't Yosemite National Park."

The road got even steeper and increasingly hard for me to make out. We slammed over low boulders and across gullies that would have stopped us if Terry hadn't attacked them with bravado.

"I always carry a change of underwear on this drive," he said.

28

The ranch was a pleasant surprise, neat whitewashed buildings set among palm, orange, and mango trees (we'd dropped back to semi-tropical elevation). I'd been expecting a tin-roofed shack. A muscular middle-aged man came out as we drove in, and I saw a woman of similar age in the garden.

"Is that Don Ramilio?"

"Don Emilio? No, he lives in Culiacan. We're renting from him. That's his cousin, Euphemio. He takes care of the place with his wife, Clara. Good cook."

"Nice. What's it cost?"

Terry didn't answer. He parked the jeep in the shade and went over and started talking to Euphemio. I sat in the jeep with my eyes closed awhile, wishing I hadn't drunk so much beer. I didn't blame Terry for resenting my sudden arrival, but I wasn't looking forward to visiting with a Clint Eastwood clone.

Finally, he turned back toward me. "Want some coffee? Clara makes great 'pan dulce'" Yes, I wanted some coffee. A bathtub-full.

The house was like a Western movie interior: tile floors, plastered walls, handmade wood and leather furniture. The woman came in with a tray of earthenware crockery smelling of pastry and fresh coffee.

"They grow coffee here," said Terry.

"Must be hard to tear yourself away from all this."

"Hm?"

"To go looking for condors."

"Hm."

"You seem to know your way around here."

"Yeah?"

"It must help to be friendly with guys like Carlos and Tito. Must be easy to get stepped on, down here, if you don't know what you're doing."

"It's not Yosemite National Park."

"Hm."

"Your friends as hungry as you?" Terry asked, watching me stuff the last pastry into my mouth.

"We ate the last of our crackers this morning."

"They'll have to make it through another night. It's too late to start today."

"Whatever." I wasn't in a hurry to introduce Terry to the parrot. I couldn't think of a way to explain her in advance, either. It was nice just to sit quietly with a full stomach and a caffeinated head. Terry went off to do something with Euphemio. I spent the remainder of the afternoon on the porch, watching trogons and tanagers in the fruit trees.

Terry was right about Clara's cooking. That night she made a chicken stew with fresh cilantro and green mangoes that I couldn't get enough of.

"Maybe you should take it easy," Terry said. "It'll go right through you if you overdo it."

"You're probably right. So, how did you get in the condor saving business?" Terry had produced a bottle of wine with dinner, and I hoped it might loosen his tongue. It was loosening mine.

"I don't know," he said. "Seemed like a wide-open field."

"You don't think captive-breeding will do it?"

"Nope." Terry was silent for a moment. "Nothing those fools up there do is going to do it. Stealing eggs and putting them in incubators, like they were chickens."

"It seemed to be working until the free adults disappeared."

"No way."

"What do you mean?"

"You think the condors need somebody to teach them how to live? They've been doing it for ten million years. They should have left them the hell alone. They don't care shit about condors. They're trying to make themselves feel good. And picking up paychecks doing it."

"How about you?"

Terry shifted in his leather-bottomed chair impatiently and swallowed some wine. "You think they send me a paycheck? I live off the land."

"What do you think *will* do it?"

"About five hundred tons of gelignite in every dam, canal, and power plant in southern California."

"I mean seriously."

"Might as well be sooner as later. The longer they go on, the worse it gets. At least in this country they know what survival is about."

"So why look for the condors?"

"I don't like to see the bastards get away with it."

"What bastards?"

Terry ate a tortilla and sat back in his chair. "You ask a lot of questions."

"Just interested."

"What do *you* do for a living?"

I told him about the South Coast Preserve. He nodded. "You know it?"

"I used to work for the Forest Circus around there. Ten years ago. I met that old guy Roberts a couple times."

"Forest Circus, eh? That's good. I used to work for them. In Shasta–Trinity."

Terry raised his eyebrows and put down his empty wineglass. The bottle was empty too. I was feeling comfortably drowsy. "We should get going early, tomorrow," he said.

"Sure appreciate it."

Terry stood up and went inside. We'd been eating at a table on a sort of patio in back. Clara came out of the kitchen and started clearing the plates.

"Muchas gracias, Señora. Me gusta mucho la comida," I said.

"De nada, Señor." Mexicans are so polite. I visited the outdoor plumbing and retired to the guest room Terry had assigned me. The bed was homemade looking, but comfortable. I fell into a deep sleep.

I awoke with a full bladder and a sense of disorientation. It was completely dark and silent, and it took me a while to figure out how to get outside. I finally groped my way out the front door. The Milky Way was a solid mass above the canyon rim. A floorboard on the porch behind me creaked, and I jumped and splashed my foot.

"Shit."

"Sorry," Terry said. "Just making sure everything's nailed down."

"You're a light sleeper."

"Light sleep, long life."

"Is that a Mexican proverb?"

"That's an American proverb."

29

"What the hell is that?" said Terry.

He was getting even testier than usual. I was having trouble finding the exact gully into which we'd fled from the train. Although we'd left the ranch at dawn, it was mid afternoon before Terry, Euphemio and I approached the rock shelter. I'd felt nervous about Euphemio coming, but hadn't been able to think of any good reason for not wanting him to.

The noise Terry referred to might have been made by a flock of jays with Vietnamese accents. It was definitely time to tell him about my friends, who at the least were likely to spook the horses. Terry had loaned me a placid mare, but I hadn't ridden since the Forest Service days, and not much then, and I didn't want to get thrown on my head. I dismounted with relief.

"I have to explain something," I said, and tied the mare to a tree. Terry looked testy, then dismounted too. Euphemio stayed on his horse, holding the other two we'd brought.

I told Terry how'd I'd come from the South Coast Preserve to the Sierra Madre. It took a while. He looked at the ground as I spoke, and nodded occasionally. When I finished, he stayed still a moment, then looked at me and raised his eyebrows.

"Far out," he said.

I was trying to formulate a response when the horses started shying. Euphemio stared beyond us with astonishment, then had to wrap his arms around his horse's neck to keep from

THE VERMILION PARROT

getting thrown. He dropped the halter, and the other two horses bolted. I was afraid my and Terry's horses were going to bolt too, leaving their jaws attached to the tree.

The parrot stood beside a tree about ten feet away. She wasn't wearing her costume. When Terry saw her, he jumped.

"Not to worry," she said. The Cretaceous sense of fun again.

"Tell Euphemio it's okay," I said to Terry. A rifle in a saddle holster worried me, but Euphemio evidently was too surprised to think of using it. Terry spoke to him, but he didn't seem reassured.

"I hope you brought food," the parrot said. "I've been thinking of eating Jill."

"Aaaaaagh!" Euphemio spun his horse and galloped away. The young parrots had just emerged from the trees. I was afraid the remaining horses would break loose. The young parrots wanted to examine them. I shooed them away, and encouraged Terry and their mother to retire to the rock shelter, leaving the horses in peace.

We had brought food, but the horses Euphemio had been holding had bolted with it. When Jill heard this, she collapsed on the sleeping platform and cried that she would not eat insects.

"Insects?" Terry asked, regarding her with admiration.

"The little ones eat insects," I said.

"They're kind of cute," said Terry, extending his hand to one of the young creatures. She bit it.

"They're not pets," I said.

"Didn't break the skin."

"Give them a few days," said Jill from the sleeping platform.

"They seem to like you," Terry observed to me.

"George is their surrogate mother," said Jill.

The parrot, who had been standing inscrutably during this exchange, caught my eye and gestured across the canyon. I saw figures on one of the buttress ridges that ran down from the other rim. The distance dwarfed them, but I could see they were small, dark men in Stetsons and denims.

"They've been there most of the morning," she said.

"Maybe this is their shelter," I speculated.

"It's time to go," said the parrot. She looked at Terry. He didn't say anything. I described the ranch to her. Terry still didn't say anything.

"I'll pay you a thousand dollars a month rent," said the parrot.

"I've got my hands full here already," said Terry.

"Fifteen hundred."

"I'm at a very delicate stage of an investigation here."

"Fifteen hundred dollars could pay for a lot of bribes," said the parrot. Terry looked a little surprised. "I'll give you three thousand in advance."

I was impressed at how quickly Terry had adjusted. I wouldn't have been bargaining about rent with the creature ten minutes after I'd met her. I wondered if he'd dropped a lot of acid at some point. He accepted the offer clearheadedly enough.

"Well, I guess you better come back, at least for a while," he said. "How are you going to get your . . . uh . . . babies there?"

"They can walk."

"That could take days," said Jill.

"Would you like to carry them?"

Terry and I found the bolted horses a few miles back along the railroad. There was no sigh of Euphemio. Terry took one horse back toward the ranch, saying he needed to explain things to Euphemio and I returned to the gully with the other. About a mile from the rock shelter, I met Jill and the parrot coming along with the young ones trailing behind. Jill fell on the food, and the parrot also ate some, which attracted the young ones' interest. She shooed them away.

"Motherhood," said Jill.

"We'll never get any peace if we feed them," the parrot said.

"What's it like to be a baby, uh, you know?" I asked.

"I don't remember."

"You don't remember?"

"We don't start remembering things until the second phase, when the brain growth starts. What do you remember from when you were a week old?"

Getting the young to the ranch didn't take days, but it took long enough. As they tired, they got irritable and started to fight, another behavior their mother refused to control. We also had to wait while they caught and devoured any small animals that crossed their path. Once, a hawk made a pass at them, probably mistaking them for a quail covey. It did an aerial double take, and fled.

"What did you do about predators with your young running around loose?" I asked.

"We didn't have that much trouble with predators."

"I thought the Cretaceous period was crawling with predators."

"There were a lot of tyrannosaurs around during migration. Following the ceratopsian herds down from the Arctic. But they didn't pay too much attention to us. We lived in the hills, and they stayed in the floodplains, for the most part. Even when they came into the Gwawactxtlopxtopleeeee we were too small to attract them. They had high excitation thresholds. It took big, noisy, smelly animals to arouse them."

"What if they did notice you?"

"If you hid awhile, they'd lose interest. The trouble with killing them was that the smell attracted more. They ate a lot of carrion."

"Why didn't you eat them?" asked Jill.

"As I said, they ate a lot of carrion. Like to eat a twenty-foot vulture? Anyway, we never went through a big-game hunting stage as you did."

"How did you learn to cooperate then?" Jill asked, ever skeptical.

"We didn't, to the extent that you do. Which is probably why our civilization had lasted fifty thousand years when the expedition left. All the leks got along so badly with all the other leks that they could never get organized enough for a real war."

"How did you get organized to invent space travel, then?"

"With painful slowness. We seem to have been the only interstellar expedition, so things may have fallen apart soon after we left. It was a very expensive undertaking."

"Why did you do it if it was so difficult?"

"I might ask the same of you."

The young creatures were slowing down, so we stopped to rest. They fell asleep, making a low buzzing sound in unison.

The sun was low. We were near the Tropic of Cancer, so dusk would be short.

"It'll be dark soon," I said.

"We can spend the night here," the parrot said.

"Here in the middle of nowhere?" said Jill. The railroad bed dropped steeply on both sides to black rock walls studded with cactus and white-barked fig trees. The figs' roots and trunks contorted into snake and spider shapes to cling to the cliffs. I thought we should reach the trail to the ranch soon, but I didn't know if I'd recognize it in the dark. "Who were those men who were watching us, George?" Jill asked.

"I don't know. Indians."

"Indians. This is like a movie. Anyway," Jill continued, "There's no place to get off the track here. We'll get run over by the train in our sleep."

I saw her point. We awakened the young parrots and drove them along until the roadbed widened. It was dark by that time. I built a fire behind a clump of cactus, and heated some beans, tortillas, and coffee.

"No tea?" the parrot said. It was the first sign of weakness she'd shown. She'd carried the bundle on her head all day. I wondered if it contained any more surprises.

It took a while to get started the next morning. The offspring seemed to get bigger and stronger every day. They definitely got harder to control. They'd started climbing things, but hadn't learned how to climb down yet. I spent the early morning extracting two from a fig fifty feet down the slope.

"The climbing phase is very important," said the parrot.

"They could get killed," said Jill.

"*I* could get killed," I said, rubbing raw places on my arms.

I managed to find the trail to the ranch. Fortunately, we met nobody on it, and straggled into the compound in late afternoon. A grandiose full moon loomed above the canyon rim. I knocked on the ranchhouse door and Terry appeared, wiping his hands on a dishtowel.

"Euphemio and Clara seem to have taken off," he said. "Any of you guys good at cooking?"

To my surprise, Jill said she was, and produced a very palatable omelette by nightfall. We ate on the terrace, watched by the young parrots.

"Try not to drop food," said their mother.

"Did they teach this in KGB school?" I asked, waving a forkful of omelette at Jill.

"KGB school?" Jill asked innocently.

"Terry's probably wondering why you're here," I continued.

"He's probably wondering why *you're* here," said Jill.

"I'm wondering that myself."

We looked at Terry. He didn't seem to be wondering much of anything as he shoveled omelette into his mouth.

"Find any condors today?" I asked, to tend the awkward silence.

"Not today."

"Come on, are there condors down here or aren't there?"

"Yeah, there are." Terry forked up the last of his omelette as we waited for him to elaborate. "Doesn't seem very important compared to dinosaurs from space."

"You're too modest," said Jill. Terry shrugged. "It must be dangerous to do this," she said. "These birds are being held by gangsters?"

"I wouldn't call them that, exactly."

"What would you call them?" I asked.

"I don't know. Creeps."

"Working for L.A. developers?"

"Yeah."

"What are you going to do?" Jill asked.

"I'm not sure."

"Maybe we could help you," said Jill, which surprised me. But she hadn't seemed to mind Terry's admiring looks.

"What do you care about condors?" I said. Jill didn't answer. Terry looked thoughtful.

"Maybe you could," he said, which surprised me even more.

30

Terry motioned me to join him at the top of the ridge. I did so, and found myself looking into the bottom of the canyon. The river looked wide and deep. A cluster of buildings stood on the bank below us. A dirt road switchbacked up the canyon side. Terry handed me his binoculars.

"Look to the right of the barn," he said.

"What barn?"

"The blue building."

I turned the binoculars on a blue building. It had some hay bales lying in front of it. I focused and scanned to the right, but I couldn't see anything except a live oak tree. I said so.

"Give them to me," Terry said. I did. "Yeah, they're there. Look toward the bottom of the tree."

I looked again, twiddling the focus ring until I realized there was a large metal cage, an aviary really, in front of the tree. The thin bars had been easy to miss.

"It looks empty."

"Keep looking."

"Goddamn." Dark shapes huddled near the top of the cage. Lower down, a bird crouched with wings outspread, the way turkey vultures do. Even at this distance, it looked too big to be a turkey vulture. I counted five of the shapes. "I thought eight condors disappeared."

"Yeah, well, they got five here," Terry said.

We'd spent the day riding downstream along the tributary on which Terry's ranch was located to get to this much bigger ranch on the main canyon. It had been a harder ride than the one to the railroad. I'd had to dismount and walk a few times, to Terry's mild amusement. Jill had wanted to come, but the parrot had insisted she stay behind.

"If I wanted to run away, I'd have done it before now," Jill had said.

"Yes," the parrot had replied, "but now you know where to find me."

A figure emerged from the barn and walked toward the house. I ducked down.

"They can't see you up here," said Terry.

"Who are they?"

"Everybody I've seen down there has looked Mexican. But there's American money behind this place."

"How long have they been here?"

"I don't know. I found them a month ago."

"What are you going to do? Call the authorities?"

"You met the authorities."

"Hmm."

"What I've been thinking is that the river might be navigable."

"The river?"

"I don't know if it's been run before," Terry said. "I flew over it once, but I didn't notice any real bad rapids."

"Wouldn't people be running it if it was possible?"

"Not necessarily around here. Too many banditos."

"What's the river got to do with the condors? You want to take them away in a raft or something?" I put some scorn into my voice, but Terry didn't seem to notice.

"They'd have trouble coming after me," he said, nodding downhill.

"They'd wait for you down at the mouth."

"Not if they didn't know I'd gone on the river. They'd assume I was driving. Anyway, the mouth of this river's a big mangrove swamp."

"Then how will *you* get out of it with five caged condors?"

"I've got a friend with a fishing boat in San Blas. He could come pick us up."

"Us?" I said, unenthusiastically. "Do you have a raft here?"

"No," Terry said, "but I'm getting one. I was in town to pick it up the day you arrived."

"But you didn't pick it up."

"No. Probably been delivered by now, though."

"Delivered how?"

"On the train. Trouble is, I couldn't raft it by myself."

"I haven't done much whitewater, really," I said.

"I can steer. I'd just need you and Jill to paddle."

"What were you going to do before we got here?"

"Hire some Mexicans. But this would be safer."

"Jill? Safe?"

"She said she wanted to help."

"She's a communist agent."

"Nobody's perfect."

"The parrot won't let her go."

"The what?"

"I don't know what else to call her," I explained. "She doesn't like being called a dinosaur and her name is unpronounceable."

"That creature can't make her stay here forever. They'll make a deal," Terry said confidently.

"What about the parrot?"

"She can stay here if she wants. She can take care of herself." I gestured downhill. "You couldn't carry that cage on a raft."

"I've got smaller cages."

"Wouldn't it be easier just to drive?"

"Maybe, at first. But if you do the expected, they get you eventually."

"Who is they?"

"Anyway, I've always wanted to try and run that river. We may be the first."

"We may be the last, too."

Terry didn't answer, and I gave up arguing. We retreated up the tributary canyon a mile and made camp for the night. After we ate, Terry said he wanted to check on some things and disappeared into the darkness. I got under the blankets and scratched the chigger bites on my calves and ankles. Something called up canyon, an owl perhaps.

I awoke in a state of amnesiac paralysis. I heard something, but couldn't turn my head to look at it. The moon had risen; at least I could see it.

"I'm back," Terry said. I remembered him.

"Find anything?"

"The watchman was drunk. There's only another man there."

"What'll we do about them?"

"Nobody's going to risk their life for a few big vultures."

"*We* are," I reminded him.

"We're gringos locos."

Terry crawled under his blankets and soon started snoring. The moon was like a searchlight, and my heart was pounding uncomfortably. I looked at the sky for what seemed hours. Sometimes lights moved across it, high up, satellites or airplanes or something.

When we returned to Terry's ranch the next day, the first thing we saw was one of the young parrots running across the yard with a chicken's head in its mouth. Its siblings were chasing it. Jill stood beside the house holding a freshly decapitated chicken in one hand and an axe in the other.

"Why don't you pluck this chicken?" she said. "I'm tired of doing all the work here."

"Is she doing anything?" I nodded toward the parrot, who was sitting in the shade of the mango with a pair of binoculars around her neck, evidently doing a bit of birding.

"She says she has to watch her brats. She is paying the rent." Jill thrust the chicken at me. Blood dripped from the neck.

"Ugh."

"That's country living," said Terry, heading for the front door.

"Where are you going?"

"To take a nap. I had a rough night."

I wanted to say I'd had a rough night too, but I didn't. I took the chicken and tugged at some breast feathers.

"Not here, George," said Jill. "Bring it around to the back."

Jill stuffed the chicken with herbs and roasted it. It was good, if a bit tough. Terry produced another bottle of wine and we had a pleasant supper. The young parrots didn't watch us as intently as they had the night before. They nodded drowsily or jostled each other in the shade of a pomegranate bush.

"I read about those dinosaur nests they discovered in Montana," Terry said. "Those baby dinosaurs lived in the nest for months, they think. Why are yours running around just after they hatched?"

"Those were anatosaurs. They had as much relationship to us as you do to cows."

"Calves start walking around as soon as they're born. Human babies are helpless for years."

"These will be helpless when their brains start to develop," the parrot said. "Now they're efficient eating machines. They need to build up strength to withstand the stress of brain growth."

"Maybe if you fed them, their brains would grow faster," said Jill.

"They get too dependent if you feed them," the parrot replied. "Their personalities don't develop properly."

"How do you know?"

"We tried it at one point in our history. Our societies started disintegrating into hierarchies. We started having ruling classes and revolutions. So we went back to the old ways."

"Social inequality comes from feeding infants?"

"Individuals that can feed themselves don't feel they have to live off others."

"But we *have* to feed our infants."

"Yes, it's too bad. But there are advantages," the parrot said. "We have a poor survival rate with our young, even though we bear clutches of up to a dozen. It makes us more vulnerable to epidemics and climate than you are. Although we never had to face your overpopulation problem, which will probably cause *your* extinction, along with your social inequalities."

"Wait a minute," said Jill. "If your young become helpless when their brains start to grow, don't you have to feed them then?"

"The basic instincts for self-reliance are developed by then. They come back after the brain develops."

"How long does that take?" I asked.

"About a year," the parrot said.

"The brain develops in a year?"

"It seems like more. They just lie there and eat."

"Don't they learn things in the process?"

"No, that comes afterward," the parrot said. "Then they learn quickly."

"I don't believe the brain could reach full size in a year," Jill said.

"I didn't say it reached full size," the parrot said. "I said it developed."

"How long does it take to reach full size?"

"About thirty-five years."

"Bizarre," I said.

"No more than us," Terry said.

"Originally," the parrot said, "we kept them in caves or tree-holes that we plastered over with mud so predators couldn't get in. Then we started building structures for them."

"I thought you said predators weren't that much of a problem in the Cretaceous?"

The parrot was unabashed. "Archosaur predators weren't. Little mammals were always slinking and slithering about, looking for something helpless to nibble on." She gave a little shudder as people sometimes do when discussing snakes. Terry guffawed.

"You're putting me on," he said.

"She's very witty," said Jill.

"What did you do before you started carrying eggs around in suitcases?" I asked.

"We put them in nests."

Jill stood up suddenly. "I'm tired of cooking all day," she said. "Would someone else do the dishes, please?"

Terry smiled and shrugged. "I've got to clean out the spring box so we have water to wash with."

"I want to take the Zzyxyvaleopits for a walk before it gets too late," the parrot said.

"I thought they needed to be self-reliant," I said.

"Within reason," the parrot replied, leading her offspring into the dusk. I was left alone to stack and carry plates. There was a tap in the kitchen, but no hot water, so I heated it on the wood stove. Jill and Terry talked animatedly in the living room. At least, Jill talked animatedly. I wondered if her enthusiasm for Terry was motivated by devious espionage or simple neurosis. It couldn't have been his looks.

At least one facet of Jill's personality had emerged clearly—she was one of the nosier people I'd met. But I couldn't tell if the nosiness was professional or just part of her personality. It was probably a little of both.

The clank of pots drowned the conversation out. I'd heard enough about Jill's sex life anyway. By the time I'd finished, the house was quiet, and it was dark outside. We all had bedrooms to ourselves now that Euphemio and Clara had fled. (The parrot slept outside with her young.) I stood in the living room a minute. Jill's door was closed, but Terry's was open. I looked in; he wasn't there. The room was surprisingly bare for a place somebody had been living in for months. I supposed it reflected Terry's personality.

I went to bed for lack of anything else to do. The wine had dulled the itch of the chigger bites, so I fell asleep pretty fast.

I awoke in the dark with a sense that there'd been a noise. A light went on, and somebody walked across the living room and opened the front door. I heard the noise that probably had awakened me, a high-pitched squawking. I got dressed and opened the bedroom door. Jill was looking out the front door.

"What happened?" I asked.

"I don't know."

We went out and saw a light in the mango trees. Terry was shining a flashlight on the young parrots. Their mother wasn't in sight.

"There are only four of them," said Jill. The small creatures' eyes were wide. One of them made the squawking sound again.

"They're frightened, poor little things," said Jill. She moved toward them, but they edged away from her, pressing themselves into a tight knot. "Where's your mother?"

"She was gone when I got out here," said Terry. "Maybe something grabbed one of them and she went after it. There are jaguars around here."

"You mean big cats?" said Jill.

"Doesn't seem like much of a mouthful for a jaguar," I said.

"Might have been an ocelot or a jaguarundi. Or a coyote."

"Let's take them into the house until she comes back," said Jill.

"You sure you want them in there?" I said to Terry.

"Do you want to be the one to tell her if another one disappears?" Jill asked. She had a point.

Getting the creatures into the house proved easier said than done. They'd never been in a house. They scattered when we tried to drive them in. They tended to gravitate toward me when I was alone, however, so I eventually was able to coax them over the threshhold. They then became curious, and started climbing all over everything. Jill and Terry took refuge in their bedrooms, but when I tried to do so, they started scratching at my door.

Pushing them away with my foot didn't work. It was getting on to 3 A.M. I finally left the door open. They trooped in, looking this way and that, explored under the bed, and evidently trapped some hapless mouse or scorpion under there, because there was a flurry of thumps and squawks. I took my shoes off and fell into bed. Of course, the creatures had to climb up and examine this phenomenon. It must have looked like one of those old lithographs of a sickbed bedeviled by the imps of pain. They seemed to like the softness and warmth. Pretty soon they were asleep around my feet. I kicked feebly at them a few times, then drifted off.

I heard a noise and opened my eyes. A dark shape loomed in the open door. The light was gray behind it: dawn was on the way.

"What is it?" I wheezed.

The shape advanced. When it was halfway to the bed, I saw that it was the parrot.

"You shouldn't have brought them into the house," she said.

"Where were you?"

The creature didn't answer. She shooed the young ones off the bed, none too gently, and out the door. Her talons dragged on the tiles. I went back to sleep.

"She should be more careful," said Jill the next morning at breakfast. "Even the chickens have a coop to stay in at night." The parrot was slumped under the mango tree across the yard, but gave no sign she heard Jill's remark. The four remaining young ones rushed about the yard, unsubdued. "And now she sits there sleeping. It's inhuman."

"She's not human," said Terry.

"She was out all night looking for it," I said.

"I'd be hysterical if that happened to me."

"She still has four," Terry said.

"If somebody killed one of your condors, you'd still have four," Jill said.

"They're not my condors."

31

We spent the next week getting ready for our condor-recovery float trip. Terry thought the raft would definitely be delivered within a week. We repaired cages, packed waterproof boxes with food and clothing, a stove, and other supplies. We studied Terry's map of the river. I couldn't see too many sudden changes in elevation that might mean dangerous rapids or waterfalls. The river twisted back and forth a lot, however, and if we couldn't run it, we'd have a hard time getting out of the canyon. The topo lines showing its walls almost touched, indicating sheer cliffs. Some side canyons opened out of the main one, but they headed in sheer cliffs too, with waterfalls.

"Must be nice in there," said Terry.

"It looks like you'd never get out alive," said Jill.

"Don't you want to come?" I said.

"I don't know," Jill replied. She'd become closer to the parrot, in a contentious sort of way, since the young one had disappeared. They had argued at length about how to keep more from disappearing. Jill had wanted to put the young in the chicken coop at night, but their mother would have none of it, saying it would make them too dependent.

"They'd eat the chickens, anyway," the parrot said.

"They won't be too independent in a jaguar's stomach," Jill replied. Terry said that whatever had carried the young one away would probably be back.

"I don't want to raise neurotics," the parrot said.

"You may not raise anything. Don't you want your species to survive?"

"Not in chicken coops."

They compromised by keeping the young parrots in the back terrace at night. It had a low adobe wall around it, and a lantern hanging from a pole. The parrot had objected that her offspring might become afraid of the dark if they were kept in a lighted place at night.

"*We* were the biggest nocturnal predators in the late Cretaceous," she said.

"I thought you said you never went through a hunting phase."

"I said we didn't go through a big-game hunting phase. We hunted small mammals."

"Our ancestors."

"It turned out all right for you, didn't it?" the parrot replied.

Jill also got closer to Terry. He started producing a hash pipe after supper, and he and Jill drifted away together into a state of drowsy hilarity. The creature never showed any interest in smoking anything, and Alec Rice had put me off dope forever.

"Come on, George," said Jill, on the third night of this, "why not relax a little?"

"I'm relaxed." She waved the pipe at me. "No, it upsets my stomach."

"Alright. Be boring." She got up and went into the house. In a little while, Terry said goodnight and went into the house too. I had become the official dishwasher, but I didn't feel like starting just yet.

"Maybe I'll spend the night out here," I said.

"In the doghouse?" the parrot said.

"Funny that there aren't any dogs here. Did you have domestic animals?"

"Some birds. The mammals and most of the archosaurs were too stupid to be domesticated."

"This experience is really good for my ego."

"There's a lot to be said for stupidity," she replied.

Terry went into town to see if the raft had arrived next morning. I peeked morosely as Jill kissed him goodbye behind the mango tree. After he'd driven away, she came up to me in a businesslike fashion.

"I want to show you something, George."

"I've seen enough."

"Don't be childish. You have to see this."

"What?"

"Come on." Jill started up the trail that led to the spring box, a windowless concrete structure that I'd seen during my idle wanderings about the place. It had a stout padlock on its door, about which I'd wondered, also idly. I'd assumed it contained tools and equipment, to be carefully guarded in impoverished Mexico.

I started up the trail too, and the young parrots appeared and followed us. They liked to follow anybody walking through the brush because they could catch any small insects or lizards we frightened. One of them had the tail of a lizard or snake hanging out of her mouth.

When I got to the shed, Jill was picking the padlock with a Swiss Army knife. "You see," she said, "they did teach me something useful."

"What are you doing?"

Jill pulled the padlock open and unclasped the door. She swung it open. It was too dark inside to see anything from where I stood.

"I thought you were tight with him," I said.

"Just gathering information. Look inside."

I stepped into the shed and waited for my eyes to adjust to the gloom. It was like a toolshed, with things hanging on the walls and piled in the corners. But they weren't lawnmowers and rakes. A large hoop strung with tangled wire hung on the far wall. A pair of leather gauntlets hung beside it. Several guns leaned against the wall. A box containing syringes, ampoules, and what might have been tranquilizer darts sat on a table. Something else occupied a big, flat box in a corner. It was too dark to see, so I put my hand in it. I felt feathers, and dry, scaly skin.

"Don't you have a flashlight?"

"No," Jill replied."

I felt in my pants for matches, but I didn't have any. I yanked on the box, but it wouldn't budge. I felt disinclined to touch what was in it again. I realized what the shed smelled like. Mothballs.

"Do you know what this is?"

"Can't you guess? George."

"What?"

"A dead condor."

"Why would Terry have a dead condor?" I asked.

"Maybe he was the one that caught them."

"What makes you think that?"

"I'm always suspicious of strong, silent types," Jill said.

"You had me fooled. Did he say something?"

"No, Terry is clever. A strong, silent type who is clever makes me even more suspicious."

"So what do you think he's up to?"

"Making some money, I suppose."

"From condors?"

"I hope only from condors," Jill said.

32

Terry returned with the raft late in the afternoon. When I helped him unload it, I realized how heavy it was.

"How are we going to get this down to the river?" I asked.

"We can probably float it most of the way," Terry said.

"On this tributary? Why don't we just take your Land Rover over there?"

"It'll be easier to surprise them if we don't use the road," Terry replied. "Besides, I want to be able to come back and pick up the Land Rover after I get the condors out. Goddamn expensive vehicle." He took a six-pack of Tecate out of the front seat and offered me one. I took it. "Where are the others?"

"On the terrace."

"Think they'd like a beer?"

"Ask them," I said. We went around to the terrace, where Jill and the parrot sat. Jill looked solemn. The parrot looked as she usually looked. Terry hesitated when he saw them, then offered them the six-pack. Neither responded, so he took one and opened it.

"There's some new gringos in town," he said. "A cowboy type and a couple of creepy goons."

"Did you talk to them?" the parrot asked.

"Nope."

"Are you sure?" Jill asked.

"Yeah, I'm sure."

"Why should we believe you?" Jill asked, in a tone I hadn't heard her use before.

"Whoa," said Terry, throwing back his head.

"We looked in the spring house," I said.

"Yeah?" Terry said.

"I think you're the creep," said Jill.

"Why's there a dead condor up there?" I asked. Terry finished his beer and took another.

"I did everything I could to save that bird," he said. "It had lead poisoning. They eat bullets in carcasses and the lead stays in their crops. One of the others had it too, but I cured it."

"I thought eight condors disappeared," I said.

"Yeah, well, I don't know what happened to the other two," Terry said. "Probably ate poisoned coyotes."

"How much did they pay you?" Jill asked.

Terry stared at her. "What do you care about condors?" he said.

"I care about not being deceived," Jill replied.

"You like to be the one that's doing the deceiving."

"How much did they pay you?"

"Who said anybody paid me?"

"They paid you to catch these condors and bring them down here," said Jill.

"Who is this 'they'?" said Terry.

"You can tell us."

Terry finished his beer and opened another one. He sat down. "They stiffed me. I was supposed to get twenty thousand a bird, but all I got was a twenty-thousand advance."

"Too bad." Jill shook her head. The parrot leaned forward a little, intrigued.

"They were going to shoot them," Terry said.

"Why didn't you tell the law about it?" I asked.

"So they could arrest them after they shot the condors?"

"What did Ricky and the Condor Rescue Committee have to do with it?"

"I was active with them," Terry replied. "Shit, I love condors."

"You volunteered to go look for them after you'd already trapped them?"

"It was a good way to get the condors away from those L.A. bastards. I was afraid they'd kill them anyway."

"Why didn't they?" Jill asked.

"Why didn't they what?"

"Why didn't they just kill them? Why pay you to catch them and take them to Mexico?"

"Because I would have told the law about them," Terry said.

"Very noble," said Jill.

"Fuck you, man. I was risking my life."

"Who are these bastards anyway?" I said.

"You want a list of names? You'd be surprised. Who owns southern California?"

"I don't know. Who does own southern California?"

"You'd be surprised," Terry repeated. Then he changed the subject. "I was going to use this place as a backup in case I had trouble at the ranch downstream. I didn't have time to move the stuff out after you dropped on me."

"Whose ranch is it?" Jill asked.

"I haven't got time to explain that."

"Why are they letting you stay here if they've stopped paying you?"

"I've been wondering about that myself," said Terry. "That's one reason I want to leave."

"But," I said, "what were you going to *do* down here?"

"I don't know. Maybe try to breed them. But there's only two females, and one of them is kind of old. It's probably a good thing you turned up."

"What do you mean?" Jill asked.

"You can take the condors back and give them to Ricky. I'll disappear. That'll put it to those pricks."

"Disappear where?" said the parrot.

"Lots of places without roads or communications along the Mexican west coast," Terry said.

"If we made it down the river," I said.

"I think I might prefer the river to Jerry," the parrot said.

"How can we believe what a criminal says?" Jill asked. Terry glared at her. Jill was awfully plainspoken for a spy.

"Why would I lie about seeing three gringos in town?" Terry said.

"How can we be sure it's Jerry? And anyway," I added to the parrot, "you seemed to handle him okay."

"I may have underestimated him."

"What do you mean?" Jill asked

"He may have more initiative than I thought."

"Your government is out of control." Jill looked at me accusingly.

"I didn't vote for him," I replied.

"That's what the Germans said."

I surpressed an urge to argue with her and turned back to the parrot. "Won't the other ... your colleagues do something if something happened to you?"

"If it happened down here," the parrot replied, "they wouldn't know about it."

"You're not telepathic?"

The parrot shook her head.

Terry finished his third beer. "Sure," he said, "I'll find a good place for you. I know a cove with pink granite cliffs and beaches south of Puerto Vallarta." Nobody had an answer to that, and the silence became embarrassing.

"How did you learn how to handle condors?" I finally asked.

"I used to work in the L.A. Zoo. I wouldn't want to be a condor in the L.A. Zoo."

"The rest of the wild condors are in zoos because you trapped these."

"They would have put them in anyway."

33

I lifted the raft's edge off a jagged rock and let it flop into the shallow pool below. It seemed the thousandth time I'd done it. My arms felt heavy as barbells. My shoulders were numb from sunburn and my legs were numb from the icy water.

"I think we're about halfway," said Terry. It was nearing late afternoon. At the rate we were going, we'd get the raft to the river around 10 P.M. Jill and the parrot and her offspring and two horses loaded with supplies had long since disappeared down the trail above the tributary down which we were arduously dragging the raft. At least, they'd have made camp by the time we got there. I wouldn't have looked forward to spending the night on a rock in my jockey shorts.

We dragged the raft over another ledge and dropped it into another icy pool. This one was fairly long, so we climbed aboard for a rest, letting the current carry us. It was a pretty place when you had the time to enjoy it. Although most of the trees were leafless, many were flowering. Gray-barked trees bore flowers resembling giant white morning glories. The parrot had said the Mexicans called them "Los palos de los muertos," the trees of the dead. A lot of trees had yellow flowers—acacias and sticklike trees with what looked like giant buttercups on top.

There was a little sand beach at the end of the pool. It promised a nice change from the rocks. I jumped onto it, and sank to my thighs.

"I don't believe this," I said, as the dank sand closed around my crotch.

"Lean forward," said Terry. "Take your weight off your lower half and you'll stop sinking."

"You have a lot of quicksand around here?"

"Fair amount."

"How about giving me a hand?"

"Then I'd get stuck too. Just lean forward and kind of swim out of it." I leaned forward, keeping my neck craned upward painfully so I wouldn't get my face in the stuff. The suction on my legs gradually eased. I flopped and waddled to solid ground.

"That's right," said Terry.

"Why didn't you warn me about that?"

"Forgot."

An hour later, a stretch of the stream became too thickly grown with reeds to get the raft through.

"We'll have to lift it around," said Terry.

"I can hardly lift my arms." We lifted it, carried it a little, dropped it, lifted it again.

"Watch out for rattlesnakes," said Terry.

"Thanks for telling me."

"It's pretty early in the year for them."

The sun was low when we got the raft back to the water. Bats fluttered in the shadows. I wondered if they were vampire bats. I thought I heard dogs barking somewhere.

"Maybe we should leave it here for the night," Terry said. "Go on to camp."

"You go first."

Even in the failing light, finding the trail was fairly easy because of the odd combination of hoofprints, sneaker prints, and giant and small birdlike prints.

"Indians must be curious," said Terry.

"You think they know about us?"

"They know about most things in these mountains."

"What would they think of the parrot?"

"You got me there."

Jill had made coffee and chili when we got to camp. It tasted wonderful.

"Where'd you learn to make chili?" Terry asked. Jill held up a freeze-dried chili packet. After he ate, Terry got under his blankets without producing the hash pipe. I fell asleep by the fire.

I awoke at dawn with a sore throat. Somebody had thrown a blanket over me. The sky was overcast.

"Rainy season's still a ways off," said Terry. "You should see these rivers then." I'd seen the tangles of straw and twigs in the branches of streamside trees.

"Well, let's get out of here before it starts."

Terry and I went back to the raft and wrestled it along for another morning. The streambed got a little gentler, but not much, and we ran into more reeds. At last, Terry said we'd come far enough, and we climbed back to look for Jill and the parrot. We found them relaxing in a grove of red-barked gumbo limbo trees, while the young ones rushed about shrieking, as usual.

"Can you quiet them down?" Terry said. "We're getting close."

"They'll get tired pretty soon," the parrot said.

"We can't get any nearer with all that noise."

"Why not?"

"There are guards there," said Terry.

"They're your guards," said Jill.

"Right," said Terry. "That's why I don't want them to know I'm involved in this."

"What do you mean?"

"Why don't you and the parrot go down and scare them away? They'll react just like Euphemio did. They're superstitious."

"Oh no you don't," said Jill.

"I've got to get something out of this," said Terry. "If you want me to go down the river with you."

"Why didn't you mention this before?" I asked.

"Didn't think of it."

"That's what you said about the quicksand."

"I've got a lot on my mind."

"What if the guards start shooting?"

"You can shoot back. Here." Terry took a pistol out of the supply packs and handed it to me.

"I'm not used to these."

"Just point it and pull the trigger."

"Give me the gun, George," said Jill. "You can stay here with the young ones."

"I don't like this," said the parrot.

"Those three gringos were well-equipped. Brand new Land Rover with a dirt bike on the back."

"Stop being so manipulative," the parrot said.

"Just trying to help."

"Alright," said the parrot. "I'll do it. But you have to come too."

"What's the point?" said Terry. "They'll see me."

"We'll go in the dark."

"Then how will they see you?"

"They'll see me," the parrot said.

34

Terry told me not to build a fire after they left because it might make the guards at the ranch suspicious. A smell of wood smoke filled the air from the Indians burning their corn patches, and our camp was at least a mile from the ranch. I was afraid that if I didn't build a fire, something would grab another one of the young parrots, so I built a small one after Terry and the others had been gone an hour or so.

They seemed to like the warmth. They rested near it when they weren't chasing some moth or beetle that the light had attracted. They seemed more insecure about the darkness than they had before the fifth one had disappeared. The Cenozoic makes neurotics out of everyone.

The parrots cast large shadows on the brush as they moved around the fire. They reminded me of the "Sacre du Printemps" sequence of *Fantasia*, the last dinosaurs fleeing across a cracking plain. I wondered if they'd had movies. Dinosaur film noir. Dinosaur musicals. What the parrot had said about their mating rituals made it seem likely. I looked in the fire and saw dancing dinosaurs . . .

"Don't move, you bastard." Somebody grabbed me so roughly from behind that I almost fell on my face. I managed to stay standing, but with both arms twisted behind me, I couldn't shield my eyes with my hands, so I stayed blind. But I knew Jerry Lester's voice.

"Holy shit!" he said. I felt the light move away from my face, and opened my eyes. He had turned it on the far side of the campsite, where the four parrots stood curiously, attracted by the commotion. "Goddamn son of a bitch, will you look at that!"

"I wish you wouldn't blaspheme so much," said Peter Eliott next to my face. He needed dental hygiene.

"The spawn of the beast," said Henry, behind me.

"I'll stop swearing," said Jerry, "if you'll shut him up."

"Jerry's here!" I shouted. "Look out!" Jerry stepped up and punched me in the stomach.

"This is the end of the trail, George."

I gasped for breath and thought about what he'd said.

"Alright," I said, "tell them to let go of me."

"Only if you promise to behave."

"I promise."

"We can't trust him," said Peter.

"Let him go," said Jerry. They did, after Henry had given me a kidney punch. "Where'd these little things come from, George?"

"Eggs." Henry kidney-punched me again, so I told them about the young parrots.

"Looks like we got here just in time," said Jerry.

"What are you going to do?" I said.

"You want to know? We're going to send them back where they came from."

"Back into space? What for?"

"There isn't room for both of us here."

"We don't have the technology to do that."

"We have the technology to shoot them past Pluto."

"They'll die."

"They should have died seventy million years ago," Jerry said.

"It doesn't make sense," I said. "Think of all they could tell us."

"We know everything we need to know from them," Jerry said. "Think of all the trouble they could cause. They're starting to breed now. Pretty soon they'll want a reservation, then a homeland. This has been debated at high levels, and finding those things," he waved his flashlight at the young parrots, who looked on with interest, "will make up a lot of minds. Survival of the fittest."

"The Russians know about it now. Jill told them."

"I know they know about it. We told them."

"What?"

"How do you think we found you?"

"Jill?"

"They tipped us off as soon as she made her contact. You think they're any more interested in getting overrun with feathered crocodiles than we are?"

"What did you do to Ricky?"

"Didn't do nothing to Ricky. Didn't need to. This situation's going to get resolved real quick. Starting now." Jerry motioned to Peter, who produced a pistol and aimed it at one of the young parrots.

"Hey, wait a minute!" I lunged at Peter and grabbed his arm. Henry clutched my neck and stuck his knee in my back. "Come on!" I shouted. "You can't just kill them!"

"Why not?" Jerry replied. "I've got to bring her back but nobody knows about them. If you kill the nits, you won't get lice."

"Hey look, I'll cooperate fully with you if you don't kill them."

"Come on, Jerry," said Peter. "Let's finish the nasty little things."

"Imps of Satan," said Henry.

"How are you going to prove they're breeding," I said, "if you don't have the young ones? You said it would help to get them sent back into space."

Jerry scratched his chin. "You may have a point."

"I'll stay with them here while you go catch her," I said. "I can control them."

"I bet you can," said Jerry. He motioned to Peter again. "Hold him still." Peter and Henry roughed me up a little more to relieve their frustrations, then I felt a bee sting in my hip.

Jerry stepped away from me, holding a syringe. Peter and Henry released me, but the strength was already leaving my muscles. I took a few steps and collapsed. I felt somebody fiddling with my arms and legs, then I felt nothing.

35

I awoke with a sense of suffocation that made me gasp. When I felt able to breathe, I became aware of thirst, and of dull pain in my arms and legs. I tried to move and discovered that my wrists and ankles were tied together behind me. It took me a while to remember where I was. It was dark, and silent except for occasional squawking sounds that seemed to come from above me. Even if it hadn't been dark, I wouldn't have been able to look up to see what was making them.

The dull pains gradually became sharp, which at least helped me to wake up. I remembered that the squawking sounds probably were those of the young creatures, but I still didn't know what they were doing above me. I found that I could ease the pain in my arms by flexing my legs, and vice versa, and kept busy doing that for a long time. The continued throbbing of the pain began to nauseate me, an alarming condition when you're lying face down in the dirt, almost unable to move. I had very little sensation in my hands or feet. I couldn't decide if that was bad or good.

I became aware that I could see twigs and pebbles before my eyes. It was getting light. The squawks had stopped for awhile, but now they started again, with a new urgency. They sounded hungry. I began to wish Jerry Lester would come back. The ground got brighter, and I felt the sun on my back, which was pleasant at first, then less so. I wondered how long someone could survive without water in direct tropical sunlight. Not long, if I remembered correctly. The squawks above me became pants and gasps. It seemed that Jerry and Peter had hung the young creatures from a tree after putting them in bags.

"Hey, George."

I was glad to hear Jerry's voice again. Somebody cut my ropes and my arms and legs flopped to the ground. They felt like sandbags, and it took me a moment to sit up and get a look around.

Jill and Terry sat on the ground in the middle of the clearing. Jill's head was bandaged, and there was blood on the bandage. The parrot, who lay between them on a crude stretcher, was also bandaged, on the shoulder. She was evidently unconscious, her eyes closed, mouth open, and tongue lolling out.

"Let the young ones down," I said. "They need to eat."

"We should leave them hanging for the ravens," said Henry, who along with Jerry and Peter stood over the others.

"Get them down," said Jerry.

"Go on, Henry," said Peter.

"Their name is legion, for they are many," said Henry, but he shimmied up the tree and let the young parrots to the ground, none too gently. Released from their bags, they looked around uncertainly, examined their prostrate mother, then went off in pursuit of a grasshopper.

"What happened?" I asked Jill.

"Ask him," she replied, nodding at Terry, who was unbandaged.

"I didn't know any more about this than you did," Terry said.

"The guards just started shooting out of pure machismo," Jill replied.

"They ran away, didn't they?"

"Just in time for your friends here to shoot us full of tranquilizer darts. Actually, I didn't see them shoot *you*."

"You were the one with the pistol," said Terry.

"Traitor."

"Shut up," said Jerry.

"I bet you made a deal with them in town," Jill went on.

"No I didn't," said Terry. "Self-righteous bitch."

"How did they happen to follow you to your little ranch, then?" Jill asked.

"Terry has a lot to learn about surveillance techniques," Jerry said. "He's a real easy tail."

"Fuck you, man," Terry said. He stood up.

Jerry made a mollifying gesture. "Listen," he said, "we appreciate your cooperation . . ."

"I'm not cooperating with you."

"But like I said, we'll shoot the goddamn buzzards if you don't stay in line." Terry didn't answer him this time. Jerry turned his back on Terry and pointed at me. "You said you could control those little things. Well get them back here, we're going."

"I never asked to get involved in this," Terry said.

"Going where?" I said.

"Don't ask questions. Just do it."

I went into the bush with Henry and Peter following. I imitated the parrot's throaty call note, but there was no sign of her daughters.

"We should leave them here in the wilderness," Henry said.

"They like it here," I said. I tried the call again, and the young parrots emerged from the bushes expectantly. One had a small rattlesnake in her mouth. The snake looked dead, and the small parrot seemed none the worse for its encounter. It gulped the snake hastily when one of its siblings tried to take it away.

"Yuck," said Peter.

They seemed disappointed that we weren't their mother, but followed us back into the clearing anyway. Jerry was tying the still unconscious parrot with the ropes he'd used on me. Jill and Terry just sat there. I wondered if Jerry had injected them with something too, they seemed so listless.

"Is she alright?" I asked Jerry, motioning to the parrot.

"She's a tough old bird."

"How can you tell what drugs will do to her? They've got a weird metabolism."

"Let me worry about that, George."

"Why do you need to tie her, anyway?"

"Let's get going," Jerry said. "George, you take the back and Jill take the front." He motioned toward the litter.

"Where we going?"

"Back to that ranch you've been staying at. Our vehicle is up there."

"You followed us down here?"

"Pick up the goddamn litter, George."

"What about him?" I motioned at Terry.

"He's not coming," said Jerry.

"I knew it," said Jill.

"Pick up the litter," said Henry to Jill. He kicked at her, and she grabbed at his foot, but too slowly to catch it.

"Cut it out, Henry," said Jerry.

"Why don't you use the horses?" I said.

"Because I want to keep my undivided attention on you," said Jerry. "Now pick up the god . . . litter." Neither Jill nor I moved. Quite apart from obeying Jerry, the prospect of carrying a litter all the way back to the ranch was disagreeable. "Alright," Jerry continued. "Since you seem so worried about these little monsters here, maybe I'll let Henry have some fun with them. Bet he used to torture kittens when he was a youngster." Henry looked flattered. I looked at Jill, who slowly stood up. Terry sat still, eyes averted. Jill and I picked up the litter. The parrot was surprisingly light.

36

The litter soon got heavier, especially after Jerry decided the young parrots weren't moving fast enough. He had Henry and Peter bag them again, and pile them on the litter. Even though they were tied on, they kept shifting around. Admirers of ancient Egypt, Peru, or other civilizations in which litter-travel was fashionable should carry one over a mountain trail for a day.

"I've got to rest," said Jill, after an hour.

"We'll stop pretty soon," said Jerry. "Pretty soon" turned out to be at least another hour of stumbling along the rudimentary trail. Carrying a weight with your arms makes you want to go fast, but of course you can't see where you're putting your feet if you're in the rear of the litter. We stopped after I tripped and pitched the litter into the small of Jill's back, knocking her down and rolling the parrot and her offspring into a gully.

When Jill and I picked up the parrot to put her back on the litter, she was limp, and cold. She didn't seem to be breathing, but I felt a slow thump when I put my hand on her breast.

"I think she's dying," said Jill.

"Don't let her fool you," Jerry replied.

"Fool me?"

"Mystery, Babylon the Great," said Henry.

"You told me you'd shut him up," said Jerry to Peter.

"He's saying the truth," said Peter.

"How did you get involved with these maniacs?" I asked Jerry. "Couldn't you get normal thugs?"

"For they have sown the wind, and they shall reap the whirlwind," said Jill, to my surprise.

"Ye have plowed wickedness, ye have reaped iniquity," said Henry. "Ye have eaten the fruit of lies."

"Pick up the goddamn litter," said Jerry.

"A scarlet colored beast, full of names of blasphemy!" Even Peter began to look a little worried at Henry's latest. He put his arm around him in a fatherly way and led him aside.

"Pick it up, goddamnit."

My arms began falling off after about forty-five minutes this time, but Jerry kept us going for another hour. When we stopped, he took out a jackknife, and jabbed the parrot's leg.

"What the hell are you doing?" I said.

"Just making sure she's out. Doesn't hurt her." Jerry replied.

"How do you know what hurts her?"

"She didn't complain, did she?" In fact, the parrot had remained quite motionless.

"What would you have done if she had?"

"Shoot her up with some more dope. In fact, I think I will anyway."

"The beast that thou sawest was, and is not," said Henry, "and shall ascend out of the bottomless pit, and go into perdition."

"Now, wait a minute," said Jerry. He grabbed Henry by the front of his shirt, pulled him close, then pushed him away violently. "He's drunk! Goddamnit, Peter."

"And he that blasphemest the name of the lord, he shall surely be put to death." Henry was flushed, but showed no other signs of intoxication beside loquacity.

"Where the hell did he get it?"

"Back at that ranchhouse, I guess," Peter said.

"You knew he was drinking?"

"He'd finished most of the bottle when I found it. I took it away from him." Peter took a bottle of tequila out of his day pack. Jerry grabbed it. "Wait a minute, Jerry," Peter said, trying to get the bottle back, but Jerry smashed it on a rock.

"You've been doling it out to him," Jerry said. Peter stepped toward Jerry and spoke earnestly.

"You've got to have some way of controlling him once he starts. I wish you hadn't broken it." Jerry and Peter looked at Henry, who'd given no sign of paying attention to their conversation. Henry was looking at the parrot and the bag of her offspring.

"The mother of harlots," he said, "and of the abominations of the earth."

"I don't believe this," said Jerry.

"It's been years since I've had any trouble with him," said Peter.

"These shall hate the whore, and shall make her desolate and naked, and shall eat her flesh, and burn her with fire."

"Pick up the litter," said Jerry. I did so almost with relief. Henry hung behind as we marched off. He'd begun to carry himself oddly, with his head down and his arms hanging limp in front of him. For awhile, I thought we'd left him and Peter behind. Then he caught up, and started talking to Jerry, who was walking behind Jill and me.

"Tell Peter to give me my gun," said Henry. I supposed Peter had them in his day packs. I was glad that Henry didn't have one now.

"No, Henry," said Peter, hurrying up from behind. "I have to keep your gun until you sober up."

"It's my gun. I want it."

"Jesus Christ Almighty," said Jerry, under his breath.

"What?" said Henry.

"No gun until you sober up," Jerry replied.

"Behold, I will smite with the rod that is in my hand." Henry picked up a stick and began whacking at plants as he passed them. Jerry was walking in front of him, and found this annoying. He spun around, grabbed the stick, and pushed Henry toward Peter.

"Shape him up or we'll leave him here."

Peter and Henry receded behind a bend in the trail. Henry's voice followed us.

"Behold, a great red dragon, having seven heads and ten horns, and seven crowns upon her heads!"

"Don't let this give you ideas," said Jerry.

37

We got back to the ranch in mid afternoon. My head throbbed from hunger, heat, and fatigue. Jill appeared to pass out after we'd dropped the litter. I started into the house to look for food.

"Hold it," said Jerry. "Where you going?" I told him. "Wait until Peter gets here. I want to keep you both in sight." He nodded at the recumbent Jill.

"Why? You've got the parrot. What difference do we make?"

"You're coming back with us."

"What for?"

"You know too much."

"What are you going to do? Lock us up?"

"That's not for me to decide," Jerry said.

"Why'd you let Terry go?"

"He has reasons to keep his mouth shut."

"How many reasons?" Jerry didn't answer. "You'll never get away with this," I went on. I didn't sound very confident.

"We'll do what has to be done."

"Who's 'we'?" Jerry didn't answer.

"You should answer him," Jill said, still not moving. "He pays your salary."

"I work for an elected government," Jerry said. "Not a slave empire."

"Elected by the rich. With advertising," said Jill.

"Your government was elected by tanks."

"Anyway," I said, to change the subject, "how about letting the young ones go free for a while? They have to catch their own food. They'll starve otherwise."

"What does he care?" Jill said.

"Alright," said Jerry, "but get them back here as soon as I say."

I untied the bag and shook the young parrots out. They looked dazed, open-mouthed. They lay still awhile, then tottered to the horse trough and drank. One seemed particularly weak.

"They may not survive this," I said.

"Nature's way," said Jerry.

"Social Darwinism," said Jill, "fossil philosophy."

The parrot remained motionless on her litter. Jerry stuck another needle into her, but it didn't seem to make any difference. The young ones eventually recovered and wandered into the brush. Henry and Peter still hadn't arrived.

"Come on," I said. "Let's go in and get something to eat."

"I'm not turning my back on that parrot," Jerry said.

"She's doped up and hog-tied."

"Still don't trust her."

An explosion of squawks came from the bush. I thought of jaguars and ran toward the noise. I found Henry in a samurai crouch over the young parrots, raising his stick to bash out their undeveloped brains. Peter stood aside, looking not unpleased. I grabbed the stick from behind, toppling Henry backward. I raised it, eager for a few satisfying thumps on Henry's fleshy parts, but Peter pointed his gun at me and told me to put the stick down. Henry rolled on his side and vomited some black stuff that looked like coagulated blood. Henry apparently had bleeding ulcers.

"Oh, God," said Peter. He leaned over Henry, who shoved him away. "Help me get him to the house." I grabbed one arm, and we led the weakly struggling Henry away. I glanced back at the young creatures. They were standing curiously over Henry's vomit.

"Alright," said Jerry, as Peter and I lowered the now semi-conscious Henry in front of him. "We're getting out of here. Put him in the Land Rover."

"He looks like he needs to go to the hospital," said Jill.

"When are we going to get something to eat?" I said.

"Here," said Jerry, throwing bags at me. "Round up those chickens again. Then you can have some canned ravioli. You too," he added to Jill. "Help George round 'em up."

"No."

"I told you, your government is cooperating with mine on this."

"I don't believe you," said Jill. "Anyway it's not my government."

"You'll find out when we get back," Jerry said ominously. "And if we don't bring 'em, I'm not leaving them here."

Jill stood up slowly and limped after Peter and me into the bush. The young parrots proved even harder to catch than before, but we were able to use their greater trustfulness of me to advantage. Jill and Peter would chase them while I stood innocently by and suddenly grabbed lone fugitives. I wondered what *this* experience would do to their development.

The sun was nearing the canyon rim when we got the Land Rover loaded and started banging up the steep track out. Jerry made Jill sit in front with him, while Peter and I squatted beside the parrot and Henry, who were both unconscious. Jerry had injected Henry with something, too. I'd begun to wonder if Jerry was working this case on loan from the Drug Enforcement Administration.

"Where's the ravioli you promised me?" I said.

"Here." Jerry threw a pop-top can of ravioli at me. I ate it with my fingers when I wasn't hanging on for dear life as the Land Rover lurched and crashed across the rocks and gullies. Henry's and the parrot's heads knocked smartly against the floor every time we took a bump.

"Shouldn't we put pillows under their heads?" I said.

"No," said Jerry. "Dinosaurs have their brains in their asses, and Henry doesn't have any."

As soon as I'd finished it, I began to wish I hadn't eaten the ravioli. Sitting sideways in the back of a Land Rover on a winding mountain road is a recipe for motion sickness. I swallowed ropey saliva for about a half hour, then gave up and threw up out the window.

"Shit, not you too now," said Jerry. Henry began to make gargling sounds, then to choke and turn blue. Peter turned him on his side, and he vomited more black stuff. It smelled strongly in the confined Rover, and a fresh wave of retching swept me. I curled myself up and closed my eyes.

When I opened them again, it was dark. The road seemed to have gotten better, and when I looked ahead, I saw lights. We'd evidently made it back to town.

"I don't want any trouble from you two," Jerry said. Peter looked at me as though he wouldn't have minded a chance to silence me.

"He still alive?" I asked Peter, nodding at Henry. Peter didn't answer.

As we drew nearer to the lights, we could see people in the streets. It looked as though some kind of market was going on. We heard the cheerful thumping of Mexican waltz music in the background, and started passing knots of denimed and cloaked men and women who peered curiously into our windows.

"Shit," said Jerry. "Cover them up with the tarp." Peter stepped over me to get to their supplies, and bumped his head. The Land Rover slowed to a walk as the street got more crowded, then to a crawl. We arrived in front of what I realized was the bar where Terry had rescued me from Carlos and Tito, the Mexican secret police. Carlos and Tito were standing in front of the bar now, along with several other men, some of whom were uniformed, their guns visible under their shirt tails. They were very interested in our appearance down a street on which the only other motor vehicle was a 1940s flatbed truck.

When we drew abreast of them, Carlos, the man with the green eyes, stepped up to the Land Rover's front window, forcing Jerry to stop. Black-haired Tito, who looked like Oliver Hardy, stepped up behind him.

"Good night," said Carlos, bending over to peer into the Rover. His eyes lit up with recognition when he saw me, and with curiosity when he saw Jill. Peter had gotten the tarp over the parrot and Henry, but they made a fairly conspicuous swelling on the floor. The green-eyed man's glance flicked over this, then back to Jerry's face.

"Buenas noches, amigo," said Jerry. His accent was terrible.

"Where you coming from?"

"Venemos del rancho de un amigo." I didn't have any trouble understanding Spanish spoken with Jerry's perfect American accent.

"What his name, your friend?"

"Terry Phelan."

"Ah, Terry Phelan." Carlos talked with Tito for a moment. "Where you go now?"

"Vamos al USA."

"What?"

"Estados Unidos."

"What you got in back there?"

Jerry took out his wallet. "Would you like to see some identification?" he said. He counted out a thick wad of pesos, put his driver's license on top, and handed them to Carlos. Carlos put the money in his pocket and handed the license to Tito, who looked at it without much interest. He handed it back and said something to Carlos.

"He want to see your tourist card," Carlos said to Jerry. Jerry counted out another wad of bills, put the tourist card on top, and handed them over. The Mexicans were conferring over this card when Jerry suddenly produced a rapid burst of excellent Spanish that was incomprehensible to me. Carlos and Tito turned to look at him as though stung, and the other men, who'd been getting bored with us, suddenly were all attention. Carlos and Tito approached the window and looked in. They looked murderous.

"What you say?" said Carlos.

"I didn't say anything," said Jerry, unconvincingly, since the Spanish had certainly been in his voice, although his head had been turned away from me so I hadn't actually seen him talking. Carlos and Tito certainly didn't seem convinced. "No digo nada."

"We hear what you say," said Carlos. Tito stepped back and waved, ordering Jerry to get out of the Rover. Jerry hesitated, and I could feel him tensing, but before he could put the Rover in gear and accelerate away, Carlos lunged into the cab and grabbed the keys out of the ignition. He pulled the door open, and motioned Jerry to get out. The Rover was surrounded now.

"Wait a minute, wait a minute now," cried Jerry, but strong brown arms reached in and began to pull him out. Peter opened his door and jumped out, but two uniformed men grabbed him.

Jill made a sudden movement. She was looking at the Land Rover floor. I followed her gaze, and saw that the tarp was moving.

"Untie me, George," said the parrot. "Hurry up."

I glanced up and saw Carlos standing in the open back door of the Rover.

"Who you talk to?" he asked. I motioned to Jill, who nodded. Carlos looked unconvinced. He motioned at the tarp. "What you got here?"

"Camping gear."

"Komping?"

"A tent."

Carlos gave me an uncomprehending look and motioned for me to remove the tarp. There was another burst of rapid Spanish. This time it was in my voice, although it didn't really sound like my voice to me. But Carlos looked at me in surprise, and responded with some rapid Spanish at me. When he stopped, my "voice" went on again for what seemed like a long time. I tried moving my mouth to the words, but Carlos viewed me with increasing bewilderment, as did the other Mexicans behind him. Finally, he shook his head and yanked the tarp off the floor.

"Ai!" He jumped back, and the other Mexicans craned their heads and pushed forward to see what had startled him. The parrot raised her head and started talking to them in a voice like a Mexican politician's or radio announcer's, very macho and authoritative, but they couldn't seem to take it in. Carlos looked at me and spoke in English as though all the fluent Spanish had never been uttered. "What the hell you doing?"

"It's as I told you," the parrot said, switching to Dan Rather–like English. "I'm a representative from the galactic confederacy to your government, and these gringos have kidnapped me to stop me from delivering an important message."

Carlos narrowed his eyes. "What?" The parrot sighed and dropped her head to the floor.

38

"Where you get this ... bird?" said Carlos. "You find it in these mountains?" He and Tito were now sitting at a table in a bar, having a drink. They didn't offer me, Jill, Jerry, or Peter one. Henry was still in the Rover with the parrot and her offspring. Carlos had made us get out, then had shut and locked it and put a guard over it, which seemed a sensible way of dealing with the incomprehensible.

"I'm not at liberty to discuss that now," said Jerry. "I need to talk to the American consul in Guadalajara."

"What for?"

"I'm on government business."

Carlos talked with Tito awhile, then both looked at Jerry. "What business?"

"It's classified."

"You a spy."

Jerry was impatient. "Come on, let me get to a phone."

"Why don't you tell us about this business if you want to come to this country? You think you can do anything you want?"

Jerry rubbed his hand across his face and shook his head. Peter looked at him uneasily.

"Don't lose your temper, Jerry."

"Shut up, Peter."

"Where you find this big bird?"

"She's not a bird," said Jill. Carlos and Tito looked at her with a trace of uneasiness, as though they didn't entirely want to know what the parrot was. "She's a sentient being."

"This woman is a foreign agent. She's in my custody," said Jerry.

"You're the foreign agent," said Jill.

"You mean she come from . . . el extraterrestre?"

"That's right," said Jill, "with a message for your government, just like she said. From outer space."

"You're going to regret this," said Jerry.

Carlos looked dubious, and held another conference with Tito. "Why from . . . houter space they want to have a message for Mexico?"

"Why not for Mexico? You are a great nation."

"What is this message?"

"You'll have to ask her."

Carlos and Tito looked uneasier than ever. Jerry and Peter eyed Jill with hatred. The bartender and the crowd of townsfolk that had spilled in from the street looked interested but neutral. In the sudden silence I could hear a donkey braying and a child wailing somewhere in the night. Big moths fluttered around the naked light bulbs that lit the place.

Carlos and Tito drank some more beer, then seemed to make up their minds telepathically. At least, they both suddenly seemed less uneasy. "Okay," said Carlos. "We take you to Guadalajara tomorrow."

"A wise decision, Señor," said Jerry.

"You're just passing the buck," cried Jill. "Why don't you talk to her?" But Carlos and Tito looked right through her.

"You stay here tonight," said Carlos. He said something to the bartender, who answered laconically. "You stay in the room behind there." He motioned behind the bar, where a door opened into darkness.

"I have to go to the bathroom," said Jill.

"Is outside." Carlos and Tito directed one of their minions to take Jill to the outhouse. I bought a beer while we waited for her to get back, but I didn't have the energy to drink it. I was as near total exhaustion as I'd ever been.

"You tired," Carlos said to me encouragingly. "You want to sleep." When Jill returned, he showed us to the room behind the bar, from which some impressive cockroaches scurried when he turned on the light. It was evidently a storeroom, because a few cases of beer stood on the bare floorboards. It was windowless.

"We're supposed to spend the night here?" said Jill.

"Shut your mouth," said Jerry. Carlos closed the door on us. We could hear him locking it. A song started up on an ancient jukebox that I'd noticed in the corner of the barroom, but had assumed was broken. The record it played took awhile to get up speed, emitting a lurching growl before the drum and accordion started their peasant dance. I suddenly felt giddy and sat on the floor.

"We ought to teach you a lesson," said Peter to Jill.

"Just try it, rotten phony."

Peter took a step toward Jill, but Jerry grabbed him by the back of his shirt and swung him aside. I closed my eyes. A harsh, sobbing voice joined the drum and accordion on the record, the voice of a woman who'd had as much as she could take of everything and had cast aside all restraint in expressing her misery. Her sorrows should have sounded odd against the lockstep gaiety of the waltz, but they didn't.

I put my head down on the floor. It was remarkably comfortable. I felt a thump nearby, and opened my eyes for a minute. I saw Jill's hip where she had sat down against the wall. The record ended, there was a scratching sound, and another record started up in the middle, as though the needle had slipped. Accordion and drum again, but this time a chorus of men's voices made yipping, trilling sounds, coyotes dancing under a desert moon. Then the lights went out, and the record stopped with another lurch and growl. I heard talking and walking in the barroom, but it seemed farther and farther away.

39

I had one of those dreams that would take a three-volume novel to describe—characters, dialogue, long, involved plots. A pre-Columbian culture in the Sierra Madre (except that it looked like the Sierra Nevada) kept condors in cages and fed them sacrificial victims. Most of the dream concerned my own maneuvers for not becoming a victim, but I eventually found myself prodded by sharp obsidian spears to climb a pyramid.

A figure loomed at the top of the pyramid, dressed in one of those feathered bird costumes that Aztec priests and warriors wore. I toiled up the pyramid with the absurd mixture of dread and curiosity that one sometimes feels in dreams. At first, the figure was just a silhouette, but I began to see detail as I got higher. The feathers were red, stained with the blood of victims which covered the pyramid steps.

The costume's large, hooked beak shadowed the figure's face until I was nearly to the top. Then the figure moved, and I could see that it was Alec Rice, which didn't surprise me. It was almost a relief to see something familiar. But then I noticed that Alec didn't look at me with recognition. I realized from its immobility that the face was a mask. For some reason, this was much more upsetting than finding Alec up there, particularly when I saw that the mask really *was* Alec Rice's face. There was blood around the eye sockets. Alec had been skinned, and the bird figure was wearing him.

"Who *are* you?" I asked the figure, but it just stood there. I heard a rustling to one side and looked down. Vultures had settled among the corpses, and one of them was looking at me.

"Ssst," it said. "George."

"What?"

"Shhhh!"

I opened my eyes. It was dark and silent. I knew immediately that the pre-Columbian welter I seemed to have been living in for the past months was unreal, You seldom remember a dream in such detail unless something awakens you in the middle of it. I listened a moment.

"Sssst!" It might have been a rat squeaking in the wall, but I crawled toward the sound. It did indeed seem to be coming from the wall. Then I felt air movement, and realized that I had crawled against the door. I heard a grunt from inside the room, and lay still for a while.

"George?" It was hard to tell from a whisper, but it sounded like Terry.

"Terry?"

"I heard your voice. Who were you talking to?"

"Never mind. Jerry and Peter are in here."

"I know. I watched them stop you, Carlos and Tito."

"That's nice."

"I'm going to get you out."

"How?" I must have sounded startled. Someone grunted and moved in the room again.

"What's that?" said Jerry, quite clearly, as though he was wide awake. But he didn't move, and about three hours later, it seemed, I could hear him breathing regularly.

"Terry?"

"I'm going to kick the door in," Terry said. "Then I'll give you a flashlight, and you point it at Peter and Jerry."

"Why?"

"Stand next to the door. Here goes." I heard Terry step back from the door and did as he said. The door crashed open and something hard thumped against my stomach. A beam of light shot against the wall, and I fumbled to hold on to the flashlight as Terry let go of it.

"Come on George!" Terry cried. I heard movement in the room and pointed the light at it. Jerry was sitting up, and Peter was already on his feet. Fortunately, Carlos and Tito had taken their guns away. I heard a "phut!" sound beside my ear, and glanced aside to see Terry holding two tranquilizer guns leveled at Peter and Jerry, who jumped, but gave no sign of being subdued. Terry rushed at Peter and knocked him down. I hit Jerry on the head with the flashlight, which went out.

"Shit, George," said Terry. "That was smart." Another light appeared from Terry's direction, a pocket flash. "Good thing I've got a spare." He flashed the light at Peter and Jerry, both of whom were trying to stand up, but with difficulty. "I gave them enough for a bear." Peter's eyes turned up, and he rolled on his back. Jerry kept staring at us, but seemed unable to move, and slowly sank backward.

"They could die," said Jill, now awake.

"You want to stay around, make sure they recover?" Terry replied.

"What made you change your mind?" Jill asked.

Terry turned and walked into the now deserted barroom. "Come on," he said. I followed him, and heard Jill coming behind. I stumbled over something, and Terry turned the pocket flash back in my direction. A uniformed Mexican lay on the floor, with a dart sticking in his shoulder. Two-gun Terry.

Terry went to the door and looked out. A dog had started to bark in back of the bar. Terry pushed through the swing doors, and I hurried after. Jerry's Land Rover stood where we had left it.

"Get it open while I get mine," said Terry.

"Why don't we just take this?"

"Because Tito's got the keys. Get it open." Terry disappeared around the corner, and Jill emerged from the door.

"Can you pick car locks?" I asked.

"They took my knife."

I picked up a cobblestone, and raised it to break a window, but wondered if I should wait until Terry brought his Rover around. I looked inside, but I couldn't see anything except the tarp, and one of Henry's hands sticking out the side.

I thought I saw movement down the street, but there were no streetlights, so I couldn't be sure. I decided to keep busy, my Forest Service training coming to the fore. I slammed the cobblestone against the car window. It was surprisingly resistant, but after bashing it a few more times, I was able to get a hand in and open the door. A figure sat up spectrally under the tarp. Frankenstein-like, Henry pulled the tarp away from his face and gazed at me.

"Behold, I am alive for evermore, Amen; and have the keys of hell and of death." He looked it. His face was almost colorless except for the purple eye sockets. His breath smelled like death, too.

"He should be in the hospital," said Jill. Henry groaned and lay down again. The parrot was on the other side of the rover. I pulled the tarp off her, but she didn't move. It was too dark inside to see if her eyes were open. I unlocked the door on that side and went around to open it. There was definitely something moving down the street.

I started trying to untie the parrot in the dark. It went slowly: whoever had tied her up was good with knots.

"Don't waste your time, George," the parrot said.

"Shit, you startled me."

"Get the young ones out of that bag. I'm not going to be able to move for a while."

"We can't leave you here."

"Who said anything about leaving me? Get the young ones."

I fumbled around in the dark until I found the bag. Its contents seemed ominously limp. I looked at Jill standing behind me.

"I think they suffocated," I whispered.

"Don't whisper, George," said the parrot. "They're torpid. It's a defensive reaction."

A light went on in a house two doors down, and Carlos stuck his head out beside that of a pretty woman. An engine started somewhere down the hill, and headlights reflected against a wall. Carlos's head turned toward that, then disappeared.

Henry sat up again, and put his hand to his forehead. "I've got a headache," he said.

"George," said the parrot, "pull the distributor cap off the engine."

"Good thinking." I opened the hood, but I couldn't see anything. I started pulling wires at random. The light down the hill grew brighter. I looked past the Rover's hood, and saw two headlights approaching. A figure stepped in front of them, arm raised, but they didn't hesitate, and the figure leapt out of the way.

Terry's Land Rover banged and rattled and slid to a stop. Jill and I opened the back door, picked up the parrot and slung her in. While Jill ran around to the passenger side, I grabbed the bag of offspring and leapt in the back. Terry roared away with a violent lurch, and I fell against the parrot, who said something emphatic in her own language. The Rover lurched again, and went into a skid. I reared up to see Terry fighting the wheel, trying to avoid an aged Mexican couple standing in the road.

"How the fuck did they get there!"

I looked behind us. More house lights had come on, and people were running about. I didn't see any headlights, which was encouraging. Terry accelerated again, and I fell on the creature again.

"A prating fool shall fall," she said.

"You know the Bible too?"

"Twenty years is a long time."

40

"Where are we going?" asked Jill, as we banged and rattled through the pine woods. The Rover seemed louder than before and the lights kept flickering out. Terry made them come back on by pounding on the dashboard.

"To the ranch," said Terry.

"Why? Why don't we just get out of here?"

"I have to get the condors."

"God," said Jill. "Why didn't you bring them?"

"Didn't know what was going to happen."

"So you decided to rescue us on impulse?" Terry didn't answer. "Jerry won't be pleased."

"Fuck him."

"He scared you, didn't he?"

"Fuck you."

"What happens when we get to the ranch?" I asked.

"We load up the condors and get out of here."

"To where?"

"I don't know about you," said Terry, "but I'm going to Guatemala."

"Oh," said Jill, "that's a nice place."

The parrot had taken her offspring out of the bag, and had gotten them conscious by making noises at them and handling them, though they were still feeble. Now I heard a gurgling sound and looked back at her. She appeared to be eating one, at least, she had it in her mouth.

"What are you doing?" I asked.

"Feeding them." It came out kind of indistinct.

"You mean by regurgitation?"

"Gross," said Jill.

"I thought you didn't feed them." The parrot removed her offspring from her mouth, and shrugged.

"Just in emergencies. It's uncomfortable."

"Smells nice too," said Terry.

I began to feel carsick again. I was glad I had an empty stomach. "But you haven't eaten in a day," I said.

"I haven't been digesting much either," she replied.

"Why don't you just let the poor condors go?" said Jill.

"They wouldn't survive down here," Terry replied.

"Why not? They eat dead things. Will they survive in Guatemala?"

"I'm not taking them to Guatemala."

"Oh, so we're supposed to take them. What are we going to do, hitchhike back to California with them?" Terry didn't answer. We'd started on the horrible track down into the canyon, so I didn't blame him for not responding. We went over an exceptionally brutal bump, and the lights went out again. The Rover skidded to the right and seemed to drop into empty space, then landed on something with a sickening bang and bounced to the left. Terry pounded the dashboard and the lights came back on. We were still on the track, but there was an awful scraping sound under the Rover. Terry stopped, got out, and looked underneath with his pocket flash.

"What is it?" I asked.

"Don't know. Bent axle maybe."

"You can't drive it with a bent axle."

"Get back to the ranch, probably."

"Then what?" said Jill.

"Dunno," said Terry. "Maybe it's just wheel bearings."

We kept going for about a half hour more, while the scraping turned into a grinding, and then an ear-rending screech.

"I can't steer anymore," said Terry, and skidded into a big thornbush. The engine roared out of gear and stopped, but the headlights stayed on. I pulled my head out from between the front seats and looked around. I could see rocks and bushes outside the headlight beams. Dawn was breaking.

"Can you fix wheel bearings?" Jill asked.

"Not here," Terry replied.

"How far are we from the ranch?"

"Just a couple of miles."

"Good," said the parrot. "I need to stretch my legs." She had been almost unable to move when we'd finally untied her, but she had recovered quickly. She still limped and hobbled when she got onto the track and started walking downhill with the young ones trailing behind. Terry shrugged and started after her, while Jill and I stared numbly at the Rover. Acrid smoke rose from beneath it.

"They'll be coming after us pretty soon," said Jill.

"Jerry and Peter? They'll be out for a few hours at least," I said.

"Those Mexicans, Carlos and Tito. They know who Terry is."

"They'll wait until Jerry and Peter come to."

"Why should they?" It was a good question, when I thought about it. Terry and the parrot had already disappeared down the track. We started after them.

We overtook the parrot before too long. The young ones had gotten their appetites back, and had stopped to persecute a small boa.

"Ugh," said Jill with a shiver. "Eating snakes."

"Rattlesnake meat is supposed to be good." I was getting my appetite back, in a queasy sort of way.

We didn't see Terry again until we got to the ranch. He was in the condor cage with a big butterfly net, chasing the condors, but without success, because the birds all stayed on the upper perches where he couldn't reach them.

"He looks ridiculous," said Jill.

"Give me a hand here, George," cried Terry.

"Why don't you just let them go?" shouted Jill.

"Shut up!"

"What are you going to do with them if you catch them? Your truck's no good."

"I'm taking them on the boat, like we planned," said Terry. He sounded a little defensive.

"With half the Mexican army looking for us?"

"Come on George," said Terry. "I need you to climb up on the perches and force them to the ground so I can net them."

"He's a monomaniac," said Jill. "You better humor him."

"*I* better humor him?"

"I'm acrophobic."

"Come on, man!"

It was the first time I'd seen condors in the flesh, close up. They didn't seem all that big, but their beaks were more prominent and impressive than they'd appeared in photographs. The birds had always looked rather gentle and benevolent, in fact, a bit dim. But as I laboriously shinned myself up their splintery dead tree perches, their eyes glittered and their heads swayed with defensive vigor. They hissed and jabbed at my hands as I tried to shoo them off their perches. They shuffled to the ends of their dead branches, where I couldn't climb. They had no intention of surrendering their fates to my hominid sapience.

"I'll break my neck up here, damnit," I whined. "Hey, where you going?"

Terry walked around the house and came back with a long pole, which he handed up to me.

"Push them down with this."

"I might hurt them."

"You don't need to pound them on the head. Just push them."

"Why don't you shoot them with tranquilizers?"

"I've run out. It's not good for them, anyway."

Terry had just fed the condors, as I discovered when one of them spat up meat at me. Condors have difficulty getting airborne at any time, and full stomachs make it even harder for them, so there wasn't much they could do once I'd maneuvered them off a perch except spread their wings and flop down into Terry's net. From that point, it was difficult and dangerous, but possible, to get them into Terry's small cages.

The parrot's entourage arrived halfway through the operation, and caused a temporary halt as her offspring climbed into the cage after scraps of meat left from feeding the condors.

"Get them *out* of here!" roared Terry, who was beginning to seem a little maniacal. He made a threatening lunge at them. They bared their teeth and hissed at him. The parrot shook her head.

"You see what this treatment has done to their dispositions," she said. "Permanent emotional damage." She made her call note, but they ignored it. "Stop threatening them, and they'll come out pretty soon." Terry slammed out of the cage and walked around the house again. I thought he was going to come back with an axe, but he returned with a broom and swept the young parrots out. Their mother's head feathers stood up, but she didn't do anything.

"Why don't I go grab a bite now?" I said hopefully.

"Later," Terry replied.

"Carlos and Tito will be here later."

"That's why we have to get this done."

"Don't we still have to bring the boat down to the river and load it with supplies?"

"I've done all that."

"You were planning this anyway!"

"Gotta foresee contingencies," Terry said.

Jill had gone into the house. She came out with some coffee and stale bread. It tasted good. I went back to poking at the perched condors and within an hour or so we had four of them caged. The fifth individual proved excessively wily and nimble, and had plenty of room to maneuver on the otherwise empty perches. Jill cheered every time it gave me the slip.

The parrot and her offspring reappeared from the brush. "I hear an engine coming," she said. We stopped and listened. The faint, intermittent roar of a vehicle winding along the track drifted down the canyonside. Terry threw the net down and walked out of the cage. I hastened after him. He left the door open.

"Okay," he said to the condor, "drop dead." The condor stayed where it was. Terry picked up a cage and started running toward the river with it. I started to pick one up, but thought better of it.

"Give me a hand with this," I said to Jill. We'd carried it about halfway to the river when Terry passed us, running the other way.

"He's going to rupture himself," said Jill. We got to the boat and put our cage next to Terry's on a pile of gear in the middle of the floor. The parrot's bundle was there. Jill put her hand on it thoughtfully.

"Come on," I said, "there's no time for that. You already went through it, anyway."

"I was interrupted."

I started walking back toward the house, and Jill followed after a moment. Halfway up the bank, we met Terry running down the path with another cage. He shouted something as he passed, but I couldn't understand it. The parrot appeared with the fourth cage on her head. She also had a piece of meat tied to a string, and was enticing her offspring to hurry after her.

"Got to run," she said. "They're here."

Terry was tying the third cage above the other two when we reached the raft. He hurriedly added the fourth.

"It looks kind of topheavy," said Jill. In fact, it looked like a Mississippi flatboat instead of a white-water raft. "Are you sure this will work?"

"What's the alternative?" said Terry, fiddling with paddles.

"I'm a little hydrophobic, actually," Jill said.

Terry tossed a life preserver at her. "Put this on, you'll feel better."

The parrot and her offspring also seemed in doubt. We heard a shout from above. She picked up two of her young ones and slung them in the boat. I grabbed a third and waded aboard, and she followed with the other.

"Shit," said Terry, "watch your claws!" The parrot looked down at her feet, which were making sharp indentations in the rubber floor. She looked perplexed, and lifted her toes.

"That's alright," he said, "just don't do any jumping around."

Jill still stood on the bank. The young parrots craned their necks over the side of the boat and looked at her. I wondered what was going on in their heads, and how it would all come out when—if—they became like their mother.

"Come on," Terry said, "we need you to paddle." Jill launched herself off the bank, and more or less fell into the boat. "Ataway," said Terry, and pushed us off. We spun around, bounced off a rock, and moved into the main channel backwards. Terry handed paddles to Jill and me and stuck his own into the water behind him, trying to get us facing forward. Something moved at the top of the bank, and I shoved my paddle into the water.

The overloaded raft moved sluggishly at first, then picked up speed. The rush of the water drowned out other sounds. When I looked up again, we were approaching a red rock cliff. The river took a bend around it, and disappeared. I glanced back at our point of embarkation, but I couldn't see anything except brush and rock. Then we slid under the cliff's shadow.

41

"Wheeee!" said Jill, "I *like* this." She paddled enthusiastically, if inexpertly. I didn't mind, because it meant I didn't have to paddle very hard to keep the raft straight. We'd left the ranch six hours before, and my arms were getting tired. It did beat throwing up in a Land Rover, though. The early afternoon sun still touched the canyon bottom, warming feet chilled by river water. The water in the river sparkled, ducks skittered before us, a fresh breeze blew upcanyon.

"Right hard!" shouted Terry. I started paddling too late, lost my balance, and thrust arm and paddle into the river. We bounced off a rock. "Pay attention, man."

"Wheeee!" said the parrot, in Jill's voice. She crouched against the baggage, holding on with her arms, obviously uncomfortable at being unable to grip with her feet. Occasionally, she lunged out to keep one of her offspring from going overboard. They never seemed to learn.

"Why don't you tie them to the baggage," said Jill. The parrot didn't answer. "Are you sure you don't want to try paddling?" The parrot nodded. "Can you swim?" Jill asked, as an afterthought. The bandage on her head had soaked off from the river water, revealing a red and black contusion. Nobody had said anything about exactly how she'd gotten it, or about how the parrot had gotten her shoulder wound, which seemed to cause her some discomfort as she held on to the condor cages. I didn't particularly want to know.

"Yes," said the parrot, "I can."

"Back left," said Terry. Jill paddled forward two strokes, then remembered and paddled backward, but not in time to keep us away from another rock. The raft dipped on my side, however, and I got splashed.

"This raft is overloaded," I said, after I finished gasping at the icy water. I could believe there was still snow on the Sierra, even though we were rafting past fig trees.

"Jump ship," said Terry.

We hadn't run into any dangerous rapids, but the boulder-choked river was no slough. I wished I had better water-repellent gear than jeans, a cotton flannel shirt, and an old rain jacket, especially now that the sun was sinking toward the canyon rim.

"I want to stop soon," the parrot said. "I want to get out of this thing for a while." She reached out her foot and snagged two young ones that were squabbling and teetering on the gunwale. "They're getting cross. They need to eat."

"It's hard to stop right here," said Terry. The riverbank alternated between sheer cliffs, reed beds, and narrow sand beaches under sheer cliffs.

"What's wrong with these beaches?" said the parrot.

"Nothing, if you want to be fossilized before your time," I said. I told her about my quicksand adventure.

"Wouldn't be any food on them anyway," she said.

"Hey!" said Terry. The parrot plucked one of its young off the cages, but made a helpless gesture.

"You can do better than that," said Jill. The parrot muttered something incomprehensible. The river took a tight curve, and Jill and I were busy paddling to keep the raft from turning sideways and getting snagged. When I looked up again, I could see that the river widened and deepened around the bend. A tributary entered there, and there was a piece of bottomland with some trees. After some bumping, we floated over the rocky delta that the tributary had deposited, and came to quiet water edged by a sand beach.

"After you," I said to Terry as we neared the beach. He jumped to the sand without sinking an inch, and beached the raft. The young creatures leapt ashore and scurried into the trees, followed less energetically by their mother.

I started to unload the supplies, and encountered the parrot's bundle. I looked at Jill, who looked at the trees. The parrot was out of sight. I picked up the bundle, looking for an opening. There were fastenings, but I didn't see how they worked.

"How did you get this open?"

"I just fiddled with it," said Jill. I fiddled with it, but nothing happened.

"To hell with it." I picked up the bundle and took it ashore.

"She doesn't seem worried about it anymore," said Jill.

"Probably full of human brains."

We unloaded and made a camp of sorts while the condors watched morosely from their stacked cages. I wondered what they felt about their boat ride. Terry took some meat out of a plastic cooler and fed them.

"What is that?" said Jill.

"It's meat."

"What kind of meat?"

"Different kinds."

"God." Jill went away to make a driftwood fire. It got dark fast under the cliffs. We boiled water for our freeze-dried dinner. Terry took out his hash pipe and stoked up. He looked glum.

"Toke?"

"No thanks."

"Well," he said, "that's a year's hard work down the tubes."

"At least they're still alive," I said. I meant the condors, as I assumed Terry did. He walked over to his duffel and came back with a quart of rum.

"Keep the chill off," he said, handing it to me. I drank some, happily. Jill puffed on the pipe a few times, but refused the liquor. The water boiled, and Jill ladled out freeze-dried spaghetti.

"Hey!" Terry shouted. "Lady Di! Come and get it!" I exchanged looks with Jill. Terry glared at us.

"This wouldn't have happened if it hadn't been for her." He motioned toward the trees.

"What wouldn't have happened?" said Jill.

"At least she could thank me."

"Well," I said, "it happened."

We ate spaghetti. A pink cloud drifted across the violet patch of sky above the cliffs.

"I hope it doesn't rain," I said.

"Might get a little rain tonight," said Terry.

The parrot emerged from the trees with her offspring, and accepted a bowl of spaghetti and some rum. Terry didn't offer her any hashish. God knows what that would have done to her.

"What did the tranquilizer do to you?" I asked her.

"Knocked me out."

"You seemed to be in a torpid state."

"That was after I came to again, when I was tied up. No sense in wasting energy."

"Wish we had some music," said Terry. He waved the rum at the parrot. "You like music?"

"Yes."

"What music? Opera?"

"Why should she like opera?" said Jill.

"I bet she can sing it, she imitates people so well. Sing some opera."

"Alright," the parrot said. She sang a duet, both parts, tenor and soprano. She also did eerily faithful imitations of trumpets and woodwind instruments. The music sounded medieval.

"What was that?" I said.

"Monteverde's *Orfeo*," the parrot said. "I like your High Renaissance best. Too bad you didn't stay with it."

"Shit," said Terry. He picked up a blanket and walked into the darkness with it.

"How can you make two sounds at once like that?" Jill asked.

"I have two voice boxes."

"Wow."

"Nothing unusual about it," the parrot said. "All birds have it, a syrinx instead of a larynx. It's down where the windpipe connects with the lungs."

I asked, "Is there any Cretaceous music?"

"You want to hear some?" the parrot asked.

"Yeah."

She began producing an incomprehensibly complex range of sounds. The bump in front of her head must have been full of air chambers. The sounds had tremendous resonance, echoing back and forth off the canyon walls. They were ventriloqual, and some of them sounded far away. There were trumpets, choirs, bass drums, thunder, and a lot of things I couldn't describe. When she stopped, it was like waking from an auditory dream. Even her daughters seemed impressed.

"We were good musicians," the parrot said. She led her young to the base of the cliff and put her head down. The fire had sunk low. The stars looked very bright in the narrow band of sky above the canyon rim.

42

I awoke with an itchy, clammy sensation. Sleeping on sand with blankets is not cushy, especially on river sand with silt in it. I couldn't see the stars anymore, but it was still quite dark. So dark I couldn't see my watch. I could see the pale sand, and the huddled shapes of Terry and Jill.

At least there weren't a lot of biting insects, just a few—tiny sand flies. A breeze blew down the canyon, rattling the tree branches of the little delta. A bird started calling in there somewhere, a plaintive, fluting sound. I wondered what it had thought of the parrot's concert.

It was raining when I woke up again, a quiet, warm, rather soothing drizzle. The water beaded the blanket like dew. I stood up and scratched. I felt an urge to wash in the river, but thought better of it when I looked at the dark, rushing water. Jill and Terry were hunched over a fire. The parrot and her offspring weren't in sight, doubtless out on a lizard-eating expedition.

"I thought you said the rainy season is a ways off."

"This isn't rain," Terry replied. He handed me a cup of coffee and I drank it greedily.

"How long is this trip going to take?"

"I don't know," Terry replied.

"Well, how far is it?"

"About seventy-five miles to the coast, due southwest. Don't know how many river miles."

"Why are we doing this?"

"It's exciting," said Jill.

I had a sense of déjà vu. I suppose it reminded me of one of the canoe trips I'd taken with my wife on the Klamath and Trinity rivers when I'd worked for the Forest Service, although I couldn't remember my wife saying it was exciting. I'd been the enthusiast on those trips. My wife would have been happy to sunbathe on the rocks. But the dankness of the early morning river bottom was the same, as was the faint incredulity that we were going to spend the day swirling through icy whitewater without needing to. Not so faint this time.

I'd been the one who'd wanted to go places. My wife had wanted to stay in Massachusetts, where we'd gone to college. Too many weirdos in California. Actually, she had adapted to Weaverville better than I had: it was not unlike the small Berkshires town where she'd grown up. But there weren't many computer jobs in Weaverville, and she'd had to make a living after moving out on increasingly weirdo George, so it had been back to Boston. I wondered if she ever went on canoe trips with her new husband.

I hadn't thought about my wife for a while. She'd been remarried for about a year. It had been a relief, in a way, since increasingly bankrupt George had been having trouble keeping up his child support payments. I'd started sending money again after I'd gotten the South Coast Preserve job, but I hadn't heard anything. Maybe she was getting divorced again.

"What's the matter?" said Jill.

"Nothing."

"You look like you're having a premonition."

"You ever been married?"

"Yes."

"What happened?"

"I got divorced," she said.

"How come?"

"I don't know. I was too young."

"I've been married three times," said Terry, walking past with an armful of gear. "Help me load this shit." Jill made a face.

"What's that smell?"

"Condor food's getting a little ripe," Terry replied, marching away. He seemed gratified. "It won't hurt them. They can digest anything but heavy metals and pesticides." The condor cages were lined up beside the offending ice chest. The birds didn't look any the worse for the previous day on the river. They didn't look any better. They looked nervous. They'd looked nervous ever since I'd seen them.

THE VERMILION PARROT

"Why don't you let them out of those little cages so they can stretch their wings?" Jill asked. Terry didn't answer. "He probably kept his wives in little cages."

I caught another whiff of carrion and glanced at the ice chest. The young parrots had emerged from the bush, evidently attracted. One climbed on the chest and was picking at the loose lid with its foreclaws. I noticed that there were only three of them at the ice chest; the fourth was still with her mother, I supposed.

I walked toward the chest to chase them away and snap the lid shut. The one on top hissed at me. I nudged it with my foot, and it hissed again. This time, it sounded like words. In fact, it sounded like "fuck off."

I saw a movement out of the corner of my eye. The parrot emerged from the trees. She was carrying the fourth young one.

"It spoke to me," I said.

"It's just mimicry at this stage," the parrot replied.

"What's wrong with that one?"

"They're not getting enough food."

"Give them some granola."

"They need fresh food. Vitamins. This one's not going to survive much longer unless it gets some." The aggressive one climbed back on the ice chest and started pulling at the lid again. Another climbed on it.

"Well, that ain't fresh," I said.

Terry came hurrying up the beach, and shooed the creatures off the chest.

"Easy," I said.

"The condors need that," Terry said, snapping the lid shut. He picked the chest up and started carrying it to the raft.

"Well, why don't you give it to them?" said Jill. Terry took the chest to the raft, returned, and picked up a condor cage. "Because they don't need it yet," he said.

"You want to spend the day on the river with a box full of stinking, rotten meat?"

"I don't smell anything. The sooner we get going, the sooner it'll be over."

The sun topped the canyon rim as we pushed off. The air stopped being dank and started being fiery. The river ran the same as the day before, winding back and forth under the cliffs so that I soon lost a sense of direction. It was like traveling on a Möbius strip. A tributary entered occasionally; then there'd be riffles and sandbars to bounce and scrape through. Toward noon, a shrieking flock of long-tailed birds crossed the canyon rim.

"Must be military macaws," said Terry. "We're getting down." He looked at the parrot, who was shielding the weak young one from the sun while holding the aggressive one down with a claw. "How come you look like a parrot?"

"You've got me."

"Is that convergent evolution?"

"I hope not," the parrot said.

"What do you mean?" Terry asked.

"I'd rather not end up in a cage, screaming nonsense." She tentatively loosed her grip on the obstreperous one. It evidently had fallen asleep.

"How about you?" Terry went on. "You ever been married?"

"Give it a rest, Terry," said Jill, who had given up paddling and was sprawled in the front. She was the kind of blonde who tans dark. She'd taken off her top, and the sparse, bleached hairs around her nipples glittered against skin that was turning milk chocolate color.

"Why don't you shave your legs, Jill?" said Terry.

"Because it turns off men like you."

"Come on guys," I said, without much conviction.

"No," said Terry, "I'm interested. We know hardly anything about this critter, and we've been with her for weeks."

"I haven't been married," said the parrot.

"You know what I mean."

"I don't know what you mean," said Jill.

"Like, you got any close male friends?"

"There's George," the creature said. Jill laughed.

"I'm serious. Don't you get lonely?"

"We're social animals."

"Why didn't any of those others you talk about come with you?"

"Maybe there aren't any others," the parrot said. "Maybe I'm the last one. What difference does it make, anyway. There's no safety in numbers."

"So what are you *doing* here?"

"Right now, I'm looking for food."

"Me too," said Jill. She sat up and put on her top. "Let's have lunch."

"We just had breakfast," said Terry. I was getting hungry too. And tired of Terry. Jill stood up and began rummaging through the baggage, making the stacked condor cages shift. The birds fluttered and scraped against the wooden bars of the homemade cages.

"Cut it out!" Terry cried.

"Where's some food?"

"It's packed. There's nothing but freeze-dried stuff anyway."

"You mean there's *nothing?* No more granola?"

"We finished that. I didn't have a chance to go to market, you know. We'll stop and have dinner in a couple hours, then float some more before it gets dark."

"Your damn birds eat better than we do."

"Help yourself to the ice chest," Terry said.

"Let's stop now, then," said Jill.

"I'm not hungry yet. We need to make some tracks. You want to run out of the freeze-dried stuff too?"

"What did you bring. Food for two days?"

"I'm getting real tired of her," said Terry to me.

"You think you're tough, but you're actually stupid," Jill said.

"Want to get off? My pleasure."

"I'm taking us to shore," said Jill, picking up a paddle. She began slashing at the river and the raft rotated for a while. Then Terry reached over and snatched at her paddle. Jill held on a moment, then let go, and Terry almost went overboard. He turned red, and a bullish look came into his eyes. Ship of Flakes.

The unsteered boat had gotten into a stretch of fairly fast water and we slid around a bend as Terry was trying to climb over my head to get at Jill. Suddenly he paused, and there was no sound in the raft but the river. It had changed. A deeper roar faintly underlay the mutterings and gurglings we were used to.

"That's not thunder, is it?" I said. Terry climbed back over my head and sat down. "I thought there were no big drops on this thing."

"I didn't see any." Terry picked up his paddle. We were still moving pretty fast.

"You flew up the whole goddamn thing, you said."

"Yeah, well, it was a little cloudy that day."

"What's going on?" said Jill.

"*Cloudy?*" I said.

"You saw the map."

"What's that noise?" said Jill. It was already getting louder.

"Could be one of the waterfalls in the feeder canyons."

"That's no tributary. That's right downstream."

"Yeah, well, okay," said Terry. "Let's go ashore, grab a bite. Check it out."

"What shore?" All I could see was cliffs and landslides on both sides of the river.

"There'll be a beach around that bend down there," Terry said confidently.

"You see it on your plane trip?"

"Want to paddle back upstream?"

We started paddling, downstream. The river definitely was getting faster. We rounded the bend. The river dropped away before us at a noticeable angle, straight as a spillway. Blocky volcanic cliffs walled it neatly, then seemed to end suddenly about a half mile downstream. The river seemed to end suddenly down there too. There was a misty look to the air above the gap, and the sound suddenly got much louder.

"Whoa," said Terry.

43

It started to drizzle again soon after the sun dropped behind the canyon wall. We'd been in shade awhile anyway, which was one of the two advantages of our position on a sandbar under a cliff. The other advantage was that the sandbar wasn't underwater— but everything else on the slippery slope leading to God-knew-what was.

We'd been very lucky to reach the sandbar, since the river had already hurried us past by the time Terry sighted it. We had to paddle to the cliff, then haul the raft back upstream by hand over very rough and slippery jumbles of rock. I had at least two mangled toenails. But I wasn't thinking about them.

The raft fit the sandbar like a glove. Two or three feet of water separated the bar from the cliff, so you couldn't even get out and sit against the rock. I kept thinking, "rub a dub dub, three men in a tub." I wondered if I was getting feverish. Terry and I had tried climbing the cliff to get a look at the rapid or waterfall or whatever it was downstream. After about fifty feet of climbable, blocky gray rock, it had become a sheer face of hard, red metamorphic rock. We tried following the bank downstream. After wading through two hundred yards of rock jumbles, the red, sheer cliff plunged into the river, forming a rushing, black deepwater stretch that reached as far downstream as we could see. Swimming down it would have been easy enough, assuming you didn't break a leg against a submerged rock or log. Swimming up it would have defeated Johnny Weissmuller.

"It doesn't really matter if we reconnoiter it or not," said Terry. "I'm sure it's not a waterfall. I would have seen a waterfall. Somebody would have seen a waterfall."

"Maybe there's been an earthquake."

"We'll spend the night on the bar, then go down in the morning. The river probably will quiet down by then."

"Why?"

"A lot of this water is probably snowmelt. It'll stop melting at night."

That was a comforting thought, until I considered that the river would probably *rise* during the evening if it was getting a lot of snowmelt. It didn't seem to be rising now, in late afternoon, but since the raft covered the sandbar, it was hard to tell.

I was sitting on the raft edge with my feet in the water, facing upwind. The young parrots weren't inhibited about excretory functions, which would have been alright if we'd been able to unload the raft and wash it out. Now it added a coup de grace to the smells of the condor cages and ice chest. Jill had stopped talking about food, which was just as well, since there was no way to cook it.

The young parrots hadn't stopped talking about food. They usually kept up a low, fussing sound as they roamed about, punctuated with squawks when they caught prey or squabbled, but the calls had become increasingly strident after we'd pulled up at the bar. They wanted to get out, at least, the three healthy ones did. The other had started making high-pitched, plaintive sounds. Their mother just sat there with her eyes sunk a little into her head. I couldn't tell if she was indifferent, or getting ready to tear all our heads off.

An explosion of squawks and thumps made me turn around. The most aggressive young one had started slashing at another with its claws, something that hadn't happened before, and blood started to fly. The parrot grabbed the aggressor by the back of its neck and held it up, still kicking.

"You're going to have to give us some of that meat," she said to Terry.

"He would have offered it if he wasn't such a dog in the manger," said Jill.

"They wouldn't be able to digest it," said Terry. "It's full of toxins."

"I'll digest it for them."

"Oh, yeah, that'll be convenient," said Terry. "Why don't you feed them something out of that bundle of yours? Why don't you synthesize some food, since your civilization was so superior?"

"It wasn't *that* superior," the parrot replied.

"I can't believe how stingy he is," Jill said.

"You either give it to us," said the parrot, "or I take it."

Terry jumped up, looking red and bullish again. "Chicken-shit!" he cried. "I can't believe this! I've been saving your asses for weeks, and what do I get for it?"

"You call this saving us?" said Jill. Terry rushed at her, and knocked her backwards into the water. The force of the blow knocked me off balance. I struggled upright. Jill sat in the water, coughing.

"You're going to have to let them go," she said. "At least *they'll* survive this."

"Oh yeah? What do you know about it? I'm supposed to give up everything for a bunch of giant chickens that ought to be extinct?"

"You could be describing the condors."

"Glib bitch."

"I won't take it all," the parrot said. The feathers on her head were beginning to stand up.

"Oh, you won't?" Terry snatched the ice chest off the baggage and held it against his stomach like a medicine ball. He looked at the parrot.

"Hey, man," I said, "the raft."

Terry snatched the lid off the ice chest and dumped its contents onto the floor of the raft. He flung the chest into the river, jumped overboard, and stormed off along the bank, to the extent possible on the slippery rocks.

The smell hit the back of my throat like a fist. I rolled over the side, and retreated to the cliff. Big flies whizzed past my head bullet-fashion, drawn to the feast. I stopped when the smell got bearable and put my back against the cliff. Jill came tumbling after.

"Terry is a perfect example of the contradictions of capitalism," she said.

"Care to explain that?" I could see the ice chest sliding away downriver. It hit a wave, flipped over, and disappeared.

"It's like a mirror at an amusement park. Every social, altruistic motive gets distorted into an antisocial, selfish one."

"That does sound a bit glib."

"I'm surprised he knew the word."

"Needling him didn't help."

"Maybe not." Jill rubbed her backside and winced. I glanced back toward the raft. The parrot was shoveling meat into her mouth with one claw and holding her offspring off with the other. From their cages, the condors watched in timid fascination.

"She's tough," I said.

"It may not be so good in the long run to have such creatures in the world."

"I don't know. Might benefit us to have some competition. Trim us down."

"*That's* an antisocial remark," said Jill.

"Like she said, there's no safety in numbers."

"Who's glib now?" Jill smirked at me in a not unfriendly way. Physical danger seemed to improve her disposition.

"You still think she's an enemy alien?" I asked.

"No," Jill replied, "I think I believe her. Anyway, she can't do much while she's got those brats."

"Maternal instincts."

"I almost admire her." Jill rubbed her arms and shivered. The air was doing its late afternoon shift from broiling to clammy.

I looked back at the raft. The parrot had stopped eating meat and was stuffing the remainder into the condor cages. Two of her young had climbed on the cages and tried to grab meat as she shoved it in.

"She keeps her word," I said.

"When it suits her. The young ones can only eat so much."

"So she's rational."

"When it suits her."

"Just like us."

"That's what worries me," Jill said, to my surprise.

I shifted my weight against the damp cliff face, wishing for a softer seat. The rock had a chalky, sparkly look, like marble. It had weathered into blocks, which reminded me of Marble

Mountain in the Klamaths, although these blocks were more regular.

I remembered reading that Mexican Sierra Madre rocks were Cretaceous in origin. It was odd to think that this petrified lakebed or reef, or whatever the marble had metamorphosed from, might have been contemporary with the parrot. It was even odder to think that we might all end up buried in silt under it. Odd, but not as scary as I might have thought. Somehow, the prospect of immediate destruction was less worrisome than the prospect of eventual destruction. Less time to worry.

44

I opened my eyes on total darkness and felt panic. Then the river noise penetrated my sleep-clogged ears and I remembered where I was, and felt panic again. The raft made rubbery sounds as I shifted my damp, itching body. Somebody muttered next to me. I focused in that direction, and saw a hint of dark gray, but nothing more. I looked upward, but no stars were visible. Not surprising, as it was still drizzling.

At least the flies had gone. Although the parrot and her offspring had been able to stomach their share of the rotten meat, the condors hadn't. They'd only picked at it. When he returned, Terry explained that vultures don't really like rotten meat that much, incensing Jill, who cried that Terry would *have* to let the condors go or they'd starve. Terry replied that condors could go days without food, and that he wasn't about to release any endangered wild animal in Mexico. The parrot and I stayed out of it. We needed Terry's rafting skills.

I realized that I could hardly smell the meat anymore, which was a relief, until I felt a stab of anxiety that Terry might somehow have taken his condors and sneaked away. I strained my eyes toward the center of the raft, and saw a faint, dark shape looming above. The cages were still there, at least.

I put my watch right against my eyes, but I couldn't see it. Cheap watch. I closed my eyes and tried to relax, which wasn't hard, since I was still half-asleep. Getting fully asleep seemed my best bet, under the circumstances. I unclenched my neck muscles and let the raft gently rock my head back and forth.

Then I was wide awake. The raft had not been rocking when we'd all curled up on it for our possible last night on earth. It had been flat on the sandbar. I twisted around toward the edge, and nearly dislocated my shoulder. When that stopped hurting, I leaned over to look for the sandbar, but of course saw nothing but darkness. I put my hand out, touched nothing, slid forward and put my hand out again, and touched water. The raft gave a slight, grinding lurch.

"Whuh?" said Terry.

"The river's rising." A flashlight switched on, directly into my eyes. I put my hand up to shield them, and the light turned toward the river. There was no vestige of sand anymore, just black water. "What time is it?"

"Four-thirty," said Terry.

"I thought you said the river would go *down!*"

"I dunno. It must be raining in the mountains."

"We're going to get carried away!"

"Don't panic, for Chrissake."

"What do you expect us to do?" said Jill out of the darkness. "It keeps going from bad to worse."

"That's the way things happen," said Terry. "Don't know why, but it is. Everytime something bad happens, like you get lost, then it starts to snow. It's like molecules work that way, bad vibes attract more."

"This is a hell of a time to get philosophical," I said.

"I think he's chronically understimulated," said Jill.

"What's that supposed to mean?"

The raft lurched again, and slid about six inches downstream. I jumped overboard, grabbed one of the handles, and tried to pull it back. It slid down a little more. The loss of my weight was helping to float it off the bar.

"Give me a hand here," I cried. "No, wait." If the others got out, the raft would float even more. A nice dilemma for Terry's new reflective mood. There was a splash, and the raft slid some more.

"Whoops," said Terry, "I see what you mean."

"Hold it!"

"I am!"

The raft stopped sliding, but began pulling inexorably at my arms. I braced my feet on the sand and bent until my ass was in the icy water, but the pull got stronger.

"Looks like we're going," said Terry, matter of factly.

"Not in the dark, for God's sake!"

I heard another splash, and the pull on my arms lessened. Jill was surprisingly strong, I thought. Terry's flashlight came on again. The parrot stood in the water at the downstream end of the raft. She bent slightly, and the raft moved a few inches upstream.

"Wow," said Terry. "How much can you press?"

The water was painfully cold until my hands and feet went numb, which was some improvement, but not much. Time seemed to stop in darkness and numbness. Then my teeth started to chatter.

"We're going to get hypothermia," I said.

"It's better than drowning," Terry replied.

"They're both fatal."

"Drowning's quicker."

"Stop it," said Jill.

"Thanks for lending a hand," Terry replied.

"She's watching my young," the parrot said. Terry said something under his breath. Nobody asked him what it was.

The raft crept downstream a few inches again. It might have been my imagination—I was too numb to feel much anyway—but it felt lighter, which would mean the river had risen more.

"Now will you let the condors go?" said Jill.

"In the dark?" She didn't answer. Terry remained silent a moment, then spoke. "No, I'm not going to let them go. We're going to get through this in one piece. What do you care about what happens to them, anyway? You just don't want to bother taking them back to L.A."

"Well, neither do you!"

"Why don't you all shut up," said the parrot.

A few minutes of silence ensued, then Jill spoke up again. "We'll capsize with those cages piled up." She had a point, but nobody pursued it.

The raft shifted downstream again, about a foot this time. I felt water running down the inside of my shirt. At least I could still feel something.

"My shoulder's getting weak," said the parrot. The raft began to twist back and forth slightly, trying to spin. I looked over my shoulder at the eastern sky, hoping for a little gray. It felt like I'd been in the water for days.

"What time is it now?"

"Almost five," Terry said. "Should be getting light."

"I think I see something," said Jill.

The raft jerked, and began pulling me to the left. I lost my foothold, and kicked out, trying to keep up with it. I didn't want to get left behind.

"Hang on George," said Terry.

"Uh."

The raft stopped for a minute or two while Terry grunted and groaned, then began moving again.

"It's floating," said Terry. "Better hop on." It was a good idea, but I found that I couldn't bend my knees enough to climb over the edge. I heard splashings and wallowings as Terry and the parrot climbed aboard. Then I was hanging on by my finger-nails as the raft spun downstream. Water covered my face, and I almost let go in panic.

"Come on, George."

"Glub glub." Something was trying to pull my arms out of their sockets. I could feel that, at least. Then I was lying on the bottom of the raft, gasping. I felt a vague sensation in one hand, I wasn't sure which.

"Here, George, start paddling."

THE VERMILION PARROT

Surprisingly, I was able to hold the paddle Terry had given me and sit up. I could even see a vague grayish-blueness when I opened my eyes. I lurched onto the side, stabbed at the water, and nearly lost the paddle.

"Not that way," said Terry, "the other way." I could see what he was trying to do. He was trying to get over to the bank and find a shallow place to stop in. It made sense, but there didn't seem to be any shallow places. I could see the pale gray marble now. The canyon walls were drawing closer together, and the water ran deeper and darker, foaming at the blocks along the perpendicular bank. A bird flitted upriver past us. It looked like a water ouzel, which was appropriate, since ouzels can walk underwater.

I paddled industriously. It made me feel a little warmer. It also increased my sense of rushing headlong toward the brink, but that seemed inevitable.

It certainly was fascinating. The closer we got to the gap where cliffs and river seemed to disappear in midair, the more we stared at it, all except the parrot. She sat against the baggage with an offspring in each claw, gazing at the rocky shore.

"Why isn't this on the map?" shouted Jill.

"Mexican map," said Terry.

"Don't be chauvinist."

"Cartographers make mistakes," I said.

"Some mistake!"

Powerful gusts of wind began to hit us, buffeting the condor cages and making a sound like sailboat rigging. The condors stirred as it ruffled their feathers. It must have felt like flying to them. Rags of mist broke away from the gap and flitted past us. Whitecaps appeared on the river surface, and the raft bucked.

As we neared the gap, the wind was actually slowing us. We entered a mist that was increasingly luminous as the sky overhead paled and reddened. It wasn't luminous enough to warn us of the massive, spindle-shaped gray boulder that appeared in midstream.

"Right! Right!" shouted Terry. I realized that I was on the right, and dug my paddle in, but we glanced off the boulder and spun. The raft lurched as Terry flung his weight into his paddle to get us turned around. Going over a waterfall backward was even less attractive than going over one forward.

We almost got straightened out, but then a gust pushed the bow aside and nearly brought us to a standstill. At the same time, it pushed the mist aside, and we finally saw what was beyond the gap.

It was one of the most beautiful sights I've ever seen. The red cliffs didn't vanish, they simply receded about a half mile on each side of the river, forming a narrow valley that extended as far as we could see to the southwest. The valley floor was an almost unbroken expanse of treetops, deep green along the river corridor, pale pink and yellow and ochre elsewhere. A ray of sunlight touched the tops of the cliffs and the swirls of mist above the river.

It was surprising how much I was able to take in during the microsecond the wind held us poised above this Thomas Cole extravaganza. Then I turned my attention to what the river was doing. It too had failed to vanish, but the view downstream was less inviting than the distant valley. The river did not thunder over a falls; it took a hard right and roared down a riparian pinball machine of gray boulders, white roostertails, and black eddies. I looked at Terry, who strained against his oar as the current gently slid us around the bend toward the slippery slope. He looked serious, but calm.

"We can handle this," he said.

45

The rapid didn't seem that bad once we got off the dizzying brink of it. The raft slid down the chute with a certain ease, headed toward a place where water boiled up and around two boulders so elongated they looked like pillars. We didn't even seem to be going that fast. I thought we'd have plenty of time to deal with the boiling water down there. I was wrong.

Abruptly the raft was half full of water. Jill lay on the bottom with her feet in the air, having flung her paddle halfway across the river, and the condor cages had nearly collapsed on the parrot and her offspring. I didn't know what had happened, except that the raft had started behaving like a rodeo animal instead of a boat as soon as we'd hit the turbulence. We might have struck one of the boulders a glancing blow.

As the river rushed us down another chute, the bottom of which was invisible around yet another boulder, Terry flung the bailing can at Jill and pushed the condor cages back upright. The raft started to spin, and I backpaddled vigorously but ineffectually against it. We hit the bottom of the second chute more or less sideways as Terry was trying to straighten us out. The effect was amazing. The raft stood up on one side like a car taking a tight curve. Jill would definitely have been jettisoned if she hadn't already been lying on the bottom. We all would have been jettisoned if Terry hadn't thrown his weight against my side to keep us from capsizing. The raft shook itself like a frustrated bronco, found chute number three without any help from its riders, and plunged down it.

Now we were all sitting on the bottom. I realized with surprise that I was still holding my paddle.

"Bail! Bail!" shouted Terry, pushing at the condor cages as they tottered once again. The condors were unrecognizable, sodden masses of feathers from which legs and wings protruded at odd angles. It took me a moment to realize what he was talking about. There seemed to be less water in the raft than before; our wheelie had partly emptied it. Terry scrambled back onto the edge and stuck his paddle back in the water. I looked warily downstream. There weren't any boulders to speak of. This chute didn't seem to have a bottom. It just turned into a sloping mass of whitewater and continued as far as I could see.

"Don't paddle unless I say so!" shouted Terry. Jill sat up and started to bail tentatively. The condors worked to right themselves from the undignified poses into which our convulsions had thrown them. The parrot had somehow stayed upright through it all, like an idol in an earthquake. She glanced at me sidelong for a moment, and I believed that she'd spent seventy million years in outer space.

Terry stood up and craned his neck at something. He sat down fast and started straining at his paddle.

"Backpaddle! Backpaddle!" I backpaddled. "Overhang! Overhang!"

"What?"

The raft came to an abrupt halt. The condor cages toppled forward this time, instead of backward, but Terry caught them before they hit. Otherwise, we sat peacefully in the midst of the rampaging water for perhaps thirty seconds. One of the condors beat its wings, as though to break out.

Then the raft shifted slightly, and the stern began to slip underwater. Since the water around us was moving maybe fifty miles an hour (or so it seemed) the raft again began to fill up.

"We're on a rock!" Terry shouted. "Shift the weight! Get down in front!"

I did what Terry said, and began to feel that I was on top of an enormous rubber band. The snagged bottom of the raft was stretching. Terry decided to move to the front too, and landed on me with both feet. I felt something give, and the raft was spinning free.

"Bail! Bail!"

It was like being in a bathtub with a manic-depressive at the height of his manic cycle. Terry put his feet on me a couple more times as he scrambled back to his poop deck. Then he turned around, and looked surprised. He had lost his paddle.

I gave him my paddle. Then I looked downstream, although it took me a moment to figure out which way it was. We were going backward now, so I could actually look downstream while I was looking at Terry, who was straining at the river again. He was so intent he didn't notice when Jill, bailing mechanically over her shoulder as she sat waist-deep in the water, hit him in the face with a can full of water. He probably thought it was spray.

Terry nearly got us straightened out, but a boulder jumped out and bounced us (I was getting confused about animate and

THE VERMILION PARROT

inanimate), so we went down the next chute sideways, with me on the down side. Since I was now facing sideways instead of forward, I didn't get a look at what was at the bottom of this chute until the last minute. By that time, all I could see was a wall of erupting water.

I felt myself go up in the air in the most dizzying way. A paddle sailed over my head, almost lazily. I felt my body beginning to part from the raft, and my hands clutched instinctively. One of them clutched on something, and my arm tried unsuccessfully to dislocate itself. I hit the raft again, but not too hard. It had started going down.

At least, my side had. Suddenly I was in water up to my chin. A dark shape loomed over me. Something slid away from it and disappeared. Then the shape began to jerk back and forth. The movement brought my eyes back into focus, and I saw that it was the condor cages. One had partly burst, and a condor's head protruded from it, and snaked back and forth desperately. Something appeared at the top of the cages, swaying as they jerked.

It was Terry's face. He looked at me a moment, but I couldn't tell if he saw me. He was soaking wet, and one of his eyes was closed. Then he looked downstream in a harried but still resolute way. It reminded me of Gregory Peck roped to the mechanical whale at the end of John Huston's *Moby Dick*.

I realized we were stuck again, which was the only reason we hadn't already capsized. I could feel the water pulling at the raft, looking for a weak spot. I craned my head around, but all I could see was water and the pile of cages with the confident little head at the top, still looking downriver as if planning a route. Then the river found its weak spot. The raft gave a mighty jerk, and pulled me underwater, throwing the looming mass on top of me.

46

I happened to have some air in my lungs as the capsized raft held me underwater, so I didn't lose my head completely. I tried diving to get away from the raft, but the turbulent water flung me about helplessly. Something banged into my head and scraped against my face, and things began to get vague. I felt myself getting smaller, spinning like a bark chip in an eddy. It had all happened so fast.

The blackness behind my eyes suddenly turned bright red. I opened them, startled, and found myself at the surface, bearing down on yet another boulder. I kicked out frantically, and managed to whiz by it. I looked around, but could see no sign of the raft or the others. I got water up my nose, coughed, and banged my foot against a rock. This gave me an idea. I would get out of the river.

Something hit the back of my head, pushing me underwater again a moment. I felt sharp pains in my scalp and shoulders, as though I'd been bitten by some aquatic poisonous snake. Something started to fasten itself around my neck. I reached back with the strength of panic and yanked a slimy, clinging object off my shoulders, pulling it forward over my head and ducking myself again in the process. After more kicking and gasping, I finally got a look at the slimy object. It was the lower half of one of the parrot's offspring, clawed feet and feathered tail. It was still squirming. I dodged another boulder, and realized that I was also holding the small creature's upper half, only underwater. I reversed it, and the parrot coughed, gasped, and wrapped herself around my neck again. I couldn't blame her, since I was wearing a life vest and she wasn't.

I remembered that I'd decided to leave the river, and looked up at the boulders hurrying past me. They looked unscalable, even if they hadn't been traveling fifty miles an hour. I kept looking for signs of the raft, but the only one I saw was a package of freeze-dried food wedged against a boulder. I plucked it up in passing, and crammed it down the front of my pants.

I looked up from doing this, and saw another wall of water ahead. I started kicking, trying to keep my feet from catching in the underwater rocks that were throwing up the water. The wall of water picked me up and flung me into the boiling eddy below it, where I stayed upside down and spinning for a surprising amount of time. When I finally kicked my way to the surface again, I found myself eye to eye with the young parrot, who was still hanging on.

"Splagh!" she cried. I could relate to that. A problem with having her for a passenger, though, was that I couldn't see ahead as well as I should have. When I finally craned around her, I found that we were headed for another brink, a patch of sky between two foam-flecked boulders, with God-knew-what waiting downstream.

One of the boulders was lying down instead of standing up. As the water swept me past, I managed to get a hand on it. A pebble turned into a pink frog and hopped away, but I didn't let that deter me. I held on, increasing my chances of hernias in later life, and eventually got my other hand on the rough marble. Then I got my hip out of the water, and finally my feet. I paused a moment to rest, since I could barely move anyway. I could see what the river did downstream now. It wasn't a waterfall, but more like a dam spillway, the water pluming down over a massive sloping slab. There would have been no way we could have handled that.

A desire to get much farther from the river agitated me. I could have climbed the recumbent boulder on foot, but fear of falling back into the river made me go up it crabwise. At the top, I found a six-foot drop to another boulder, and somehow managed to make the jump without breaking an ankle, although I probably should have because my joints were frozen stiff from the water. After more boulder hopping, I finally found myself at the base of an earthen bank. At the top were trees, their roots snaking out to anchor them to the eroding bank. They were the biggest trees I'd seen since we'd left the South Coast Preserve, although they had little in common with the redwoods. They were broadleaved trees, angiosperms, although many were seasonally leafless. They were full of epiphytes. A blue, crested bird landed on a branch and eyed us jauntily. It might have been a Steller's jay, except that it had a tail two feet long.

But it was too early for birdwatching. The young parrot's stranglehold was no longer necessary, and I tried to disengage her gently.

"Fuck off," she hissed. There was no mistaking the words now. It even sounded a little like Jill's voice.

"Watch your mouth," I said, searching her eyes for a hint of understanding. But they just blinked, as inscrutable as the blue bird's. "Can you imitate me too?" I shook her gently. No response. "Where's your mother?"

This was pointless. I felt a strange fullness in my abdomen, and clutched it, fearing some bizarre injury. It crackled, and I remembered the freeze-dried food package. That was reassuring, although I wasn't hungry just yet.

I didn't feel like scrambling up the bank just yet, either, although the exertion would have helped to keep me warm. I'd stopped being numb, and had started to shiver. I could see sunlight on the treetops now, but the shaded boulders remained chilly. I looked at my watch, which had kept on ticking. It was six forty-five A.M.

I put the young parrot on the ground. She looked up at me a moment as though thinking of climbing back aboard. Then a small lizard shot up the bank, and she turned her attention to the fauna. Within short order, she had caught and eaten a large cricket and a small frog.

I started walking downstream, which seemed the most likely way for finding other survivors, if there were any. The young creature tagged along, which raised an unnerving prospect. I didn't want the responsibility of bringing up the first dinosaur born on earth in sixty-five million years.

"Hey!" I shouted. "Heeeeyyyyy!"

I could barely hear myself above the river noise. The creature cocked her head at me, but there wasn't any other response.

47

I started getting hungry around midmorning. The young parrot had filled up on lizards and grasshoppers by that time, and gotten drowsy, so I had to carry her as I wandered in search of her mother and Jill. The forest was quite dense, although many of the trees away from the river corridor were leafless, so I could only see a few yards in any direction. The roar of the rapids made shouting pointless.

I recognized fig trees and Indio desnudo trees, but I'd never seen most of the trees in the forest. Some of the commonest bore brilliant orange or yellow, trumpet-shaped flowers, accounting for the colors I'd seen in the forest canopy as we hovered in the raft at the beginning of the rapid. Other trees had pink, pea-shaped blossoms or feathery white ones. Several times I stumbled into an intensely prickly, fragrant shrub with orange flowers. Patches of eight-foot-tall bromeliads obscured the forest floor.

The long-tailed, jaylike bird came back with some friends and investigated me for a while. They made plaintive, whispery sounds instead of jaylike screeches, and they had little plumes on their heads, like quail. A larger bird with electric blue and green plumage landed on a branch overhead for a moment, then flew off as though oblivious to my presence. It too had a long tail, which was shaped somewhat like a squash racket. I wished I'd brought a field guide. A four-foot-long lizard, its body banded with yellow and gray, regarded me balefully, then disappeared into a hole in the rocks.

The grayish limestone or marble that had lined the bottom of the gorge above the rapids formed the bedrock of the little valley. I supposed the rapid had formed when the river cut down through the harder volcanic rock to the soft limestone. The forest floor was a jumble of the gray stone, white tree roots snaking through it. If it hadn't been a seventy-million-year-old Cretaceous deposit, I'd have though it was the ruins of an unknown, pre-Columbian city.

I put the sleeping parrot down and took a closer look at the rock around the lizard's hole. How would a limestone building block look after it had been lying under a volcanic mountain range for seventy million years? I supposed it would look cooked and squeezed, like any other block. Lying on the surface, it would also look eroded and dissolved. I bent down and scraped and scratched at the natural-looking blocks. There might have been a certain regularity about them, a suggestion of joints, flutings. There weren't any chisel marks, carvings, keystone arches, plinths, or lintels. There certainly weren't any electric outlets, picture windows, porcelain fixtures, or hi-fi consoles. How would *they* look after lying under a mountain for seventy million years? Like nothing, I supposed, little bits of black stuff.

The lizard peeked out of the hole, saw me, and ducked back. I thought I felt a draft, and put my face into the hole. There was a slight pull of air, suggesting cavities down there. Vaults bearing bas-reliefs of archosaur heroic ages? A metamorphosed matrix of Cretaceous high-rises and shopping malls? It was like something out of H. P. Lovecraft. I inclined an ear into the darkness and listened. Was there a faint, seaside sound, separate from the rapids?

"That's not a problem-solving attitude," said Jill. She was close enough to startle me, and I scraped my scalp withdrawing my face. "Whoops. Sorry."

I straightened up. The parrot was standing a little way off with two of her offspring. When they saw the one I'd rescued, they attacked it, not too ferociously. It could have passed for a sisterly greeting.

"I suppose you knew about this," I said.

"Knew about what?" said Jill.

The parrot shrugged. "Of course I knew about it," she said, "I lived here."

"Right *here?*"

"It's hard to be sure about the exact location. But I studied at Tweztlesik Sipzeep, which was in the northwest of this subcontinent. The name means 'white limestone town.'"

"You mean all this rock was a city?" Jill said. "I thought it looked weird."

"This is why you came along on this?"

"Not at all," the parrot said. "Purely coincidental."

"Oh yeah."

"What would I want with this pile of rocks?"

"Why come here if you didn't want something?" said Jill.

"I didn't know I was coming here. Any more than I knew I was returning to this planet after seventy million years."

"Hell of a coincidence," I said.

"ZZzzzzzeeeop gwa tsyxyoptl," said the parrot.

"What's that mean?" Jill asked.

"Life is strange."

"At least this proves she existed," I said.

"I don't need proof," the parrot said.

"Maybe it's not a city after all," said Jill. "If these cities really existed, somebody would have found one."

"I told you," said the parrot, "we lived in the hills. Fossils don't get formed in the hills unless volcanoes erupt on top of them, as in this case. We didn't have that many cities, anyway."

"Sounds like you're protesting too much," I said.

"You're right," the parrot replied. "You can think what you like." She turned and started to walk away, followed by her three daughters.

"Where's the fourth one?" I asked Jill.

"We couldn't find it," Jill said.

The parrot paused and looked up. A large shadow slid across the forest floor. I caught a glimpse of wings overhead, then the canopy hid them. They looked dark, with white markings.

"Maybe it's a king vulture," I said.

"What's a king vulture?" Jill asked.

"A big vulture that lives in the tropics."

"Not enough white for a king vulture," said the parrot. I knew better than to ask how she knew about king vultures.

"Maybe Terry let the condors go," said Jill.

"Did you find Terry?"

"No," Jill said.

48

Jill and I spent the rest of the day looking for jetsam from the raft. We found a lot of stuff: more freeze-dried food, a paddle, a blanket, an aluminum pot, a partly waterlogged roll of toilet paper in a plastic bag, and, most surprisingly, a plastic container of raisins. These we promptly gobbled.

"I wonder what else Terry had that he didn't tell us about," Jill said.

"Looks like we'll never know." We found no sign of Terry or the cages.

"He may turn up again."

"I don't know," I said. "Did you see that last rapid?"

"We went down it," Jill said.

"In the boat?"

"In the water."

"Geez."

Unfortunately, our finds didn't include dry matches, so building a fire to cook the freeze-dried food proved difficult. I had a lens attachment on my Swiss Army knife, and I tried burning some tinder with it, but it was getting late, and the focused light didn't seem hot enough to ignite the bark and leaves. Or maybe they weren't dry enough.

"Unable to start a fire when we're sitting on an ancient civilization," said Jill. She turned to the parrot, who was now frankly eating grasshoppers and cockroaches, popping then in her mouth like salted peanuts. "Can't you find something that will help us?"

"What?" the parrot inquired.

"There must be something besides rocks under here."

"There probably is, if we had some dynamite to get at it with," the parrot replied.

"Dinosaur Dynamites Dinopolis," I thought, idly.

"You'd dynamite your own city?" Jill asked.

"Just a manner of speaking."

"If there's nothing here you want," I asked, "what are you doing here?" Jill nodded approvingly.

"Well," said the parrot, "it's a very interesting place. Do you know what this is?"

"What what is?"

"This is pristine tropical dry deciduous forest. Very rare now. Magnificent habitat."

"We're not even below the Tropic of Cancer here."

"I know," said the parrot, "that's one of the unusual things about it. This must be a relict stand growing in this isolated valley."

"How do you know all this," said Jill, "if you were shut up in Washington and California for twenty years?"

"I read about it. That biologist in Costa Rica who wears dishtowels on his head. Anyway, it was a lot like this when I lived here. The animals were different, but a lot of the trees were similar. I told you that."

"So it's pristine tropical dry whatever," said Jill. "What are you going to do?"

"There's plenty of food here, and it's quiet. I think I'll just stay here."

"What about when their brains start to grow?" Jill pointed at the offspring, who were watching their mother eat insects.

"I'll build a shelter for them. There's plenty of building material."

"What about the Mexicans?" I said.

"I don't see any Mexicans."

"What about the Indians?" Jill said. "I bet you'll see some Indians."

"I think I can make some accommodation with them."

"How?" I asked.

"I think they have a more flexible view of reality than you people."

"You think they'll make you into their god Quetzalcoatl or something?"

"Don't be so literal-minded, George," the parrot said.

"What about Jerry Lester?"

"Jerry's not catching me off guard again."

"Sounds pretty iffy to me."

"I was here first," said the parrot. "Anyway, I'm tired." She herded her daughters beside a leaning boulder and put her head down. The sun had set, and dusk was fading fast, but I was still too hungry to be sleepy. I dipped river water into the pot and emptied a pack of beef stroganoff into it.

"How are we going to cook it?" Jill asked.

"Guess we aren't."

"Ugh."

"You got a better idea?"

"We should learn to eat grasshoppers."

"I think I'll go back to California instead," I said.

"That sounds nice."

"It's home."

"I guess I'll stay here though, for a while," Jill said.

"Why?"

"Somebody has to watch her."

"You think you're going to discover her secrets?"

"It's what I do."

"What if she doesn't want you to stay?"

"She said I could. She wants help with the young ones. Listen, don't tell Jerry about this."

"Gimme a break."

"I'm not just doing this for world socialism, you know. I'm doing it for humanity."

"You putting me on?" I dipped up a handful of soaked stroganoff and put it in my mouth. It was like eating a cellulose sponge.

"I know it sounds corny."

"Hoo. What about your bosses? They want to send her back to space."

"You believe what Jerry says?" Jill didn't sound as though she altogether disbelieved what Jerry had said.

"You believe what your bosses say?"

"Not always," she said.

"What if they do want to send her back into space?"

"Then they're not true socialists."

"So you don't think intelligent dinosaurs are a threat to humanity anymore?"

"They're a resource."

"To be exploited?"

"Shared," Jill said. "This could be the beginning of a new age. Think what her knowledge could mean for the underdeveloped countries."

"If you can get her interested." A large green grasshopper landed on my leg, a katydid actually. I grabbed it, pulled off wings and legs, and popped it in my mouth. It tasted faintly shrimplike, but the chitinous carapace made it hard to swallow. I chased it with more cellulose sponge.

"Ugh," said Jill. "She's going to have to learn to cooperate."

"You're going to have to learn to eat grasshoppers." I coughed and swallowed hard. "They're probably better cooked."

"Probably less nutritious, too," Jill said, already arguing with me, although she'd yet to ingest her first katydid. I thought I might miss her a little.